PRAISE

TWIST OF FAITH

"This well-crafted tale builds to an unexpected, chilling ending."

—*Publishers Weekly*

"There are so many twists and surprises . . . The plot is great as well as the depth of characters."

—*Tulsa Book Review*

"A steady build of intrigue and tension shrouded in a dark mystery that began decades before."

—*Novelgossip*

SILENT REDEMPTION

ALSO BY ELLEN J. GREEN

Absolution

Twist of Faith

The Book of James

SILENT REDEMPTION

ELLEN J. GREEN

This is a work of fiction. Names, characters, organizations, places, events, and incidents are either products of the author's imagination or are used fictitiously. Any resemblance to actual persons, living or dead, or actual events is purely coincidental.

Published by Thomas & Mercer, Seattle

www.apub.com

ISBN-13: 9781542008402
ISBN-10: 1542008409

Cover design by Rex Bonomelli

Printed in the United States of America

For my mother, Edith Judith Green

PROLOGUE

Anais

Saigon, July 1968

The air was heavy with sweat and human breath. She was standing, squeezed next to two women and at least three children that she could see. There might have been more by her legs or under the seats. The bus jostled and weaved down a small winding path through palm trees and jungle brush. The dirt beneath one wheel or the other seemed to give out at times, and the bus would tip at a startling angle, then right itself and continue down the road.

The heat was excruciating—more than the intense sunlight, it was like the air was filled with so much moisture that each breath coated her lungs. Her hair was wet against her scalp, the perspiration dropping from her cheeks onto her shirt.

Anais looked around at the Vietnamese women near her. Dressed in their light clothing, straw hats on their heads, they didn't seem to notice any of it. They were breathing, moving, talking in a language that was lovely and difficult at the same time. When she'd first arrived in Saigon, she thought it sounded like fighting cats—loud, screeching. It made her angry and frustrated. But the longer she stayed, the more it sounded like a rhythmic song, lulling the people from moment to moment. Because if they stopped singing, they'd have to look at what was happening to their country. War after war. No respite.

The bus lurched, and everyone was thrown forward. Anais found herself on top of a small woman no older than she—maybe eighteen, nineteen. In turn, Tommaso had fallen on top of Anais, Philomena on top of him, and Tommaso's three-year-old sister, Adrianna—called Na—was thrown against all of them. Stacked like that for so many minutes, Anais thought she might get brain damage from heatstroke.

One by one the people righted themselves, the girl under Anais cursing her in a vulgar tone. "We're getting off the bus," Tommaso said. "I can't take any more of this."

Anais—and Philomena, Na's hand in hers—followed his lead, stepping down onto the muddy trail. Only later would Anais learn that he'd planned to get off at that exact stop anyway. That the whole time he acted lost, he was searching the road for the farmhouse on stilts. It was there, set back from the road—vines growing along the sides, the back filled with animal pens, and farmland in the distance.

"What are you doing?" Anais whispered. "Why did we get off the bus? We could've just stayed on until we reached Bu Non."

"We're going to ask for water. That's all," he answered. He was only thirteen years old, all legs and gangly arms, dusty blond hair and freckles across his nose, but he acted so much older. Oftentimes she forgot he was just a child.

He was walking in front of her, muttering in English heavy with his Italian accent. Sometimes he tired of speaking in halting English and lapsed into his native tongue with Philomena. They were both from similar regions of Italy, and Anais, with her French, usually felt left out.

The three of them had been plunked down in this violent corner of Asia for different reasons, and had then clustered together over commonalities. Anais was a diplomat baby—her family was always attached to one embassy or another; it didn't seem to matter where. Wealth and privilege followed. Philomena's parents had arrived in Indochina on a whim—a business venture investing in rubber—and never left. Tommaso was a different story. He'd shown up fairly late in the game. His father's occupation was cryptic—retired Italian military intelligence, attached to a US advisory committee. Tommaso made up details of his father's supposed importance and changed them daily.

They were side by side, walking around the house. Anais followed behind the other three. Her head was beginning to pound. Her throat hurt. Na was screaming, sweat running down her face. The sound of the child's wails felt like claws against Anais's flesh. Piercing, endless.

A Vietnamese man appeared in front of Tommaso, startling them. He was short and talked fast. Tommaso replied in halting French and English, but despite understanding the words, Anais was confused. They seemed to know one another. And they weren't talking about the heat or about water.

A woman appeared on the raised platform that ran around the exterior of the house. She had a baby strapped to herself, its little face toward her chest. An infant of maybe two months. The woman started yelling at Tommaso too.

Anais took Na's hand from Philomena and backed up. "He knows them," she said to Philomena. "We're not here by accident. It has something to do with Tommaso's father. Tommaso keeps saying, 'Give me the name. I need the name.'"

What came next seemed to happen in slow motion. The man turned his back on Tommaso and returned inside the house. Tommaso charged up the steps after him. He held a long knife in his hand—where it had appeared from, Anais didn't know. She'd never seen him with a knife before. She heard the screams, but they were so improbable, it was if they meant something else. None of them moved until Tommaso flew down the steps with the baby under one arm.

The infant was wailing, and Na's cries reached a new pitch. Philomena stumbled backward when he thrust the baby at her.

"Shut it up," Tommaso screamed. "Shut it up now. Before people start coming. We need to get out of here."

Na let go of Anais's hand and ran toward the road, nothing more than a brown, muddy scar through the brush and weeds around them. Stunned, Anais watched Philomena. She was completely still, not moving, clutching the baby to her. It continued to cry, its wails muffled in the folds of her shirt.

"Tommaso, what happened? Are they dead? You killed them. What happened?" Anais looked around. "Where's your sister?"

The tall grass by the side of the house came up to their thighs. Everything was still, silent, except for the baby's wails. Philomena put her hand on the tiny head and pushed it farther into her chest. *What's wrong with you?* Anais wanted to ask.

"Shhh, be quiet," Philomena said, eerily calm. "Go get your sister," she told Tommaso. "Go. She just ran down the road."

When he didn't move or answer, she said, "Fine, I'll go get her. Take the baby."

Anais saw the knife then, dangling from his fingertips; the blade was coated with blood, some of it sliding off the tip into the grass.

Philomena reached out and gently took the knife from him, slid the baby, quiet now, into his arms, and disappeared around the front of the house in search of the missing three-year-old.

Anais stared at Tommaso. His bloodied hand was pushing the back of the baby's head so hard against his shirt, his fingers turned white. "Listen, Anais. Carefully. Those two people in the house, yes, they are dead. We need to get away from here now before neighbors show up. Follow my lead." He lowered the baby into the grass. The cream-colored blanket she was wrapped in was nearly obscured by weeds.

"But she'll die there, Tommaso. There's no one here to find her. She'll die. She's sleeping now; we can drop her in town somewhere. At least do that much."

He put his mouth next to her ear. "She's not sleeping, Anais. Let's go."

When Anais looked down at the baby to see what he'd meant, Tommaso yanked her away so hard she stumbled and fell. When she looked up he was already on the road, leaving her. She started to turn, to reach for the baby, but she heard the chattering of voices in the distance.

They would catch her here, and they would blame her.

Pushing to her feet, she raced to the front of the house and saw the two of them, Tommaso and Philomena, in the distance. When she approached them, they began speaking Italian in quiet, nervous tones. Tommaso told Philomena to shut up, be quiet. That much Anais understood. As she drew closer, she saw the knife in Philomena's hand; the metal edge caught the sun's rays. The two of them were shoulder to shoulder, like a fortress.

"Where's Na? Where is she?" Anais asked.

"She's gone," Tommaso said brusquely. "People are coming." He pointed toward the horizon.

"Gone? There's nowhere to go. Is she on the road up ahead?"

The rain started at that moment, almost as if on cue. The sky just ripped apart, the storm coming down hard. Anais had become used to these torrential rains that made it seem as though the world were ending. Tommaso took off his bloodstained shirt and lifted his face to the sky, letting it wash him clean.

But he wasn't clean. After what had happened here today—and what was that? Anais still didn't know—none of them could be clean ever again. A sob escaped her, and she pressed her hand against her lips. "You brought us here knowing you were going to kill those people. Now Na is gone? Oh my God, what are we going to do?"

Philomena said nothing. She hadn't moved.

"You did this on purpose. Did your father send you to do this for him? And you dragged us along? For what? As witnesses? As a cover? To make it all seem innocent?" Anais was hysterical now.

Philomena finally stirred. “Where’s the baby? The little baby, Tommaso?” She was trembling so hard, her legs rattled against one another. Then she burst into tears.

Tommaso lunged at Philomena, scratching her face with his fingers. He grabbed her arm and Anais’s too. “Nobody knows what happened here. Nobody. Just us three. We need to walk to town; it’s three miles up the road.” He glared at them. “This never happened. It never happened. My father told me to do whatever I had to. And I did.” He took a breath, then stepped back from them, cool now. “And the baby? That was you. You killed it, Philomena—smothered it while you held it in your arms. Now keep my secret and I’ll keep yours. Let’s get moving.”

“But Na. What about Na? We have to find her,” Anais said.

“We will,” he answered. Then he tossed the knife as far as he could into the grass and started walking. With no idea what else to do, Anais followed. She dared to look back every few feet, hoping to see Na appear from the brush. But the only thing she saw—the thing that stayed with her for sixty years, that she was never sure was real or if she’d conjured it—was a shoe.

A little girl’s shoe, tipped sideways at the edge of a mud puddle, its tiny buckle shining with rainwater.

PRESENT DAY

CHAPTER 1

AVA

Vicenza, Italy

I couldn't help but notice the hand-painted pasta bowl, the ceramic swirled in bright colors of red and orange, like looking down into an open poppy flower. I picked it up and tried to read the maker's mark on the bottom without spilling the contents of the *cassoeula* all over the table. The woman across from me, who was not really my grandmother, would not be happy with that.

"Philomena, where did you get these bowls?" I spied the rest of the set on the shelves of the cupboard. I'd seen them before, or ones like them, in a shop window in Milan. Eighty-five euros for the simple pieces. Artisan pieces. The entire collection must have cost at least four thousand euros.

Philomena glanced up at me with just a flick of her eyes before looking back down again. "I don't know, Ava. Don't you like the cassoeula? It used to be your favorite." A quarter-inch-thick line of gray traveled down the part of her hair, giving away her age. "And call me Nonna. I prefer it."

I didn't remember seeing these dishes when I was here last week. It was the least of my concerns what the DeFeos chose to eat and drink out of, but it was causing me anxiety now. Mostly because I had been here for two days and Philomena had yet to produce the money I'd wired into her account before I left the States. We'd planned it out. Wire the money to her account, then travel here, retrieve the money, and . . . the rest hadn't been decided.

I'd arrived in Vicenza on Sunday morning. The banks weren't open, so I'd relaxed into the day, Mass followed by a large meal of veal and pasta, and then some wine to close the evening. Monday turned out to be a bank holiday, and I'd found it harder to calm myself as the day was whiled away. This morning, there had been nothing preventing us from getting in the car and heading into town to transfer the money to my account—maybe not all of it, maybe I'd leave Philomena just enough to have made all of this worthwhile. But she'd been stalling from the minute she'd poured her coffee into her brightly painted red poppy cup this morning. Then she insisted on making this cassoeula—buttery hot cabbage with pork pieces hidden within the folds—that took hours to simmer in her cast-iron pot on the stove. I couldn't remember ever liking this. The sight of the cabbage, shiny with butter and pork fat, was making me ill.

"I used to eat this?" I asked. "When I was three?"

She nodded. But she didn't look up.

I was born here, or somewhere in the vicinity. I'd lived in this house with the woman sitting across from me until the age of three. I had some memories, little pockets of sudden familiarity, but most of it was just a blank page, filled now with things I'd been told but didn't know. One blank page turned to another—to the morning my mother, Adrianna, ripped me from my bowl of cassoeula and took me first to Tuscany, then to Philadelphia, where she was murdered. I'd spent my life trying to find out where I belonged, where I'd come from, who my mother was, and why she'd been killed—and finally, where the rest of my family might be. My life was filled with nothing but blank pages and questions.

But here I was, staring at the woman who believed she had given birth to my mother, but who wasn't my grandmother, the woman with the stripe of gray down her part and the expensive dishes. The woman who had at least a hundred and forty thousand euros of my money secreted in her bank account in Vicenza.

I pushed the bowl to the middle of the table. "Philomena, you've spent the entire day making this. I was hoping we'd get to the bank, but it's too late now. Everything is closed."

She hesitated, settling back in her seat. "You've been so quiet since you got here. Are you all right?" she asked.

I shook my head. Another stall. "What do you mean?"

"You've been out of our lives for so long. This must be so strange. Sitting back at this table. Here."

I frowned. "I don't remember this table, Philomena—"

"Your mother, Adrianna, looked like Victor," she blurted. One way to keep me distracted was to talk about my mother; Philomena was getting to know me well. "She was dark. Dark hair—his hair is gray now, but it was black once. And they had the same light coppery eyes too."

I half smiled and stared into my bowl of cabbage and pork. I remembered my mother. Fragments of her anyway. Sudden bolts of clarity coming to me when I wanted to sleep. Of her being killed while I cowered in the corner of the church. The look on her face as the men stabbed her. Her bloody black shoe almost touching me, connecting with me while she died. I'd served justice, vengeance, on those men, and I didn't want to talk about this anymore. "My father must have been lighter, then? My eyes are green."

I felt a tug in my stomach. Butterflies had settled in and nested. He'd disappeared from my mother's life the minute she'd decided to travel from Tuscany to the States, or so I was told. He'd returned to Vicenza briefly, but that was where my information ended.

"Your father's name was Davide Tosi."

"Davide Tosi. Do you have a picture of him? Can I see him?" I whispered it, feeling it slide across my tongue and out of my mouth.

She stood up and disappeared from the kitchen. Five minutes later she returned with an album in her hand and opened it to a middle page. "Here he is. It's the only one I have, just this. It was taken out back here."

She put it down in front of me. A jolt shot through my stomach. It was my mother in black and white. It was sometimes hard for me to remember her whole face because it only came to me in bits. But I never forgot her eyes. She was laughing in the picture, mouth open, straight teeth, the corners of her mouth nearly reaching her cheeks. The boy standing next to her was laughing too. Handsome, with dimples and short hair, he was looking at Adrianna like she was the only woman in the world. "How tall was he? He looks huge."

"Victor used to say he must have German blood in him. He was six two at least. Loved sports. He played rugby here for the local team."

His shoulders were broad, his arms thick, his hands were stowed in his pockets. There was nothing but happiness emanating from either of them. I dropped the album onto the table with a thud. This was my life, the one that had never happened.

"They were in love, you know," Philomena said. "Though they shouldn't have been. If they'd met even three years later, things might have been different."

"They were, what, fifteen, sixteen here?" I asked.

There was no answer, and my head jolted up from the photograph in front of me. Victor was standing there, behind me, where seconds before he hadn't been.

His eyes were on the photograph. *"Philomena, cosa stai facendo?"* His Italian was thick with the dialect of the northern provinces. *"Ne abbiamo parlato. Nessun Adrianna, e nessun Davide."*

He was admonishing Philomena for speaking about my parents. Then he reached down and closed the album. "Giada, how long are you staying?" he asked. "Have you made other plans?"

Philomena shook her head, eyes down, wiping at her nose. "Victor, stop. She's your granddaughter."

I was. I truly was his granddaughter, and I was sure he knew it. I could see some of him in me, when I let myself look long enough. But what did he see when he looked at me? A reminder of sins he'd committed long ago? Of his affair with Anais Lavoisier, Philomena's lifelong friend? Of the night Anais and Philomena both gave birth, but only one of their babies survived? Adrianna, my mother, taken from Anais and placed in Philomena's arms, not by Victor, but by another man. Neither woman told the truth.

Or maybe he thought about none of that. How many other indiscretions had he committed against his wife? I didn't know, but I found him mysterious, awkward, abrupt. I had no idea how he'd kept two women—Philomena and Anais—on a string, yearning for his company for years. I'd had enough after two days.

I stood up. "Maybe I should find someplace else to stay, Philomena. I'll be back in the morning to get my money. Once I have it, I'm leaving town. Give me two seconds to get my things." I edged around Victor and out of the kitchen.

My heart was heavy, though I was trying to ignore it. Though Philomena wasn't my biological grandmother, she was in spirit. And I was certain she still didn't know the truth. At least she gave no indication she did.

After tossing a few items into my duffel bag, I returned downstairs. With the cash I'd be getting soon—my hard-won inheritance from Grand-Mère Anais—I could rent a nice little room somewhere and figure out my next step.

"What's wrong with you, Philomena?" The voices came to me in the hallway.

"It's natural she'd ask about her father. Her life's been a mess with those people. She has no family but us and them. I'm not going to hide it."

I peered around the corner. "Philomena, I'm ready."

She patted the table. "Sit for a minute, Giada."

"Ava," I said. I was Ava now. Giada died with my mother.

"I need to tell you about your father before you go. It's important."

I obeyed, feeling my fingers tighten around the handle of my bag near my feet.

"Davide came back to Vicenza after leaving for Tuscany with Adrianna, but he was different, don't ask me how, he just was. He stayed away from everyone, wouldn't talk about her—we were worried sick about where she'd gone, was she safe. And then one day he just vanished too."

I felt my head tilt to the side. "He followed her to Philadelphia?"

Philomena nodded. "We always thought that was the case. It's what made sense. That Adrianna had run, and Davide had decided to go with her. The two were inseparable, so they had to be together. But now—"

"Now what?"

"Her body has been identified. It was her in the church for sure, and he hasn't turned up."

I opened the album still sitting on the table. The look in my father's eye, hands in his pockets, the smile. "He wasn't with us. Not that I remember. I have no sense of him ever being there."

"You were three years old, Giada—Ava. How can you know for sure? Think harder."

"I know he wasn't because he would have turned up after Adrianna was killed. He would have identified her body. He would have brought her home. He would have found me. How could he not? Look at them. They're in love." I ripped the picture from the album and put it in my purse. Then I stood and pushed my chair in so hard, its straight back smashed against the table. "He wasn't there. That's why none of that happened."

Victor was leaning against the counter, his face blank of expression but his eyes watching me intently. I saw the glance that passed between them. A look of knowing, of having some information that I didn't.

"About your money, Ava. Something's come up, and there's going to be a delay." It wasn't Philomena saying those words, it was Victor.

My money was my freedom, and right now it was my life. The expensive hand-painted mug was winking at me. The swirls of red and orange blinking on and off. I picked it up and studied it. "What's the problem?"

"Your grandmother transferred the money to my account. It's safe, but it'll be a few days until we sort it out. That's all."

My gaze went from Philomena to Victor, but their eyes wouldn't meet mine. I felt the cup slip from my fingers, and I didn't try to hold it. It fell onto the table, smashing in half, bits of ceramic exploding everywhere.

CHAPTER 2

MARIE

Camden County Jail, New Jersey

Marie was flat on her back, staring up at the sheet of metal of the bunk above, only twelve inches from her nose. *Fuck u Melissa* had been scratched onto the surface with something sharp. Someone, lying in the same position as she was now, had spent at least an hour on the project, using some sort of contraband—a paper clip, a sharpened toothbrush, maybe even a knife—to scrape through layers of dull paint to deliver her message. Marie turned sideways and stared at the cream-colored cinder-block wall, but it was littered with so much graffiti it was hard to see the exact tint underneath.

Ava had left this building three days ago, and Marie had only moved from the cell twice since then. Once to be taken upstairs for a first appearance in front of a judge, to be told she was staying in jail until her parole hearing—date unknown—and the second time to be taken down to the mental health office to sit in a plastic chair and be interrogated by a chubby, middle-aged, balding man with glasses. He'd introduced himself as Lonnie or Lance, she couldn't remember. He'd sorted through papers endlessly, moving them from one side of the desk to the other until something caught his eye.

"So you were a nun?" he'd asked. Marie just nodded. Her days in the convent seemed so long ago, she'd had to think for a minute. "Well, let me ask you something," he continued. "Why'd you want to be a nun? You don't look like a nun."

"How does a nun look?" she'd countered.

"But you'd be good-looking if you weren't in jail. Why would you want to be in a convent?"

That was a question that couldn't be answered in five minutes, so she'd said nothing, just watched him shift more papers until he'd gleaned new facts about her long-forgotten past.

"So, you were in a psychiatric hospital before? Huh. In Switzerland? I never heard of that before." His eyes slid down her arms looking for scars. "When's the last time you cut yourself?"

Having her entire psychiatric history trotted out by this stranger was humiliating. She shrugged. "So many years ago it's not important now."

"So you're not taking any medication?"

She took a breath before she spoke. This man had looked back and forth between his papers and her breasts too many times. "I'm not interested in any mental health treatment here. So, can we end this now?"

In the end he'd had her sign a refusal slip while discussing her housing options—mental-health housing in a quiet block alone, or suicide watch with no clothing in a noisier one if she developed any thoughts of harming herself. She'd opted for the quiet block alone. That epitaph scratched into the bunk above her should read *Fuck u mental health. And fuck u Ava,* she thought. This was all Ava's fault. Marie could pin her ousting from the convent on her, her ongoing mental instability, her legal problems, all of it could be linked back to that girl.

That skinny niece of hers had had the nerve to come to the jail days ago, papers in hand, and sit across from her, the remnants of a smirk still etched at the corners of her mouth. She'd won this round of their little game to track down Anais's money, calling Interpol on Marie and informing them that she was in Italy, in violation of her parole in Camden County, New Jersey, knowing they'd haul her home and stuff her back in this crummy place to await a hearing. Oh, but there was more. Ava had cracked the code to Anais's bank accounts, figuring out the pass code. The pass code they'd spent the past month circling Europe and each other to find.

"It was right in front of us, Marie. So simple." Ava had held her hands out to her sides like an innocent child. "I'm shocked you didn't figure it out first."

Ava had sucked her teeth, and it was all Marie could do to keep herself in her seat. It was just the tiny thought of adding more charges to her current violation that prevented her from smashing the girl's teeth in so she'd never suck them at anyone again.

"So, just one thing, Aunt Marie. It's funny—you really are my aunt. Blood and all. I need you to sign these papers so I can get the money from the account in Philly." She held up her hand. "No, hear me out—"

Marie had studied her, bit by bit, every inch of her face, hair, arms, hands. The dark hair pulled back with just tendrils falling along the sides of her face. The fair skin, no makeup, no flaws, that now seemed slightly tinged with yellow, as if she were ill. The green eyes clear, with just the slightest circle of gold around the edges of the irises. Those piercing eyes had fixed on Marie. The thick eyebrows rose, as if she were entitled to an answer to a question that hadn't been asked. Sitting so close to Ava made her skin crawl.

Marie sorted through all the facts as if they were in a card catalog in her brain, each drawer containing the details of a particular betrayal. The most cluttered drawer was filled with murders. So many Marie had almost lost count. A priest asphyxiated; the Owens couple—man and wife—bludgeoned with a hammer; Jack Quinn left to die on a dirty green carpet from a heart attack, while Ava watched his breathing slow to a stop; Michael Ritter, a forgery man hired to obtain fake driver's licenses, stabbed in the bathroom at the house in Haddonfield. That had been a clever one because Ava had framed Marie for the killing, and so her legal troubles had begun.

And Ross Saunders. Marie's father. All of that death was what Ava deemed justice for the murder of her mother.

"You're not my blood, Ava. You're a stray my father dragged home, and he paid the price for it. What's the code? How could it hurt to tell me now? I'm not going anywhere."

Ava shook her head. "So many things you don't know. But look, let's wrap this up. Here's my offer. You sign the papers, I get the money. I buy you a really good lawyer and leave your half of the account with him. Or . . . sort of half. You know what I mean—"

Marie pushed herself up far enough to lean across the table. "Explain to me why I'd do that? Let you take all the money."

Ava put her hand on Marie's. She felt Ava's cold lizard flesh against hers and ripped it away, falling back into her chair.

"I said I'd leave your half. We have to work together. So here's the thing. We're stuck, like it or not. I have the pass code to all the accounts. You have the knowledge that I'm alive." Ava looked around to make sure no one could hear them. "If you told them Ava Saunders was alive, I'd be arrested."

"They'll figure it out when you withdraw the money," Marie snapped. "You can't pretend to be Joan Smith, Karen Rogers, or whoever the hell you are today when you go to the bank. And moving that much money. Won't it perk up the ears of the IRS?"

Ava nodded. "It will eventually cause ripples. But I'll have time to get out of the country. And at least empty three or four accounts in Europe before they catch on. And maybe they never will. I'll figure it out as I go. So look, I'll leave you your part. An agreement. You don't enhance their knowledge of my whereabouts, I give you half as I go along."

"And how can I know what you're up to when I'm in here?" Marie's arms were folded, pressing the wrinkled orange jail jumpsuit against her stomach. She felt her hair matting to her head, and it itched.

"Focus, Marie. Geez, are they giving you sedatives? Your fancy lawyer will confirm it for you as I go. He'll keep tabs on all Anais's accounts. If I don't wire your money on time, and exact paperwork, you can dime me out. And they can follow the money trail to find me." She stopped talking for a half minute, but Marie didn't feel the need to jump in. She was scrambling the facts, figuring how she could make all this work to her advantage. "If you turn me in, I will get arrested, but then the money stays where it is. Because you, unfortunately, don't have the code. And you'll never get my signature at that point to make any withdrawals. Ever. We both lose."

"Anais left twelve million. You don't need all twelve million to live. I sign the papers, you leave, you can empty three or four of those accounts and disappear. You can leave me here to rot. And I'll never see any of the money because I don't have the code. So, even if I turn you in, it won't matter."

Ava's leg swung back and forth. It looked the size of a broomstick, and Marie stared at it, wanting to snap it in half. How many times had Marie beaten her already? Twice? One more time should do the trick.

"True. But you're forgetting a few things, Marie. I'm greedy. I'd never leave any of that money sitting there so you could potentially step in and take the rest of it. Never. And two, if you tell them I'm alive now, there'll be a hunt. I wouldn't have time to enjoy any of it, not really—on the run, looking over my shoulder, changing identities, staying under the radar. That time in Paris, in my shitty apartment, doing odd jobs, whoring myself out, counting my pennies, it almost killed me. I'm not going back to that. Ever."

Something had changed in her; Marie had seen that when she'd appeared at Anais's cottage after the funeral. Ava had been battered, hardened by life.

"Do we have a deal, Marie? Here's the lawyer's name." Ava pushed a business card over to her. "Andrew Baldwin. He's the best. The perfect lawyer for this job. I knew him when I worked at the courthouse. I already gave him a retainer, so . . ."

Marie picked up the card and looked at it. Her head hurt, and she couldn't afford to make a mistake on this. The Librium they'd given her to help with the supposed withdrawal she'd have from drinking a few glasses of wine every day was slowing her thoughts. She stood up.

"Have the lawyer come here to meet me. I'll give you an answer after that. Tomorrow."

That conversation with Ava had been days ago. Baldwin, in his gray suit, wrinkled white shirt underneath, and crew cut from the 1950s, had come and gone, but she didn't trust him. Not really. Anyone who knew Ava was working with her, as far as Marie was concerned. Though Ava had kept her word and left a hundred and twenty-five thousand dollars in an account with Baldwin, she was going to screw Marie down the line, take all the money and pin some other crime on her so she'd never have freedom again. That's the way it worked.

Marie turned from the cinder-block wall to stare at the slab of metal above her again. All of this was going to end. Marie had help now. Someone on the outside. Someone who was going to send Ava on a wild-goose chase looking for her dead father. It wouldn't end well, and with some patience, luck, and good timing, Marie would be out of here to claim all the money for herself.

She took a pencil and scratched a letter into the paint over and over. It was invisible at first but became clearer with every pass. *A.* Twenty minutes later her message was complete. *Ava Saunders is alive.* And soon the whole world would know it.

CHAPTER 3

AVA

Vicenza, Italy

I counted it all twice, lingering with each bill to make sure it was right. Five thousand one hundred twenty-two dollars and thirty-seven cents, and four hundred and ten euros. That's all I had to my name. I'd have had nine euros and fifty-seven cents more, but I'd splurged on a pack of cigarettes and a cup of coffee after I left Philomena's. I sat at a table outside the café and lit one now, watching the smoke billow up into the cold air.

Philomena had betrayed me by giving my money to Victor. No amount of explanation of bank accounts or fear of the police coming to their house smoothed it over. None of it had made sense. The money was clean. It was mine. I'd endured being beaten by Marie to get it, traipsed across Europe for it, almost got arrested in France for it, betrayed Russell for it. And it was so cleanly taken from me. I couldn't reconcile why I'd been so stupid as to trust a woman I really hardly knew. A woman who'd raised my mother until the age of nineteen, nothing more. A woman with a complicated past and shady entwined connections to Anais Lavoisier from the time they were children. A woman with an oily husband with a history of deception. In a moment of impulse, I'd thrown my lot in with the two of them and lost, not everything, but I'd lost.

I rolled the money again and stuffed it deep into my pockets. "How could you have been such an idiot?" I muttered under my breath before sucking what was left of my cigarette and stamping it out under my foot. But it wasn't all for nothing. There was more money to be had. I could get to Switzerland in the morning and empty the account there, another nine hundred thousand, if I moved fast. Four hundred thousand for Marie, to shut her up, and the rest for me.

When I went to stuff the cigarettes back into my bag, I saw the picture I'd taken from the album. My father smiling down on my mother. I pulled it out and studied it like I'd missed something the first go-round. A hidden message. Something that could help me now. Adrianna was staring into the camera lens, and her eyes disturbed me. I knew them in life and in death. My time was short—I needed to get on the train to Geneva, but I had to meet the people that gave birth to this boy. The missing half of my life. My other grandparents.

I didn't have an address, but Philomena hadn't told me they'd moved. They had to be close. I did a quick search on my phone. *Tosi.* Not an uncommon name, judging from all the entries that came up, but not overwhelming. I could do this. I flagged the waitress over and parted with another two and a half euros for another cup of coffee. Thirty minutes later I thought I had it. An address on the other side of Vicenza. Not easy walking distance. I'd have to part with more money for a cab or spend half a day on foot getting there.

◆ ◆ ◆

The house was average, weathered stucco, a row home on a long, crowded street littered with mopeds, children's plastic toys, and bicycles. If this was the right place, they didn't have money. Not DeFeo money and certainly not Lavoisier money. The Tosis were on the lower end of middle class. I hesitated slightly and pushed the doorbell, my insides quivering. All my usual certainty and confidence were gone.

"Yes?" a woman said, opening the door just a crack. She looked to be the right age, in her late forties, maybe early fifties. Grayish hair, long enough to be pulled back from her face. Pretty, elegant even, from the little I could see. She didn't belong in this house.

"Salve, mi dispiace disturbarla. Questa è la residenza de Tosi?" I waited.

"Sì. Lo è," she responded, opening the door a little more. "How can I help you?"

I shifted from one foot to the other. "Are you Davide's mother? Davide Tosi?"

Her eyes scanned from my head to the bottom of my scuffed boots. "Davide? You know Davide?" she asked.

The look on her face, the way her head dropped, the weary but hopeful expression told me everything I needed to know. She had been in torment for years. I put my hand to my chest. "I'm sorry for coming here like this, but I had to see you. Do you have a minute?"

Francesca Tosi opened the door and stepped out, looking up and down the street, and then she pulled me in and shut the door behind us. "Oh my God. Oh my God. Do you know where Davide is? You have some information for me?"

"I don't. I'm . . . I don't know how to say this. Signora Tosi. Do you know me?"

Her head shook back and forth. "N . . . no. Should I?"

The house was dark and closed in. The woman in front of me was dressed from head to foot in black, as if she were still in mourning. Her gray hair was held at the back of her head with a metal clasp, leaving the ends to curl neatly along her neck. She looked at me but was saying nothing.

"Giada—actually, I go by Ava now. I'm Adrianna and Davide's daughter."

For a second I didn't think she'd heard me. Her head tilted slightly, and she seemed to be considering my words. "How did you find me?"

An odd question. "Victor," I said, only because his face came to my mind first. "Philomena too."

"Victor sent you here?"

"Not exactly. They just told me about Davide. So, I found you. Google search."

She seemed startled and confused. "What did Victor say about me exactly?"

"He said . . . nothing—"

"I heard they'd found Adrianna—identified her, I mean. I just didn't know . . . I'm sorry." Her words were muffled. "It must have been terrible. Your mother and all. But you're home now? With Philomena?"

"I'm heading to Geneva very early tomorrow morning. I have to go. But I needed to see you first."

"You look like Davide. I see it in your eyes, and the shape of your face. His grandmother had green eyes." She sniffled and then took my hand. "It's like I'm seeing part of him again." She let it go and studied me. "Do you know where Davide is?"

"I have no idea," I answered.

I followed her to another room, more open, the walls painted in a lighter color, and we sat on the edge of the sofa. "He had to have been with you in Philadelphia . . . Ava, yes? He lived for you and your mother. He left here to go find you. I know that."

"Do you know that for a fact? Because I don't remember him. And he wasn't with me when my mother was killed. He never claimed her body. He never looked for me."

Her fingertips were playing all along her lips, and I knew she was about to cry. "You were too young to know. Maybe he was murdered too? Maybe he saw what happened to your mother, and they chased him and murdered him?"

I shook my head. "The men who killed my mother weren't hired assassins. It was four drunk men. If that were true, that they killed Davide, someone would have found his body. It would have been connected to my mother's. There'd be a file on it. There wasn't."

"How do you know? How can you possibly know that?" she said angrily.

"Because I have spent my life figuring out what happened that night and who I am. And why do you want your son to be dead, Signora Tosi? I'd rather my father was alive. Out there somewhere than dead in some unmarked plot in Philadelphia. I've been through that already."

Her fists were clenched. "I want something to make sense." A stream of tears rolled down her face. "Enough is enough."

I pulled the pack of cigarettes from my purse. "Tell me what happened between the time Davide came back from Tuscany and when he disappeared. I need every detail. Can I smoke?"

"Of course, outside."

We moved to a table and chairs on a broken concrete patio at the back of her house. "When he left with Adrianna that night, to take the train—to Tuscany, to the house of Enzo Martinelli. You know this already?" I nodded. "We didn't know he'd gone. We only found out a few days later when he called." She took one of my cigarettes and lit it. "He had a job at a restaurant downtown—La Cucina—and usually came in late at night, so it wasn't unusual that we didn't see him."

"What did he say when he called?"

She pulled on her sleeves, adjusting them slightly before speaking. "That he was coming home on the five o'clock train."

"Did you like Adrianna?"

She held her cigarette near her lips and shook her head. "I'm sorry, but no, not particularly. She was brash." She used the Italian word *insolente*. "Too fast for Davide. He could have finished university. He was a very good rugby player. Instead—"

"Instead he met her, had sex, and had me. All at the age of sixteen."

She gave a slight nod.

"And he came back on that five o'clock train alone that next day?"

She nodded. "He got to the house around eight or so."

"And then what? Did he say what happened in Tuscany?"

"He said that Adrianna was going somewhere, and he wasn't going with her. That she took the baby . . . you, with her."

I was trying to think. To put together all the facts I'd gleaned from Anais's letters—letters she'd left for me to find after her death. "He didn't know she was going to the States?"

She shrugged. "If he did, he didn't say." She leaned quickly toward me. "Look, Ava, his father and I wanted what all parents want for their children. He had a future. University—he was smart, had good grades, was athletic, loved to travel. He was tall and good-looking. When Adrianna showed up, his whole future changed in a matter of months. So, I can't say I was sorry when he said she was gone."

"And that the baby was gone too?"

She snorted. "That's unfair. You, grown-up, sitting here with me, and baby Giada are not the same thing. It's not the same. We just couldn't take care of a granddaughter. And we wanted more for him. So, yes, I wasn't unhappy that the baby was gone too. I just . . ."

I shuddered a little inside. I was the baby. Me grown and the baby were the same—just some horrible years had gone by to separate us. "Just what?"

"I just thought Adrianna and . . . and the baby would come back. I didn't know they'd be gone for good."

"Tell me about those days between when he returned and when he disappeared. Everything you can remember."

The cigarette between her index and middle finger wobbled a bit. She cleared her throat. "He came back and wouldn't talk about what happened in Tuscany. But he was different. I don't know how—kept his head down, didn't go out so much. Work, practice, then home. Wouldn't talk to us. Something was going on. He locked the door to his bedroom, which he'd never done before. He missed practice a few times too—"

"Rugby?"

She nodded. "The only thing that Davide would say to us was that Adrianna was in trouble. Upset, I think. And I would say, she should be upset, being a mother at such an age." Her forehead lowered into a scowl. "I didn't know what I was saying. I didn't know he needed me."

"He said Adrianna was in trouble or was upset?"

She rubbed the cigarette out in the ashtray. Then she pressed her fingers to her temples. "In trouble. Or was troubled. I don't remember."

"When is the last time you saw him? My father." I added that so she'd remember I was family.

"It was a Saturday night, the twentieth of July. He said he was going to practice. He left, just like nothing was wrong. But he never showed up. And he never came home."

"But—"

"He left with his bag, like always. We thought it had his sports things in it, but maybe it was clothes and he'd been planning to leave town. I don't know." She shrugged. "He was nineteen, had finished school. There was nothing we could do to keep him here."

"And no one saw him after that? In town? Or at the station?"

"Only two people, confirmed. A woman who worked at a convenience store on Piazza Castello said he came in and bought some water. He's on the surveillance tape. He didn't talk to her at all. Just bought the water and left. That was at 6:53 at night. The second person was a man in town who was walking his dog near Parco Querini at around nine thirty at night. He said Davide was at the phone booth on Contrà Marco—near the bus station. He hung up and started moving so fast the man almost bumped into him. There were no cameras, so we aren't certain it was really Davide, but the description matched, right down to the color of the sports bag he carried. He yelled to him to slow down or stop, but Davide kept moving like someone was after him. Or following him."

"The way you said only two confirmed—you think there might be someone else that saw him?" I checked my watch. I needed to leave soon if I was going to find a decent place to sleep for the night.

"I do. I think he saw someone else." She was whispering as if it were protected information. "I just know it."

"Who?" I whispered back.

"The DeFeos."

CHAPTER 4

Philomena

Vicenza, Italy

The wind was rattling through the tree branches so hard Philomena feared one of the limbs might break off and hit the house. She sat in the spare bedroom, Adrianna's old room, watching the storm collect. And waiting. Victor would come upstairs to look for her eventually. The fight between them had been particularly nasty this time, though, so it might take him longer. Stealing Ava's money had been his idea. He said he feared the police would come when they discovered she was alive, that they would be implicated in aiding and abetting a fugitive. That they should pull all the money out of that account in the form of a cashier's check made out to cash and hold it somewhere safe until he could find a way to launder it through his business. If the police came, they could say she got the check and left. That they'd had no idea what was going on. Play dumb.

Philomena knew it was not only a stupid idea but also unfair to Ava. Any officer who made their way to the house would certainly follow up with the bank and know Philomena had requested the cashier's check. Victor had left her to take the fall and to accept Ava's wrath. And she had. Her granddaughter had grabbed her bag and darted through the door before Philomena could gather the words for an explanation. There wasn't one. Why not just give Ava the check and send her on her way? Why complicate things by withholding it? It made no sense, but Victor had insisted on it in a way that frightened her.

Philomena pulled a throw into her lap and began to roll it between her fingers. Twenty years ago it had belonged to Adrianna—not a special blanket, or even her favorite one, and the smell of her sweet perfume had long evaporated, but it was something. The rhythmic sensation of the plush cotton against her skin was soothing, though her heart was racing; she could feel it against her ribs, pounding out the uncertainty of what Victor might do next.

She heard his feet on the stairs and then doors opening and shutting. He was looking for her. She kept her eyes on the sky—the dark clouds forming in the distance. No rain, just a wind that threatened to take the shingles off the roof as it passed by. Ava was out there with her little satchel, with only the money in her pocket. Headed probably to Switzerland to try and access another account.

"Philomena, non abbiamo ancora finito di parlare." He was in the doorway, demanding to finish the conversation they'd started downstairs.

"There's nothing to finish," she responded. "Things will never be the way they were before Ava came back to us. We can't hide anymore."

"Giada." He said it like it came from the back of his throat.

"Same child, Victor." She whipped her head around to face him. "Why do you despise her so?"

"Davide brought something to this family. Something we didn't need or want."

This was true but had nothing to do with what they were talking about. "That might have been true before the child was born. Not after. And if you had nothing to do with Davide's disappearance, as you swore to me back then, why shouldn't she know her father? There was nothing wrong in letting her see the picture."

He stared at her so long she had to look away. His eyes were almost black, the pupils melting into the irises, creating a solid circle of darkness. "If she reaches out to his mother, and of course she will, it's going to be terrible."

Philomena just nodded, her fingers kneading the blanket harder. The night Davide disappeared was something they never discussed. Not after the initial investigation was over. They'd talked to the police, cooperated, answering what was asked of them, but there was so much not asked. So much they could have added. So much Philomena wanted to say but didn't.

Victor had told her his story—that he hadn't seen Davide for weeks. That he didn't know if the boy had followed Adrianna, had no idea where she'd gone, and hadn't spoken to her since she'd left for Tuscany. Philomena had repeated the words her husband wanted her to say. And when the police questioned people in Tuscany, everyone who'd seen Adrianna there denied knowledge of her whereabouts.

It had upset Philomena at the time. But there were more important things that deserved the focus of her ire. That night that Davide had disappeared was not ordinary or quiet. Adrianna had been gone for three weeks and two days by then. No word from her. Philomena hadn't slept, barely ate. Her nerves were raw. She'd just wanted Adrianna and Giada home. Davide had shut down, wasn't speaking much, not even to his mother, demanded to be left alone. But then one night, he'd called their house, late, after eleven o'clock, and before Philomena could say hello, she'd heard his sobs.

She'd held the phone to her ear, listening. "Davide? Is that you? What's wrong? What happened?"

"He's going to die. Oh my God," he'd said. "Help me."

Victor had torn the phone from her hand. He listened for a moment, then hung up and ran out of the house. Philomena had stared at that old wall phone for ten minutes before picking up the receiver and pressing the numbers to call back. It rang at least six times before someone answered. Then she'd heard screaming. It seemed like a dream now. Something she'd made up in her sleep, but it wasn't. She had no idea where the call had come from—inside a building or phone booth—but the voices, the yelling, in terror almost, went on for minutes, as if the receiver had been lifted and then set down without disconnecting the call. Philomena could never be sure, but for one brief second she was convinced one of the voices she heard on the other end of that phone belonged to Victor.

He was standing at the doorway now. "We're not keeping any big secrets, Philomena."

Philomena felt the flinch, as if she were somewhere else, watching her body react to his words. He was still lying. He'd told the same story over and over again so many times that it had become his truth. But it wasn't *the* truth. She knew the phone call had been real. That Victor had gone to Davide while something terrible was happening. But when she'd questioned it, he'd acted like she was insane. There never was a call. He'd made her seem crazy and fragile, so distraught over the loss of their daughter and granddaughter that she'd concocted an event that never occurred.

"Why I despise Ava, now that's the question you asked." He turned his back to her, looking out the window. "She's a dark force, and she's going to take us all down. Mark my words."

Philomena stood and dropped the throw onto the bed. "Like grandfather, like granddaughter, that's what I always say." She was watching him carefully for any sudden movements or unpredictable rage.

"Lolo?" It startled her. He hadn't called her that nickname in so many years.

She lifted her eyes to him. "Victor."

"We need to be together in this to protect ourselves. Protect what's ours. Understand?"

"I don't know what I'm protecting. You, me? This house? The story of our daughter and her boyfriend? What happened years ago? What are we protecting, Victor?"

"Maybe Ava's gone, and there's nothing to worry about."

"She's not gone. You took her hundred thousand euros. If you wanted her gone, you would have given her the check, instead of taunting her with your thievery and then telling her to leave. Of course she'll be back."

She knew it was coming but was surprised anyway. He took her wrists in his hands and squeezed hard enough that she felt the skin bruising; her bones ached beneath his fingers.

"And when she does, you're going to turn her away. And don't mention Davide again. We have the upper hand. She's supposed to be dead, remember? Wanted in the United States. I could turn her in if she makes trouble." He let go and pushed her at the same time, and she fell back onto the bed.

She got to her feet and rushed to the doorway. "She's the only child I have left. The one thing that's left of my only child." She stopped. "And remember, Victor, she's only pretending to be dead because she's wanted for murder. Multiple murders. I'd say she's an even match for you."

CHAPTER 5

Russell

Cherry Hill, New Jersey

Gin always made him angry and ready to fight, but he was drinking it anyway. It was better to sit here and drink the gin and tonic than to turn it away. The woman was trying to be nice. She was pretty in a tired sort of way. Too much makeup. Her skin was getting rough around her eyes and mouth, and she was trying too hard.

She reminded him of Juliette. It was something in the way she walked over to him and sat down without asking. And how she kept talking, though it was clear he wasn't interested in conversation. Then proceeded to buy him a drink of her choice, not his, and presented it to him like it was an enormous favor. A favor that now needed to be repaid with God knows what. The longer he looked at her, the more her features shifted to match those of his ex-fiancée.

Juliette had been dead exactly five weeks today—an anniversary of sorts. He didn't want to think about it, that's why he'd come to the bar. Juliette dead in their bed with a needle mark in her arm. He closed his eyes and took a gulp of his drink, feeling the bitter tonic sliding down his throat. She'd killed herself, of course. But that hadn't come to light until after his arrest, after his career was completely destroyed.

The thought of her suicide, the despair and lies that led her there, combined with his joblessness, depression, bitterness—there was plenty of blame to go around for all of it. His name had been all over the news. Even after he was exonerated, nobody would hire him. Not even Home Depot or Target. Once a Navy SEAL, then a police detective with the Prosecutor's Office, he was now getting by on bit private-investigator jobs handed to him by lawyers, and a part-time security-guard job at Virtua Hospital in Voorhees.

"You don't remember me, do you?" she said.

He turned to the woman who'd bought his drink. "No." Enough said.

"I'm Isabelle Marek. Sheriff's officer? And I remember you very well, Russell Bowers." She laughed, too loud.

He drained the rest of his glass, trying to picture her in the uniform, and where their paths might have crossed. He shrugged. "I don't know you."

"I'm on leave. Disciplinary. So yeah, we have something in common. Though I wasn't accused of murder." She winked at him.

Then he remembered her. She was Joanne's friend. The two would meet up and eat lunch together occasionally. They'd gone out for a drink once, and Joanne said Isabelle consumed way too much. "You talk to Joanne recently?" he asked.

She motioned to the bartender for another drink. "She's not at the courthouse anymore. Quit. And I'm not there either, of course. I texted her last week to see what she was up to."

It was the first bit of this conversation that had interested him. Joanne had, once upon a time, been probably his best friend, confidante, even partner in crime. They hadn't spoken in weeks. She blamed him for Juliette's death, and she wasn't wrong.

"She said she's taking it easy. Living off her savings for now."

He chuckled. Joanne's savings was a bag of cash Ava had left for her—she'd dumped seventy-five thousand on her living room floor and then hightailed it to Europe. Ava, who'd sealed the friendship between him and Joanne and then destroyed both their lives.

For someone who was legally dead, she'd created huge problems for everyone around her. But all he could think about was an image of the last time he saw Ava on the street, in her little blue dress, her hair done, carefree and laughing—like she hadn't murdered so many people; like life was just one adventure after another.

He'd hugged her good-bye that day, felt her smallness against him. Fragile and brittle, yet made of iron. There hadn't been a day he didn't wonder about her. He still had the American Airlines record locator for the ticket she'd purchased for him so they could meet in Tuscany. Share some fantasy of a life together. He'd stood her up. She'd known he would, but buying the ticket—first class—and giving it to him had been just another in a long series of provocations on her part.

"Are you seeing her anytime soon? Joanne?" he asked.

She shook her head. "She did say something that I thought was interesting."

"Yeah?"

"She didn't know I was on suspension and said she was coming to Camden and said we should meet out in front of the courthouse. Get lunch. So, I asked her why she was coming. I didn't know if she had court or needed to finish something for the judge."

She pushed a drink to him, but he waved it away. He definitely didn't want any more to drink this early in the day. It wasn't even two o'clock. He started to get up from the bar stool.

"But it was neither of those two things. She said she was going to the jail. To visit that nun who's being held on a parole violation. You know, the case you were involved in?"

He stopped. "Marie Saunders? Did she say why?"

"She said the nun sent her a postcard. From the jail. You know those postcards they give them when they go in? Yeah. And that she needed to go see her for something."

"That doesn't make any sense. What'd the postcard say?" His mind was ricocheting through everything he knew about the two women. Joanne had seen and talked to Marie only a few times. Marie—a conniving psychopath not so unlike her niece, Ava—wasn't above stealing, beating someone, maybe even killing if it served her purpose. He'd seen what she'd done to Ava firsthand, smashing her in the head and leaving her in a heap in the cemetery.

Isabelle smiled and swirled her drink. "We didn't have a long conversation or anything. Just a few texts back and forth."

"When is this visit taking place? Did she say?"

"Today."

Russell slid his empty glass onto the bar and headed for the door. He could hear Isabelle saying something, but he didn't bother to respond.

It was risky going to her house. She might call the police. Or throw him out, or worse than either of those things, start to cry. He'd never admit it to anyone, but he'd stalked Joanne a little bit since she'd cut him off. Not really stalked, more like driven by her house for no reason just to see if her car was there. She'd taken a vacation with Ava's money, then boom, one day her car was back in the driveway. He knew she'd appeared in court for her hearing. Her charges had been dismissed—all of them, obstruction of justice, tampering with evidence—but she'd opted to leave her job with the judge's chambers anyway. Too much had happened.

Her car was in the driveway, the house was still, the blinds were drawn. Russell pulled up out front and waited. He closed his eyes. The person he cared about more than anything, more than his family, his other friends, maybe more than Juliette and Ava, was behind that door. Their relationship had been forged through the worst experiences, and she'd been steadfast through it all. But when Juliette died, when Joanne found out he'd taunted his fiancée with his knowledge of her affair, told her she should kill herself, even got the vial of potassium chloride from her medical bag, Joanne had had enough.

He hadn't meant it, of course he hadn't. But Joanne was right to be disgusted with him. And he knew he'd spend the rest of his life paying penance for the way he'd treated Juliette. Yet he needed desperately for his best friend to absolve him.

He saw Joanne's front door open. He hadn't wanted it to be like this. He'd wanted to take his time and go to the door, plead his case. Before he could decide how to handle it, he saw a male figure walk out onto the front porch with Joanne. The house was less than twenty yards from the street. He could see them clearly, Joanne with her arms folded across her body. The man was not her ex-husband, Tim, or her son, Steven. It was Andrew Baldwin, a lawyer. Everyone who worked in the courthouse knew him, but Russell was surprised Joanne knew him so well.

He slid the passenger's-side window down and held his breath. They didn't notice.

"Look, I'm just the messenger, Joanne. The middleman. Don't kill the middleman."

"Being a middleman for Marie might be a fate worse than death. In fact, it might literally kill you. Be careful."

"She just asked me to plead with you to visit her. Nothing more. I've been paid, this job is done."

"What does she want from me?"

"I think she wants to clear things up. And she has something important to tell you about the postcard she mailed you." He headed down the four steps to the sidewalk without a look back and walked right past Russell's Jeep without a glance sideways. Joanne turned to go back in her house, and Russell bolted out of the car to her door before she could get inside.

"Joanne—"

Her eyes went wide. “No, no, no. Uh-uh. Not this time.”

“Don’t go see Marie. Why would you do that?” he said.

Her shoulders slumped, and she went inside, holding the door for him to follow. She said nothing but went to the kitchen table and picked up a small postcard and handed it to him.

He scanned it twice. Then he read it again. Seven sentences. “Shit” was all that came out of his mouth.

“Now get out” was her response.

“Wait, what does this note even mean?”

CHAPTER 6

Ava

Vicenza, Italy

I stared back at Davide's mother, who was so afraid someone might overhear what she was saying that she was whispering. The wind was picking up, rattling the trees and dropping debris down onto us. Francesca Tosi didn't move to go back inside, so neither did I.

"Why do you say that—that you think the DeFeos saw my father that night?"

"They denied it. And I have no proof, but after Davide disappeared, I took his room apart looking for any clue where he'd gone. All his clothes were there, I think—it's so hard to know if a few things were missing. He was starting university in September, so he had books. But I found two things that were interesting. A string of numbers on a piece of paper."

"A telephone number?"

She shook her head. "Too long." She half laughed. "I had nothing but time to figure it out, but finally I found the other piece. A bank slip mixed in with some papers in a bag. I connected them and went to the bank. He had an account there, in a bank we never used, on the other side of town."

"And?" She was telling the story too slowly for me.

"It still had the equivalent of fourteen thousand two hundred and twenty euros in it. Apparently he'd withdrawn ten thousand euros two days before he disappeared."

"And you have no idea where it came from?"

"No. We don't have that kind of money sitting around."

"But why do you think it had something to do with Victor?" I was confused.

"Where else would Davide have gotten money like that from? He worked as a busboy in a restaurant. Sometimes as a waiter. So, I think it was from Victor. I just don't know why. But there's more. Philomena looked odd, caught off guard when I asked her about it. She started to say something but stopped herself."

"What'd she say?"

"She said Davide had called their house that night—the night he disappeared. But then she stopped talking. She wouldn't say another word."

I stood up. It was getting colder, and my legs felt frozen to the metal chair. "You told the authorities so they could investigate them? Interview the DeFeos?"

She was shivering but didn't move. "The police talked to them, interviewed them over and over, and came up with nothing. So who am I to say? But they know more than they're telling."

"But what about the account, the money?"

"The account was opened six months before with a deposit of forty-eight million lire—about twenty-five thousand euros. Davide was eighteen at the time, not a minor, so it was only his signature on the account. He signed the card. I know his writing. It was his writing."

"Did they find where the money came from? Transfer from another account, anything?"

"Untraceable. The police got nothing."

"And the fourteen thousand left in the account? Nobody ever tried to reach out for it?"

"You mean did Davide or someone posing as him try to withdraw or transfer any of it? No. Ten years after his disappearance, we filed with the courts for a death certificate, and the money was given to us." It suddenly occurred to her we were both freezing. "I'm so sorry, I got lost in my words. Come in. Have something warm to drink." Her eyes scanned my body as she was speaking. I knew an offer of a meal was next. I'd forgotten to eat these past few days, and my clothes were even looser, if that was possible.

I refused everything but coffee, black. She took me through her living room, showing me pictures of Davide growing up. I felt my skin tingling. The resemblance to me was unmistakable, down to the shape of our faces.

"Do you think he's alive?" I asked. "In your heart?"

She stared a long time before answering. "I want him to be. I do. But I can't. His passport was missing, so I think he went to find Adrianna. I think he was with you and your mother and was killed."

"Did the police check his passport to see if he left the country?" It seemed so obvious to me.

"This isn't the United States. He could have gone to France and then anywhere in Europe before leaving for America. It makes it harder. And a nineteen-year-old missing person who ran away with his girlfriend isn't high priority for the police. They supposedly exhausted all leads."

"What about your husband? What does he think?"

She shook her head. "Benito passed away almost five years ago." Her eyes were glassy. "He lost hope that Davide was alive. And in the end it was probably too late for him to open his arms to you." She dropped her head. "I'm sorry."

I nodded. I was a pariah to both sets of grandparents.

I felt light-headed, and the jolt of caffeine wasn't helping. Davide had taken the money because he knew he was leaving, but not all of it, because presumably he expected to come back. I needed Russell. Someone who would know where to start unraveling this and could try and pick up a trace of him in the States.

I turned on my phone, hesitating, unsure I wanted to draw Russell Bowers into this. He and I had a sordid past, a one-night drunken stand, a weird destructive connection that hurt us both. But when I thought of him, my heart always stood still for half a second.

My phone started ringing in my hand.

"Ava, are you still in Italy?" Philomena.

"I'm still in Vicenza," I responded.

"Then come back here first before you leave town. To the house. I need to talk to you. To give you something. It's important."

"Tonight? What's wrong?"

"Yes, tonight. The back door will be open. Come in through the mudroom. You don't want to leave Italy without talking to me. Promise me?" Her voice was shaky, slightly off. "There's something you need to know."

"Is this about my money?"

"Much more important than money. It's about your life."

CHAPTER 7

RUSSELL

Haddon Township, New Jersey

Joanne had thrown him out. The look in her eye hadn't changed in the two weeks since he'd seen her last. She wasn't ready to forgive him for being a scumbag. And it wasn't only what he'd done to Juliette. It was more than that. It was the sleazy way he'd hooked up with Bridgette, Marie's parole officer. It was the way he'd glommed onto Ava, even after knowing she was a manipulative murderer. It was the way he'd carried himself over the past six months, lying, scheming, hiding.

She'd held him up as her version of what a good guy was supposed to be. Her good guy always treated his girlfriends with respect, was never chauvinistic. He cheered them on when they got a promotion, did the dishes, vacuumed, washed their lingerie in cold water and hand-wrung it to air-dry. He complimented his women endlessly, even when they lounged in dirty sweats for three days in a row and their hair looked like greasy straw. Good guys were always ready with a shoulder or foot massage or a hug.

Good guys never asked for sex. They waited for it to be freely given, and when it was, they were only finished when she was finished. Or they were finished when she was finished, even if they weren't. They never even glanced at other women in public. Never considered cheating. And they never ever said or even thought that a woman's ass looked fat in those pants.

He wasn't the good guy Joanne had wanted him to be. He'd been selfish, angry, self-indulgent. He'd resented Juliette for the hours and pressure medical school and her residency had put on them, on their relationship. He drank too much sometimes, he looked at porn. He thought about having sex more than he'd admit. And he'd cheated on her first with Ava, and then Bridgette. But it was Ava who counted. Ava had crawled into his brain and never left.

That's why the postcard Marie had sent to Joanne upset him. He was surprised the jail hadn't pulled it before it left the facility. It should've caught someone's attention. The words were simple, not lost in a complicated paragraph.

> *Ava is going to kill again. I know who and I know where. I need to tell you in person. Come and visit me at the jail. If you don't, you'll hear about it on the news. And you'll be sorry. It doesn't have to happen.*

Ava was in Italy or France, or maybe Asia by now. There was no way Marie could have any idea what she was up to. But he knew Joanne couldn't ignore the message either. She had options. She could take it to Internal Affairs at the jail and let them deal with it. Marie could then say it had been a joke, or that she'd just wanted to bother Joanne. Neither of those things would sit well with the parole board, and Marie was smart enough to know that. So why risk it?

There had to be enough upside to make the risk worthwhile for her. Maybe Marie wanted to hurt Joanne and was using the card as bait. But that didn't make sense either. Anything Marie did would fall right back down on her. He needed to fix this.

He picked up his phone and dialed Joanne's number. She answered on the second ring. "I don't want to talk, Russell. That's why I asked you to leave."

"Don't hang up, Joanne. We need to figure this out."

"There's no *we*. I'm going to see her. See what she says. I'm going to let the officers know I'm afraid. I won't be alone with her—"

"Those visits are all virtual now, Joanne. The only contact visits are lawyers, doctors doing psych evals, or cops. You're not going to see her face-to-face."

"So—"

"You have to make an appointment, and then either go in and use the jail's equipment for a virtual visit—you're in the lobby, she's in the unit—or I think you can do it from home if you have the right setup. I'm not sure that's what Marie had in mind."

"And there's no way to get into the unit?"

"I don't think so, Jo. You got in last time because they thought you were a cop. And now that you're an ex-inmate, that's going to be a definite no."

"I'll call them—"

"But I think if you set up the visit from your house, you should let me come over."

"No—"

"I'm not the person you thought I was. I know. I'm not. I'm shitty. Shittier now than ever. I drink, I'm angry all the time. I didn't treat Juliette right. I get that. I'm sorry. It wasn't about hurting her, or you—"

"You fucking told her to kill herself and left the needle and the potassium chloride next to her. What is wrong with you?"

"You really think I thought she'd do it? I was angry. Joanne, she lied and cheated too. And got pregnant by another man. I can't rehash this with you. We went over all of this before. There's no place lower for me to go now. You have no idea how sorry I am for all of it, and if you don't think I've paid, you're wrong. But I miss you . . . and you can't handle Marie on your own. You know that. Let me help you."

"I need to think about this. Maybe I'll just turn the postcard over to the police and be done with it. I don't want to be involved in round three with this family." There was a moment of silence. Then, "But you do."

"Who would Ava want to kill, do you think?" he asked, ignoring that last statement.

"She doesn't just randomly kill people. There's always a reason, even if it only makes sense to her. So it's hard to know what she's doing out there, wherever she is. Look . . ." Her voice slowed and then stopped.

"I know things between us aren't going to be the same. But let's just do this one thing together. Call and arrange the visit. My house or yours. Get it all set up, and see what this woman has to say. We've got nothing to lose, really. Please, Joanne? And then turn it over to the police."

His phone was buzzing that he had another call. He looked at the number. It was a bizarre string that he knew immediately was international.

"I gotta take this. Think about it?"

The voice started speaking the minute he clicked onto the call. "Russell—" The line was as crackly and broken as the voice. It was a female with a bit of an accent. And the background noise provided an extra layer of commotion over everything she was saying.

"Who is this?" But he knew who it was. Ava.

"I didn't know who else to call. Don't say anything. Just listen. I'm still in Vicenza, but I'm leaving for Geneva tomorrow. I need your help."

"What's happening? What's wrong? Have you done something? Marie said—"

"Forget Marie."

"She said someone was going to die. Whatever is going on, Ava, don't do it. Don't do it—"

"I have no reason to hurt anyone. I'm headed to Geneva in the morning, but I need to see Philomena tonight. The reason I'm calling is I need you to help me find my father. This is crazy. He disappeared—I need you to come here, to Italy."

"It's a lot to ask for someone to just jump up and fly to Europe," Russell responded.

"It's not that hard. I'll pay you back for the ticket at some point. If you hear the story about my father . . . poof, gone, right around the same time my mother vanished . . . it's interesting. Right up your alley—"

The connection broke, and Russell just stared at the phone for a few minutes trying to put it all together. He knew in his heart this was just the beginning of something horrible.

CHAPTER 8

Victor

Vicenza, Italy

If only things had been different that night. Like maybe he'd been closer to the phone when it rang so that he answered it and not Philomena. And he'd just picked up the receiver and put it down, without hearing a word. Many nights he'd dreamed about it. Or that they hadn't been home at all when the call came, that they were out to dinner like Philomena had wanted. She'd suggested it, that they go have a bite in town, get out of the house. He'd ignored her.

It was almost like she had known what was going to happen and didn't want to be there. Adrianna had been missing for three weeks and more by then. The worrying, the waiting for word, was making both their nerves taut, stretched to the point of snapping. But the phone rang, and Philomena was standing next to it. He saw her hand reaching for it, slow motion in his mind, though it had only taken a second.

When he put the receiver to his ear, he heard the screaming. Davide, out of breath, running. Why was he calling them on the landline? Something had gone very wrong.

The boy had spoken so fast his words blurred together. He kept saying the same thing over and over, until Victor hung up and raced out of the house:

"Come to Cresole. The park."

Cresole was a village about a fifteen-minute drive north from Vicenza proper. Victor made good time getting there that night—the roads had been relatively empty—driving past the smattering of buildings, the Rangers rugby field where Davide played. His head was spinning. Philomena answering that phone had created an unnecessary complication he thought he'd deal with later, but never really could.

When he pulled his car over next to the park in Cresole, there were voices in the distance. More than one person, but he couldn't see anything. He got out of his car and walked onto the green, looking out into the distance. Then he saw him—Davide. He was on the ground, his phone next to him, the screen on, as if he'd been taking a call when he fell and the person at the other end never hung up.

He'd gone over and seen that Davide was breathing, then gingerly pushed the "Off" button on the phone, but not before realizing the person listening had been Philomena. She must have called back. He looked up from the glare of the phone screen, his eyes adjusting to the dark. There were other people in the park. Most were just shadowy figures running away. But one caught his eye.

"Adrianna?" he'd called. He knew it was her. She was standing there, her back to him, but he'd know her anywhere. The child in her arms was the giveaway. But how could she be there? It made no sense. He started to run toward her when he was tackled from behind and forced flat onto his stomach. His last glimpse of his daughter and granddaughter was of Adrianna slipping to her knees, then getting up and trudging forward out of view.

He looked up. It had been Davide that had tackled him to the ground. "What's the matter with you?" he sputtered. "That was Adrianna. She's not gone. She's here."

"No, it wasn't," he'd responded. "She was never here. What is wrong with you?"

"It was!" He was on his feet now. "What's going on, Davide?"

"I called you, but you got here too late."

"For what?"

"It's over. You need to get out of here now. I mean right now, before they blame you."

Davide, in one swift move, threw his bag over his shoulder—his clothes were stained with dark matter, either from playing rugby on a muddy field, or something that had happened afterward—pulled a knit cap down onto his head, and charged out of the park.

Victor had been stunned, confused. Blamed for what? He'd wandered through the park in the direction he'd seen Adrianna go. The park was poorly lit, so he was stumbling up the hill but then stopped. A neon-pink squeaky toy. People brought plenty of dogs to this park, but this wasn't a dog toy. Philomena had bought something like it for Giada at the supermarket where she did her weekly shopping. The baby had seen the toy and wouldn't let it go. It ended up mixed in with the groceries on the conveyor belt.

He picked it up and inspected it. It was covered in teeth marks. From a little dog or a little child? And all of this wouldn't have mattered at all—so what if Adrianna had come back from Tuscany? So what if they were in the park together?—except there was a man killed in that very park that night. A man from a prominent local family, stabbed six times. Witnesses said they saw people running from the park out onto the street.

Victor had waited as the police investigated, waited for someone to report his license plate or give his general description. It never happened. And he never saw his daughter, granddaughter, or the boyfriend again.

The murder in the park was never solved, but the murdered man's wife kept pressure on the police to find the culprit and hired a private investigator to search through every bit of information. Every so often, Victor would see the man's death in the headlines again—that police had a clue, or a new witness, or a friend of the man remembered something—but it amounted to nothing. Not even twenty years was enough time for it all to go away, though. The man's wife had enough money; as long as she was still alive, she would never forget what happened that night.

And Victor sat back, kept his mouth shut. He'd stuffed the child's toy and Davide's phone into a drawer in the spare bedroom along with a written account of everything he knew, everything he remembered from that night in minute detail. From the blue car that was driving slowly when he was trying to get to the park—a woman behind the wheel—to the temperature outside, to the way Adrianna looked as she was running up the hill away from him. He did it so he could remember everything if he needed it. Or maybe he thought he could figure it all out if he went over it enough. Either way, the papers and the toy had been there, exactly where he'd put them, until Giada, all grown up, had shown up at the door with a new name. Ava. Did she remember anything from that night? Her eyes gave away nothing.

He was in the spare bedroom now. It was in disarray. Drawers were spilled across the floor. He'd hidden the things well, but then, nobody had been looking for them. Other than Philomena, the only person who had been in here recently was Ava. Ava DeFeo Tosi Lavoisier Saunders. The girl who came from nowhere, out of nowhere, like Athena springing from Zeus's head—smart, edgy, with a chip on her shoulder. Philomena had invited her to stay and made her a space in this room before Victor even knew what was happening, before he could protect himself.

It seemed she'd burst through the door, after a twenty-year absence, with questions and money. And unnerving Tosi eyes. She was a ghost, and it made him shudder every time he had to look at her. Her eyes always seemed to hold the same expression as Davide's that night in the park. Terrified, arrogant, angry. If she'd taken the things from this room, he needed to get them back.

He looked at the clock. Almost eleven. He felt a sharp pressure in his chest. His phone dinged, and he was sure it was Philomena texting him, wanting to rehash their fight, but it wasn't. The number came up as unknown. *It's a countdown. How long will you live, Victor?*

He heard a noise and peered out the window and saw Ava's slim shape pressing against the door of the mudroom.

CHAPTER 9

Joanne

Haddon Township, New Jersey

She hung up the phone and looked at the postcard again. Mailed from the Camden County Correctional Facility. Marie was trying to drag her back into the melee, and she didn't want to go. She read the words on the back, neatly printed in pencil.

> *Ava is going to kill again. I know who and I know where. I need to tell you in person. Come and visit me at the jail. If you don't, you'll hear about it on the news. And you'll be sorry. It doesn't have to happen.*

Russell wanted to get in on this, sit in on the visit with Marie, sop up all the information he could about Ava, because for him it was always about Ava. She tried to think back to the days when they were working in the courthouse together. Ava was just a translator. Russell was just a detective for the Prosecutor's Office, and she was just a secretary for Judge Simmons. She used to try and push Ava and Russell together, even knowing that Russell had a fiancée. She had wanted Juliette out of the way and for Ava and Russell to find each other.

Little did she know how her wishes would come true. Juliette was dead. And Russell had wrapped himself so completely around Ava that he'd lost his career, his grounding, his life. Ava was pretty in a very skinny way, with a good face and big green eyes. Sophisticated, preferring head-to-toe black and simple jewelry. And she was smart and resourceful like no one Joanne had ever met. If Joanne were ever arrested in a third-world country, she'd want Ava by her side, hands down. But Ava was also reckless, crazy, unpredictable, and not above killing anyone that got in her way. A frightening, edgy, brilliant nightmare.

Joanne couldn't sit by and watch Russell descend into her clutches again. So, she was going to go on this visit herself, and no matter what happened, she'd deal with it. She dialed the number to the jail and waited. After being put on hold and transferred three times, she was told to come in and register in person. There was a potential spot open at 4:00 that afternoon. She was going to have to trek to Camden, to her old stomping ground, and wait in line with all the other visitors, in the cold, if she wanted to see Marie.

It was almost like her brain was on automatic, driving onto Route 70 and taking the cutoff to Admiral Wilson Boulevard, then the exit to Martin Luther toward the aquarium. For the past seven years she'd done this drive to the courthouse, only this time her nice little parking pass was no longer valid. She was going to have to pay at a meter and walk.

Her feet hurt, and she was nervous as she stood in line waiting for the big industrial green metal doors to the jail to open. Ten minutes later she was processed and led into another room filled with computers. The machine in front of her suddenly went on, and Marie's face was there, larger than life. It filled the screen, and Joanne picked up the telephone and pushed back in her seat automatically to get away. Marie was gaunt and pale. Her hair looked frazzled and greasy, but her features were still strikingly pretty, even with no makeup and probably no sleep.

"Hello, Joanne. I'm so glad you got my postcard. I was surprised when they said you were coming to visit." Marie had an odd expression on her face. Hard to read.

"I'm here. But I'm not sure why. If you think Ava's going to kill someone, tell the police. Why go through all of this by sending a postcard to me?"

"You need to go to Tuscany. I can't do it, obviously."

Joanne started to laugh, but it caught in her throat. "There's no way. No way in hell that I'm getting involved in any of this. But thanks for the invite." She started to put the phone back on the hook.

"Don't you even want to know who's going to die and why?"

Joanne shook her head. "No."

"What if I said it was someone you know?"

Joanne's arm went out to the side. "Who do I know that knows Ava? You? Russell? Me? She's going to kill one of us now?"

"Okay, okay, maybe it's someone you know *of*."

"Enough games, Marie. Enjoy county." She pushed herself up off the seat. "Here's a tip. Save the fruit and bread from your tray. It might be all that's edible, and you'll be hungry later."

"Ava is going to kill her grandfather Victor. You need to warn Philomena. I can't. I can't call long distance on these pay phones. And mailing a letter would take eons."

"Tell the police—how about that? Tell your lawyer."

"No. By the time the US police contact the Italian police, it'll be too late. You have to stop it."

Joanne sat back down. "How can you possibly know this, Marie? You've been in here since you got back in this country."

"Life with Ava is chess, not checkers, Joanne. Don't take your eyes off your king—"

"Meaning?"

"I know more about that family than you do. I know just about everything about the DeFeos—growing up with Anais helped. Ava's father disappeared right after her mother came to the States. Right around the same time her mother was being murdered. Poof, gone. Never seen or heard from again. Did you know that?"

Joanne's head was spinning. How many more cracks could there be in Ava's life? It was a cesspool of murder and intrigue. No wonder she was so screwed up. "Seriously? A report Russell got on the family weeks ago, when we were looking for Ava, said he was living in Vicenza. That's not true?"

Marie shrugged. "His family is. But not him. And Victor might be at the center of his disappearance. Anais always thought so. It's just a matter of time—Ava asking questions about him, putting pieces together, Victor there, refusing to answer. Ava takes revenge. I give it maybe a week, and he'll be dead. Mark my words."

Joanne leaned in and put her hand to her face. "You have it all figured out, but it's all just speculation. You don't know anything. But send a postcard to Russell. He'll go there, I'm sure."

Marie cackled, and it took Joanne by surprise. "Aww, Joanne. Still lovesick over that man? Can't forgive him for loving Ava? Tsk, tsk. Sad, really, what you've done for him, and he's chased after that little tiny woman—he must like them skinny—and destroyed your life."

Joanne couldn't help but run a hand over her sweater, pulling it down. She suddenly felt fat and dumpy. She pushed up again from the chair. "I'll call Philomena. That's what I'll do, no more, no less. None of this is my business. Bye, Marie, good seeing you." She leaned in to put the phone on the hook.

"Good move, stealing my purse the last time we met," Marie spat. That was true. Joanne had gone to the parole office and walked off with Marie's purse and had then given it to Ava. "It's because of you that Ava got the code from the letter in my purse and accessed my money.

But don't worry, we'll settle that score later, Joanne. Bye for now." The screen went blank.

She sat back down for a minute, her breath gone. Just like that, she was pulled back in with this family and felt angry, anxious, worried. Not this time. Ava wasn't in the United States. Joanne didn't need to get involved. As far as she was concerned, this little visit never took place.

CHAPTER 10

PHILOMENA

Vicenza, Italy

She sat in the car. Her hands were shaking, and she clasped them together to still them, then turned on the engine and headed out into the street. She was going to try one more thing. One more. She had no choice. Victor would never tell her what happened that night that Davide called the house. He had never admitted it was really true. But she had a feeling things were going to start again. And not because of Ava.

It was cyclical, coming around again every seven years or so. The unsolved murder in the Cresole park. An article would appear in the paper, then the interviews would begin. The dead man's wife would be front and center, witnesses' testimony would be dissected. And a footnote to all of it, just a line in fine print at the bottom, that a nineteen-year-old boy, Davide Tosi, disappeared the same night Tommaso Lacroce was stabbed in the park and left to die in the dark.

There was a connection between the two events. Philomena had always known that. From the minute she'd heard on the news that Tommaso Lacroce had been found dead, she could think of little else. His brownish hair, the way his mouth twisted when he was angry—an expression he'd had even at thirteen. She never told anyone she'd known the man years before. Tommaso's image had been all over the pages of her photograph albums until she'd ripped them apart and threw them in the trash, trying to forget that they had spent a turbulent year together in a foreign country and shared horrible secrets.

Her introduction to his wife, Olivia, had happened after Tommaso's death, in the midst of the investigation—the two events, dead man and missing boy, weren't necessarily linked, but the police brought them together to see if there was a connection—both events occurring on the same night in the relatively small town of Cresole was odd.

The wife was younger than Tommaso by many years, with short reddish hair, and very alert, inquisitive, smart. Philomena knew then, in that instant, that Olivia would never let his death go. Ever. And the uncertainty of whether Tommaso had mentioned Philomena, or spilled their secrets, made her acutely uncomfortable.

She rounded the corner and parked on the road in front of the house. The neighborhood was full of tall fences with locked gates, surveillance cameras, private security. She'd ventured there only once before, and that was upon invitation so Olivia's private investigator could pick her brain, ask questions. Uninvited doorbell ringing might be a less satisfying experience.

She rang anyway and waited. From what she could see, a few lights glowed from windows in the upper floors. She was rousing Olivia, who, no doubt, was getting ready to retire for the night. Finally, the intercom crackled.

"Yes?"

"Olivia? Is that you? It's Philomena DeFeo. I only need a minute, please?"

There were a few seconds of delay, and then the gate popped open. Philomena wasn't sure it would. Olivia Lacroce appeared at the door in a pale robe tied tight at the waist. Her hair was combed back, her face was cleaned and unadorned. She looked older than the last time Philomena had seen her.

"What's happened? Why are you here so late? You have some information about Tommaso?"

She shook her head. "Why would you assume that?"

"Because there would be no other reason for this visit. Not at this hour."

"No. I don't know who killed him if that's what you mean."

"Then what?" She wasn't moving from her doorway to let Philomena in, so Philomena just stood there, rubbing her hands together.

"I just need to talk. It's been so hard since they identified Adrianna's body. I knew you were the one person who would understand."

Olivia finally moved and waved Philomena in. They took a seat in a small parlor. "I understand the pain of losing your daughter. I heard the news. But it's late for a visit, and her death had nothing to do with my husband being stabbed six times and left to die in the dirt twenty years ago. Does it?"

Philomena's head whipped back and forth. "No. Other than they happened within a short time of one another, I don't believe so. But your husband died the same night Davide disappeared."

Olivia pushed back in her seat. "Ah, yes. Davide Tosi. Is he dead too? Did they find his body?"

Philomena shrugged and felt tears welling up in her eyes. "I don't know. How can I know that? Nobody has seen him since then, so I can't imagine he's out there somewhere and doesn't call—"

"So why are you here at this hour? What do you want from me?"

She cleared her throat. "Hearing about Adrianna has brought so much back to me. And I was thinking about the last report of Davide being seen near the pay phone, at the bus line to—"

"To Cresole. You think Davide was in the park when Tommaso was killed?"

"Is there a connection between them? Did Tommaso know him? Know of him? Somehow?"

Olivia leaned in toward Philomena. "I've had a private investigator looking into my husband's death for the past twenty years. Every witness, every report. He's interviewed them all multiple times—the woman who found him in the park and tried to stop the blood with her hands, who called the ambulance at exactly 11:12. The witnesses who saw a group of young people running down the street around that time. The residents in the houses all around there. He even got footage of the street from surveillance cameras—maybe not as good as they have now—but still, nothing came of it. The angle was wrong. He went through Tommaso's phone. Incoming, outgoing calls—"

"But—"

"In nineteen ninety-six the phones were not so sophisticated, but it was enough. We've been through everything, and if I thought for one minute that Davide Tosi had something to do with his death, I would have been at his family's doorway long ago. Besides, Tosi has nothing to do with you really. Other than he was . . . with your daughter. Her boyfriend?"

"We always assumed Davide went to join Adrianna in America. But if he didn't, then where did he go after that night? Why? I think the two of them are connected somehow. I want to help you." She noticed the quizzical expression on Olivia's face as the words came out of her mouth.

"How, Philomena? How can you help me? Do you know something—" She swallowed hard. "Tommaso left me to raise my son alone. He was only forty-one when he was killed. His life was taken—"

It was the first time she realized Olivia was at least ten years younger than Tommaso. "Adrianna's life was taken too. And maybe Davide's. And they *were* connected in one way—"

"They played rugby, I know. Tommaso was a coach for another team." She waved a hand dismissively. "The teams may have matched against one another at one point, maybe Davide and Tommaso even met after a game, but my investigator found nothing—"

"There's something else, Olivia."

"Anais Lavoisier?"

The name brought a chill to Philomena's heart. "Yes."

"My husband may have known her years ago, my investigator said. But it's a thin connection—"

"Thin? Your husband knew her. I spent time with her too. She knew my husband, Victor, too. I believe in my heart that she had something to do with Adrianna being in Philadelphia, maybe even her death. And, in turn, your husband's. We have to find the connection together."

"What connection could Anais have to Davide? You think we know more than police? Than investigators?"

"What if I have some information that has been hidden?"

"What information, Philomena?"

"I need your word—"

"Why?" Olivia looked weary now. "Why the secret? If you know something, turn it over."

"Because Victor is connected to this. I know he is, and I want to figure it out on my own. Please?"

She nodded. "Yes, yes. Anything to find out who killed my husband. Just between us for now."

Philomena pulled out the old Nokia phone that had belonged to Davide and placed it on the table. It landed hard and spun around before stopping. Both women stared at it without saying a word.

CHAPTER 11

RUSSELL

Cherry Hill, New Jersey

Russell went home and surveyed things from the doorway. The disarray matched what was left of his life. The living room was filled with clothes taken off and dropped onto the floor. Dirty dishes, silverware, papers, mail opened and put down. His house looked like Ava's had when he'd first started spending time with her, not long after her adoptive mother, Claire, had died. Now he had an idea of what was going on in her mind at that time. He was distracted, disinterested, angry, anxious, remorseful. But he hadn't gotten to the point where he'd kill someone yet. He wasn't exactly like Ava.

Ava's phone call was bothering him so that he couldn't think of anything else. Ava had gone off, free and clear. She had money, everything she'd wanted, almost. Yet Marie was predicting she was going to kill again, and Ava was reaching out asking him for help. How could things have gone so wrong?

"Are you going in or out?"

He turned around. Joanne. "I can't believe you're really here—you're not mad at me anymore?" He reached out to hug her.

She pushed past him. "I'm not here to make up with you. Or to make small talk. I just came from the jail—"

He followed her in and shut the door. "You saw Marie, then?"

Her eyes scanned the room and then locked onto his. "Your life is literally a mess. Yes. I saw Marie, and I didn't want to come here. I swear to God, I was going to keep going. But I can't live with what she said. I'm not like you and Ava. Cheating, lying, killing—it all makes me sick. I can't pretend I don't know—"

"Enough of the moralizing, Joanne. We all know you're better than us—"

"Not better, Russell." She moved up so she was a couple of inches from his face. "I'm just not a scumbag." She dropped her purse onto the floor.

"Okay."

"Okay." Then she was silent. "Look, never mind. Marie said Ava is going to kill her grandfather." She sat down. "Get this. You're not going to believe it. It's blowing my mind. Ava's father? Not a simple story. He disappeared off the face of the earth shortly after her mother disappeared."

"That's not possible. The reports I got said he was living in Vicenza. Remember?" He searched through a pile of papers on his coffee table until he found the ones he was looking for.

She shook her head. "His family is in Vicenza, yes. Not him. He's not been seen or heard from in twenty years."

"Hmmm. So, they both vanished around the same time. But look, right here." He showed her a page. "This says Adrianna was killed in that church a year after she vanished, not weeks—"

"I don't know who's doing your intel, Russell, but that's not true either. She wasn't missing that long before she was killed. Maybe a month at the most."

His brow was scrunched as he stared at the pages. "Did he follow Adrianna here, then? Is that what happened? And then got killed too?"

"That's why I'm here, Russell. It's too interesting not to tell you about it. That, and if Victor DeFeo dies and I never said anything, my house would look like this, and I'd be sitting at the bar all day too."

He ignored that comment. "There was nothing in any reports about Adrianna's murder that indicated another body was found that might be connected. But maybe the cops weren't looking for it."

"We know who killed Adrianna. The four men—Saunders, Quinn, Owens, and Connelly. All of them are dead. And Adrianna was never really the target; they were there at the church that night to kill the priest, and she just happened to show up. It's hard to believe they would've just randomly killed Davide too."

"And when could they have done that?" he asked. "After Adrianna was killed, it seems Ross Saunders just grabbed Ava and left, then dropped her off with Claire."

"Are you still in the good graces of anyone on the force that can look into it?"

He shrugged. "Maybe. Just maybe. But here's the thing. Ava called me, when I hung up talking to you—"

"And?"

"It was short. She said I needed to come to Vicenza. It was urgent. She needed me or something like that."

Joanne shot him a side-eyed look. "But she didn't say why?"

"To look into her father's disappearance. Then she just hung up."

"Don't go to Vicenza. Call the Italian police, Russell. Let it go. Stay here and look into Davide. Please don't get drawn into the Ava stuff again. Please?"

He dropped his head and ran his hands over his hair. "Joanne—"

"What, Russell?"

"I can't call the police. She hasn't done anything for sure. They'll know she's alive. And I promised her I wouldn't do that."

"So by all means let her kill again. She catches you in this trap *every time*. Think back to the beginning. It was 'I can't turn this in because of Ava.'"

"I can't—"

She picked up her bag. "You're obsessed with her. That's the reason you let her go twice, knowing she's a murderer. The reason you gave up your career for her. The reason you'd rather let another person die than report her."

"Joanne—"

She opened the door. "Not now. I'm going to soak my soul in a glass of wine and decide if I'm going to call the police in Italy. Because I'm not sure I can live with myself any other way."

"Meet me here tomorrow? Let's start by rereading the reports on Adrianna's death. See if there's anything in there that we missed? And bring a bag—a few days' clothes. Basic toiletries, just in case?"

"Whatever, Russell." She walked out and shut the door behind her.

CHAPTER 12

Philomena

Vicenza, Italy

Ava. She'd forgotten Ava. She'd called her to come back to the house. That was before the fight with Victor. Before she'd come in and found him in an uproar pulling apart the entire house. Before he'd accused her of trying to destroy him. She'd wanted to make it up to Ava for her abrupt departure earlier. She wanted to bring her back, give her everything she'd need to find her father, along with some money, maybe not all the money that was in the account, but some. She wanted to make it right. This girl was the only grandchild she'd ever have. She wasn't going to see her lost in the world without at least trying to give her an edge. But instead Philomena had fled, opting to visit Olivia to rehash events from years ago.

The back door was now unlocked and slightly ajar. She couldn't remember how she'd left it when she'd raced out earlier. She flipped the switch and watched the light flicker several times and then go on. It was an old incandescent bulb in need of changing. She'd meant to do it before and had forgotten. The mudroom was empty. She started for the door at the other end of the room and stumbled on the pair of dark-green wellingtons Victor had worn when he'd cleaned the shed earlier. Her ankle turned; her hand reached for a shelf to steady herself.

"Dannazione, Victor," she muttered.

Something sharp sliced at the skin on her hand. When she pulled her hand back, there was moisture on it. The light was dim; she wiped her hand on her pants and kept going through the door to the living room. There was no sign that Ava had been there, no glasses on the table, nothing had been moved. No indication Victor had had company.

"Victor?" No answer. "Victor? Where are you?"

The lights to the hallway were off, but she hesitated in turning them on. She sensed someone was there. The sounds of shallow breaths came to her from somewhere above on the staircase.

Turn the light on. She said it over and over to herself, but her hand wouldn't obey. "Ava? Are you here? What's happening?"

She heard the sound of a cough and labored breath and raced up the steps, hitting the switch as she moved. Victor was on his side in the hallway, his head on the carpet, blood-tinged foam pouring from his mouth. She knelt beside him and turned his head. "What happened?" she whispered. "Can you talk?" She put a hand to his chest and felt it rise and fall beneath her fingers. "Hold on, let me call the ambulance." She picked up her phone and dialed the number, her voice cracking as she gave the address.

"Victor?"

His eyes were wide; he shook his head but didn't speak. She saw the cut just above his collarbone, long, deep, seeping dark-purple blood onto his clothing and the floor.

"Oh my God, Victor. I'm sorry. Just stay there. Stay there." She ran into the bathroom and grabbed a stack of towels. "We're going to do this together. Hold on." She pressed the towels on the wound and held them there to stanch the flow. "Just breathe. I'm so sorry. So sorry."

His breathing became more labored, and she feared he would die on the floor. Then the door opened below and she heard yelling.

"Up here!"

Huddled in the corner with her back against the wall, a white towel in her lap spotted red, she watched as three men loaded her husband onto a stretcher and carried him down the stairs. The police had arrived too, and were waiting for her.

Philomena sat on the couch, rocking slightly. Her hands clasped in her lap, her fingers still covered in blood. "I don't know who did this. I was out. I wasn't here."

"Where?" The youngest of the officers seemed to be taking the lead.

"I had errands to run. I came in and found him like that."

"Errands? A bit late for that. Nothing is open. What errands?" he asked.

She ran a finger over her cuticle. This was tricky. "I went to see Olivia Lacroce. I've been meaning to for a while." She looked up into the officer's eyes. "Her husband was killed twenty years ago. My daughter was recently identified in the States. Murdered as well. Nobody can understand what that's like. So I went to talk."

"You know her well?"

"Yes and no. We've talked on and off over the years."

"Fine. Was your husband expecting anyone tonight? Anyone at all?"

"No." She couldn't tell them about Ava. Ava was dead. Ava wasn't supposed to be here. She couldn't give her up now. The thought was there, not too far from front and center in her mind, that Ava might have arrived here before her. "I don't know."

"Is anything missing from the house that you notice?" The officer wearing glasses and sitting across from her was speaking.

"How can I know that? This just happened."

"Two bedrooms upstairs are torn apart. Like someone was looking for something? Money? Jewelry?" Glasses again.

She shook her head. "I don't know right now." But she did. Victor had been searching for the phone and toy she'd taken. She knew it. "Is he going to be okay? Tell me. Please?" She stared at her fingers to keep her thoughts from spiraling. It was Victor's blood on her hands. Literally. She should never have taken Davide's phone. It was stupid, impulsive.

"We found the murder weapon in the back room. Or what we think is the murder weapon. Forensics will determine that."

Philomena looked up and wiped at her face with the back of her hand. "What weapon? What was it?"

"A knife. Found in the back room, just tossed on a shelf. Did you come in that way?"

She nodded. "I did. The door was unlocked and open a little. I thought it was strange. But—" She stopped talking. She was going to say she thought Ava had come in that way.

"But?"

She shook her head. "Nothing. Sometimes Victor doesn't close it, especially if his hands are full. I've told him before. And his boots were in the middle of the floor, so I thought that's why the door was open."

"When's the last time you saw him?"

"Ummm, about eight-thirty. Nine o'clock. I left the house. He was upstairs."

"Did you have a fight? Or disagreement before leaving?"

"No. I just left. He was upstairs." She knew she was repeating herself. Her stomach was twisting, and she felt a huge amount of acid reflux in her throat. It always happened when she was very upset. She put a hand to her stomach just below her ribs and pushed. "I don't feel well."

"We're almost finished. Just a few more things. Has your husband had any disagreements with anyone?"

"I don't think so."

"Was he involved with something? Was he afraid of something?"

Her eyebrows went up. "What do you mean?"

Glasses was looking down at something in his hand. Victor's phone. "It looks like someone texted him this evening. Probably very close to the time he was attacked."

Her throat was screaming like it had been doused in acid. "Who? What did it say?"

He turned the phone toward her. The text was clearly in the box with *unknown* typed above it. *"It's a countdown. How long will you live, Victor?"* The message stopped.

Her heart froze, and for a second she thought she might pass out. "I need my medicine."

Glasses nodded. "Of course. But who would have sent that, do you think? Have you noticed he might be involved in something? Was he behaving differently?"

She was weary, but her heart was picking up pace. "You're guessing. But I don't know who would have sent something like that. I don't."

He nodded to the other officer. "We will get the incoming number. It's just a matter of time. Did anyone have a key to the house?"

She shook her head. "No. Just the two of us. My medicine, please." It felt like a blowtorch in her throat.

"Tell us where it is; we'll get it."

"My purse. Back room. I dropped it when I fell on his boots."

A minute later he returned with her purse. She couldn't help but notice he was wearing latex gloves. "Did you go back to your purse for anything? To grab your phone? Anything after you found his body?"

"I don't think so. No. My phone was in my coat pocket."

He held up her saddle-brown leather satchel. "I can't be one hundred percent certain, but I'd bet my career this is blood." He pointed to a dark wet stain near the top of the bag. "How'd it get there?"

CHAPTER 13

Olivia

Vicenza, Italy

"New evidence? What do you have, Olivia?" The private investigator had been roused from his sleep and was dressed in a wrinkled sweater, jeans, and boots. "It's very late for this."

"I saw Davide Tosi's phone. Philomena pulled it out of her pocket before she left. It exists. He was in the park that night. The Cresole park. The same park where Tommaso was killed. That's something."

"Well, give it to me, then."

She'd waited only ten minutes after Philomena left to call her private investigator. "I don't have it, but I saw it. There are numbers on his phone that need to be investigated. They may connect to Tommaso somehow."

"I've been looking into this for years, Liv. This Tosi boy—he disappeared that night too. Nobody has seen him. Money in an account has been untouched. Davide's probably dead too. It doesn't bring us any closer to who actually killed your husband."

She stood up and started circling the room. "This *is* something new. At least it's an avenue."

"And what avenue might that be?" He sounded tired and frustrated.

"That Victor DeFeo—" she responded.

"I know the DeFeos. I've interviewed the DeFeos more than once. I've sat with Victor to go over his statement to the police—just trying to see if there was a thread of something related to Tommaso. Now you're saying he's withheld information?"

"His wife was just here. She looked a mess. I think that woman is tormented. But she found this phone, Davide's phone, hidden in the spare bedroom in her house. Victor had to have put it there. Why would he do that if he wasn't with Davide the night he disappeared? If he wasn't trying to cover something up? Maybe Victor and Davide planned to meet there. You don't know."

"Can you make some coffee? I want to go over this with you bit by bit." She nodded and left the room, returning five minutes later and putting the mug in front of him. "So, going over everything you remember from the night your husband was murdered. Everything—"

She sighed as if she were being asked to redo a scene in a play she'd practiced fifty times before. "Tommaso came home that afternoon—late afternoon. Around four thirty. Maybe a little after. But it wasn't five o'clock yet. I yelled to him from upstairs because he was early from work. It was unusual."

"And then?"

"He didn't answer. Tommaso stayed downstairs. I didn't see him or talk to him for a few hours. Then Maximo came home from a friend's house. We were all home for dinner. We ate dinner together."

"Was anything different or unusual with Tommaso? We've been over this before, but think hard."

Olivia pinched her bottom lip with her fingers. "No, I'd have to say no. Not that I saw. He didn't talk much, but I didn't think anything of it. He left the house, but I don't know the time. He told Max to tell me he was going out."

"Where?"

"He said he left something at the office. But he didn't even bring his briefcase with him. Just his jacket and his phone."

"Go on."

"The last time I saw him alive was at dinner. He never came back that night. The police called at twelve thirty"—she wiped a tear from her eyes—"to tell me my Tommaso was dead. But you know all of this. The woman who found his body in the park and called the ambulance and police—"

"And the only real credible witness we have said she saw a few people—she thought they were younger because of the way they were dressed—running down a street in that area," he chimed in. "But we don't know if they were even involved in the stabbing."

"The police think that group of thugs stabbed him. Six times."

"What did Philomena say exactly? Tell me again."

"She wants us to use this phone, work together to find the connection between Davide and Tommaso. Why she cares, I don't know, but learning that her daughter is dead seems to have roused her to find out what happened to Davide. The only connection to Tommaso, other than that they both played rugby, was this woman, Anais—"

He rubbed his face. "Anais Lavoisier died a few weeks ago. Her daughter Marie is in jail in the States on a parole violation. Her granddaughter, Ava Saunders—"

"Tommaso was always so secretive about his childhood, but I think he must have known this Anais back then. He never wanted me to speak to anyone in his family, to his mother," she jumped in.

He seemed to be thinking it over carefully. "We went over his past—"

"I just know one of them—Davide or maybe Victor—stabbed my husband. They were together that night; the cell phone proves it. And

Davide was seen near the park." She finished her sentence and waited for him to say something. "Well then, what's the next step?"

He swallowed his coffee in one gulp. "I go interview Victor. Again. If that will make you happy."

"Interview him and bring that phone to me."

CHAPTER 14

Ava

Vicenza, Italy

Victor had been so angry—rageful is more like it—when he saw me standing in the doorway of the mudroom. The look on his face is one I'll never forget. I'd interrupted something, but I'll never know what. He was flustered too. Bumbling, his eyes narrowed so much it looked like his bushy eyebrows almost touched his cheeks. I was stunned. I'd done nothing but come to the back door as Philomena had asked.

"What are you doing here?" he barked.

"Philomena asked me—"

"She's gone. Not here."

I took a step into the room. "She made it seem like it was really important. Is she okay?" That's when I noticed the knife in his hand.

I put my hands up and started backing away. "I've interrupted something. I'm leaving."

He shook his head. "No. Maybe you can help me. Since you're here."

"With what?"

"Did your mother—I mean Claire. Or Marie or even Anais—did they ever mention anyone named Tommaso? Or the name Lacroce?"

I knew that name somewhere; it clicked. "I'm not sure."

"Is it familiar?"

"No."

"What exactly do you remember about living here in this house when you were little?"

"Bits. Not much."

"Funny you remember the incident with Adrianna in the church, but nothing before that."

"I can't explain how memory works. But I don't remember you much. Philomena only a little. My mother more, and my father not at all."

"Philomena was giving you information about your father. Why? Why now?"

I was stunned. *Why now,* he was asking. "Lord knows I didn't ask her for it. She volunteered it. I didn't know anything about who I was before this. I never had a chance to ask questions because I didn't know what the questions would be."

"A man named Tommaso Lacroce was killed the night Davide disappeared."

I stood very still. Victor was looking deranged. "Who was Tommaso, then?" I asked. More murder. More destruction. "You think my father killed him?"

His face was blank. The knife dangled loosely from the fingers of his right hand. "I don't know. Maybe he saw the murder and ran away. Did your grandmother—Anais—ever tell you anything about Saigon? About what happened back then? It was the late sixties—"

I was lost in his words. "No, she didn't. It never ends with this family. Never. The tangled mess of secrets and murders. What does Saigon fifty years ago have to do with my father's disappearance?" I watched his fingers clutch the knife harder. "Or with this man's murder that same night?"

"I was there, in Saigon back then, sort of. I visited Philomena." His eyes were sliding back and forth with his words, but he wasn't making sense. "I think things have come full circle. I know they have."

"Wait—say that again. How so?"

Victor was still holding his knife in one hand, his phone in the other. His face shocked me, but what shocked me more was the person coming up behind him, the shape taking form in the darkness. It was a woman, of that much I was sure, watching me without Victor knowing someone was standing there, just behind his left shoulder. Her eyes, as well as his, were pinned on mine, but the rest of her face was covered in a black hood. It made the hairs on my arms go up. Victor's eyes were wide, questioning, angry. The other set of eyes, the whites visible in the dark, were expressionless. It suddenly dawned on me what was happening.

I intended to back up to the door. To twist the handle without turning around and then run. But it didn't happen that way. I was frozen in place, wondering how many times I'd been in this predicament before. I felt those eyes burning into mine even in that moment when I closed my lids for two seconds, to breathe. They were the things nightmares were made of. When I opened my own, madness ensued.

The roads were empty and dark, shiny like they were covered in a thin sheet of ice. But that wasn't true. It was just water. There was blood. It was all over my hands, hair, on my pants, my jacket. Victor's car keys hung from my fingers. I opened the garage door, careful that my sleeve was covering my hand. There was enough trouble already. No leaving bloody prints. Victor's Volkswagen was parked where he'd left it. The engine started smoothly, and I jerked the car backward and then into the street. I kept the lights out, glad he'd chosen the color midnight black for his automobile. It would help me disappear into the night.

Once someone discovered the scene inside, I had an hour or two maximum before they started to track down the car. And Philomena might blame me; might tell the police I was alive. I was in a dangerous time crunch. *Think, Ava, think.* My resources were almost nil. It was both too late and too early to be knocking at doors. And even if I had the money I'd wired to Philomena, I couldn't check into a hotel, not looking like this. There was nowhere to go, but I had to keep moving. Then it dawned on me. Anais's cottage in Cherbourg. It hadn't been sold after her death. It had been left to Marie and me, so it was technically mine, even if the courts said I was dead and the title defaulted to Marie. It was safe, warm, away from everything. But it also meant I had an exhausting fourteen-hour drive—at least—in front of me with the police on my back, covered in blood.

Shit, Philomena, why'd you ask me to come back here? I'd be in a hotel sleeping now if you hadn't called. All I wanted was to come to Vicenza, find some family, get my money. Geneva? Five hours away, maybe a bit more. Lots of train stations with restrooms there, parking lots in which to ditch the car. Get the money that was there, then catch a train to Paris, get the money from Anais's account there, then another train to Cherbourg to Anais's cottage. Not for the first time, I cursed her for these charades, for the enjoyment she must be getting even from hell at the thought of Marie and me chasing each other from bank to bank around the globe.

I hoped Philomena wouldn't turn me in. As long as I was legally dead, they wouldn't be looking for me. They'd be looking for the car.

I massaged my temples. Victor was a fool, even if he was an actual blood relative. He never saw it coming. He never saw the woman's eyes behind him. He'd been talking about Tommaso Lacroce. Tommaso. Why hadn't Davide's mother told me someone was killed the night my father disappeared? She went blathering on about bank accounts and sports bags, phone booths and surveillance cameras. She never said,

Oh, by the way, Davide may have had something to do with a murder that night.

What Victor was trying to say, I think, before the bloodshed, was that my father's disappearance wasn't simple. Did he head to America after my mother—which seemed to make the most sense? Or was Anais involved, somehow, in some sort of mystery that stretched back half a century? I was afraid I was going to end up following a trail of dark-red violent drops to the answer.

I'd wanted to shake Victor and say no. *No. Not this time.* I had been dragged to Philadelphia and witnessed my mother's death. That was more horror than any one person should be allowed to see in a lifetime. I wanted to tell Victor that, but I couldn't because now he had a two-inch gash just above his collarbone, deep enough that he'd bleed to death if someone didn't call the ambulance. And if he lived? What would he say? At this particular moment in time, I didn't care. I'd be gone by then.

CHAPTER 15

Joanne

Haddon Township, New Jersey

His hand brushed against her. It was a mistake. An accidental grazing against her breast. But when she looked at him, she knew it wasn't. The man with no face reached for her, and she let him kiss her. His lips were warm, searching. She was hesitating, resisting a little, but not. She knew this was all so wrong. But he was kissing her and fumbling with the buttons on her shirt. The cold tips of his fingers prodding underneath, flirting against her stomach, reaching for her zipper. When she looked up again at his face, she saw it was her ex-husband, Tim. Then it shifted, and it was Russell. Her eyes jolted open, staring at an empty room, a blank ceiling. It had been a half-asleep dream. Her mind had drifted when she'd closed her eyes for a second.

Aww, Joanne. Still lovesick over that man? Can't forgive him for loving Ava? Tsk, tsk. Sad, really, what you've done for him while he's chased after that woman—and destroyed your life. Marie had been talking about Russell, but her words had bothered Joanne so much they were fueling sex dreams about her ex-husband and Russell. She couldn't even come up with something original in her sleep.

Was it true what Marie said about her and Russell? She liked him, cared about him, felt protective toward him, trusted him, brotherly loved him. She'd been rankled not by the naked Bridgette pictures themselves, but her own reaction to them. It had hit her in her gut. She'd become angry at Russell over it, but she'd had no right. Juliette had the right to all the feelings Joanne had experienced over the past few months, and it bothered her. Stirred something inside her so now she was having semi–sex dreams. She'd just woken up too soon. Dream sex was better than no sex. Even if it was with Tim.

Her phone started ringing. She looked at the clock on her bed stand. It was just after six at night. There was nothing good coming from the other end of that call—she could just feel it. She took a swallow of the wine she'd been drinking before drifting off, and reached for the phone anyway.

"Joanne, just listen. It's important. So important I may not be able to contact you again."

Joanne pushed herself up in bed. She hadn't thought she'd ever hear Ava's voice again and certainly not so soon. She could feel the wine still controlling her brain, making it fuzzy, hard to think. "Ava?"

"Listen, I'm heading out of Vicenza. I need something from you. You're the only one I can ask. You or Russell, and I'd rather it be you."

"I went to the jail and saw Marie, Ava. She said some horrible things about you. When is all of this going to end with you? Why do you keep dragging me in? I was going to call the Italian police—"

"Don't do anything, Joanne, until you hear everything I have to say."

She was fully awake now. "I can only imagine—"

"Listen, I stumbled into something, and I'm sort of on the move. This involves my father—"

"Marie told me he disappeared years ago—"

"I stepped in shit in this life from the very beginning, Joanne. It's not all my fault. A man, Tommaso Lacroce, was killed the night my father disappeared. I only have a small thread connecting them. I need your help."

Joanne sighed into the phone. "I don't want to help you, Ava. Is Victor dead? Marie said you were going to hurt Victor. Is that why you're on the run?"

"I didn't stab Victor. Why would she say that? How could she possibly know what was going to happen?"

"So, she was right? Oh my God, Ava. I can't believe this is happening again."

"No, I didn't stab him. But someone did. I was there, okay. Philomena asked me to come back to the house. I just walked in on it. I was on my way out of town. I had no reason to go after the man. But how exactly is Marie involved in this? You need to—"

"Oh wait, you're serious right now, Ava? I thought this might be one of your jokes. We all know how funny you can be."

"I'm on the run, Joanne, for something I didn't do." There was silence. "Joanne? Are you there?"

"Barely. Of course you were in the room, of course you witnessed this man's murder. And again, of course you didn't have anything at all to do with it. What is this, body number eight at your hands?"

"Oh my God, listen. My blood is at the scene, and they'll connect it to me eventually. I don't have anyone else I can trust. If Marie knew this was going to happen, she has information. She's up to her graying hair in this mess. This involves my father, Davide Tosi, this involves Anais—"

"Anais? Again? Really?"

"Yes. There's a man named Tommaso Lacroce—he was killed the night my father disappeared, July twentieth, nineteen ninety-six—there's so much more than what's on the surface, and I need you and Russell to look into it for me. Please? I can't do it from here. Start with Marie."

There was silence.

"I'm turning my phone off now," Ava continued, "after I hang up, so you won't be able to reach me. Remember those names, Joanne. If you can find out what happened to Tommaso, maybe you can find my father. Shit, I need to hang up. I'll be in touch. Tell Russell I want to see him." The line clicked off.

Joanne stared at the wall for a full minute until her bladder told her she needed to move. "She had nothing to do with it, she says," she muttered as she walked into the bathroom. "Old Victor is probably dead with his head cut off, or stabbed a million times, her blood is all over the scene. But she had nothing to do with it."

Through the sleepy fog in her brain something was coming to her. That name. Tommaso Lacroce. Did she know that name? Had she read it somewhere in one of those endless reports she and Russell pored through when they were searching for Ava's mother's identity? It meant something. She still had those boxes with most of the reports in them. They were in her garage, right by the door, stowed for the moment, until she could figure out what to do with them.

"Ugh." The garage was a separate structure. It meant getting dressed and going outside in the cold and dragging them all in, all five or so boxes, and filling her living space with Ava Saunders's life history again. Going over every detail from her adoption, her time growing up in twenty or so different towns across the US. She looked up at the ceiling, contemplating her choices.

Thirty minutes later she was on the floor, papers scattered by her feet. Maybe it wasn't Tommaso Lacroce. Maybe it was just somebody else Lacroce she remembered. Her eyes were weeping with exhaustion, but she couldn't stop. Piles began to fall and scatter about the room, and when Joanne looked up, she saw the clouds to the west were the color of pewter against the night sky. Tomorrow was promising to be another cloudy winter day.

She stood, her muscles screaming from lack of movement. She poured water into the coffeepot and turned it on. Coffee in hand, she went back to the papers with a renewed energy. She rifled through them, pulling out pages and tossing them aside, until a one-page notation caught her eye. It was about Marie Lavoisier-Saunders's movements around the time a woman's body, later determined to be Adrianna DeFeo—Ava's mother—was found in the church in Philadelphia. Russell had gotten the information from a police officer friend in New York who was also a friend of the Catholic Church. She wasn't sure how, but in any event, they were records pulled from the convent where Marie had been assigned at the time.

Marie Saunders had arrived at Sacred Heart Convent in Brooklyn, New York, on a requested transfer from France in the spring of 1996. She was there only a few months before she took a trip overseas. Date: July 16. There was a notice of arrival and request for lodging at the Vatican. One night. The night of the 17th. But she didn't report back to her convent in Brooklyn until the afternoon of the 21st.

Marie had been in Italy around the time Ava's father disappeared and this other man was murdered. Ava had been right—Marie knew something.

Joanne stared at the pages, trying to convince herself she didn't care. She didn't care. But there was a tear in the fabric protecting her rational thought, and the bits of sorrow she felt for Ava and everything she'd been through would leak in. Joanne pictured her in some small car, driving down some road in Europe in the middle of the night, alone. With nowhere to turn. No one to turn to.

Joanne needed help with this. But that help was going to have to come from the one person she hated right now. The one person she'd wanted to avoid. And she knew that by calling, she would open up a door and be sucked through a vortex into a world where murders were swept under the rug, and the lies were the brooms that brushed them there.

She checked her clock. Almost nine. Perfect time to call Russell and pull him from whatever bottle he'd latched on to. She dialed the number.

"Hello?" He answered on the fourth ring, sounding like the bourbon was still making its way through his system.

"Russell, listen, it's Joanne. Can you concentrate for a minute? Do you know the name Tommaso Lacroce? Think hard."

She heard muffled sounds through the phone. "I don't know. Why?"

"Put away the booze, and get over here now. It's urgent, urgent."

CHAPTER 16

PHILOMENA

Vicenza, Italy

The wall was an off-white color probably named *nube di nebbia—cloud mist*—or something like that. The random thoughts kept coming in and out of her mind because she'd been sitting in this chair for hours. She was too weary to pull out her phone to see the exact time, but she knew it had to be approaching dawn. Victor was in surgery, and all she wanted to do was go home. But she knew that if she did she would be seen as uncaring, unconcerned, unmoved by her husband's plight.

The police were suspicious enough. They hadn't accepted her account of coming in, falling over the boots in the mudroom, and reaching for the shelf to steady herself. The knife that had been sitting on that very shelf, left there by a would-be killer, had cut her hand. That's what she'd told the investigator. It had to be how her purse had gotten a nice blood smear on one side, as well as her slacks, her fingers. The police hadn't been concerned about the latter two because that was explained away by her handling *the body*. That's how they referred to Victor. He was still alive, but to them he was a body.

She couldn't account for Victor's car being missing from the garage either. His key ring, always in his desk drawer, was gone as well. They were tracking the car. Testing the blood. By the time she'd been allowed to climb in the ambulance beside her husband, men dressed in white from head to toe were crawling all over her property. The forensic team, she was told. She chewed her lip at the thought. Whose blood would they find at the scene?

She wanted to scrub those walnut planks in that upstairs hallway until the blood was gone, washed away. But the memory of Victor struggling for his life would never go away. *Ava.* She shuddered. She'd called the girl to come to the house, and she'd tried to kill her own grandfather. All of this was Philomena's fault.

"La signora DeFeo? Possiamo parlare?"

She was startled. "Yes, we can talk."

The man sat next to her, and she knew he was a police detective just from the cut of his suit, the way his hair was combed. "We have some preliminary tests from the scene, and I wanted to ask you some questions, if I might."

"Okay."

"There were two blood types at the scene. One was A positive, which we assume belongs to your husband—that's his type. There was also an O positive sample taken. What is your blood type? Do you know?"

"O positive. I'm O positive. And I cut my hand, so that makes sense." She scanned her hands and arms. "I was putting pressure on his wounds, so that makes sense both our blood types would be there."

"Of course, we are doing DNA tests. Those results won't be back soon, so I want to try and—"

"His car is gone. I didn't take it, so you know there was someone else there." Philomena stood up. "I need to go home. Are they finished at the house yet?"

He scowled. "No, they'll be there for the rest of the day. Can you stay elsewhere tonight?"

She said nothing. She'd invited this granddaughter, Giada-Ava, into her life, and piece by piece it was falling apart.

The detective slapped his knees. "A few more questions. Who knew where Victor kept his car keys?"

She shrugged. "I don't know. Just me. It wasn't something we talked about." She sat down again and pushed back into the seat.

"Hmmm. The spare bedroom was ransacked. Was it like that before?"

Could she tell them Victor was looking for Davide Tosi's phone that he'd hidden away for twenty years? That he was at least peripherally involved in the boy's disappearance? "It wasn't like that the last time I was in there." That was true. She had to be truthful because if she lied, they'd blame all of this on her.

"Which was when?"

"I'm not sure. Yesterday afternoon."

He looked at his watch. "Afternoon? You mean around twelve hours ago?" She nodded. "Have you had any visitors staying in the room recently?"

She thought about that for at least thirty seconds. "No." So much for telling the truth. "Victor sometimes sleeps in there. If he's up late and doesn't want to disturb me. Did you find his car?"

"Not yet. There's a bath towel on the rack and a hand towel on the sink. That was from Victor?"

She tried to keep her face still, show no reaction. She should have done the laundry. Moved the towels to the hamper. Something. Ava's DNA would be all over it. "I can't be sure. Are we done?"

"Actually no, if you don't mind. You left the house to see Olivia Lacroce at what time?"

Philomena looked up into his face. He was just getting started. "Around nine-thirty, I'd say."

"So, we spoke with Mrs. Lacroce. She said you rang her bell an hour later than that. Her surveillance footage backs that up. Did it take you an hour to get there? Did you stop anywhere?"

Just then a doctor approached. "Mrs. DeFeo, your husband made it through surgery. He's in recovery, still groggy. Would you like to see him? Just for a minute?"

Philomena jumped up. Anything to be away from this bulldog detective. She didn't look back as she followed the doctor through the double glass doors into the recesses of the hospital.

Victor was in the corner bed, on his back. He had an IV attached to his arm and an oxygen tube connected to his nose. A tube went down his throat, helping him breathe. His eyes were closed. His face was swollen, and all the injuries she hadn't seen before in the dim light of the hallway were on display.

Both eyes were swollen, but the left protruded so much that she knew he couldn't open it. His arms were dotted with black-and-blue marks. His hands crisscrossed with knife wounds. He'd put up a fight, even if he lost. He was bandaged across his chest all the way up to his chin.

"He looks terrible," Philomena commented.

"The cut above his collarbone missed his esophagus by a millimeter. He's lucky. There was damage to his vocal cords; we stitched him up. If his vitals hold through the day, and he seems to be getting stronger, we'll know more."

"Has he lost his voice for good?"

"Not necessarily. One step at a time."

"But he'll be able to write?"

His head tilted sideways. "Meaning?"

"To tell what happened to him?"

"Let's just concentrate on tonight, Mrs. DeFeo. We'll be taking him to his room in a few hours."

She sat in the chair by his bedside and watched the doctor walk away. "You've done it this time, Victor. Do you know what happened to Davide? Is that what all this is about? Did you hurt him and Tommaso Lacroce? If you did, I'll find out, and next time I'll really kill you."

CHAPTER 17

Olivia

Vicenza, Italy

She was forcing the tea down her throat, sip by sip, waiting for the call. The logs she'd placed in the fireplace had burned to sparks and embers, but in the time it took to reduce wood to ashes, she'd still heard nothing. Her private investigator had left long ago, with a list in his pocket. Interview Victor was on the top, next was getting Davide's phone from Philomena. She'd only been able to see the old flip phone for a second before Philomena had closed it and stowed it away. A taste, a tease, a way to try and bribe Olivia for help, maybe even money, she wasn't sure. But she'd made it clear, if the investigator was able to procure the phone, he needed to bring it to her first.

Tommaso's eyes were in front of her. They always were. She saw them in her sleep, when she was preparing dinner, or standing in the grocery line. Not his whole face. Just his eyes following her. She'd been tormented for twenty years because of things she'd never say out loud in order to protect her husband. Not even to her PI. She'd convinced herself that she didn't need to tell him, that the withheld information meant nothing and had nothing to do with his search for information. But now she wasn't so certain.

She looked up and saw automobile lights near the gate. Then the bell rang.

She pressed the buzzer, and the gate swung open. A silver Ford Fiesta circled around the driveway to a space near the door. The investigator jumped out and leaned on the doorbell.

The wind came in with him, and she stepped back out of the cold.

"What are you doing here so late—"

"Things are escalating, Olivia. Sit down."

"What happened?"

He shut the door and went to the fireplace, rubbing his hands back and forth. "Victor DeFeo was stabbed tonight—"

"The police came by. Asking a few questions. Who stabbed him?"

"They don't know. He's not dead. He's in surgery. So if he makes it, we might get that answer, but the timing is interesting."

"You know what else is interesting? Philomena lied to the police about when she was here. She said it was an hour earlier than it was." She put another log in the fireplace and prodded it with the poker. "I might have backed her up if I knew to, but they would have asked for the camera footage anyway."

"You think Philomena lied because she stabbed her husband?"

"Think about it. She comes here with proof her husband saw Davide on the night he disappeared. He's lied to her for at least twenty years. What if he had some sort of proof that Davide was involved in Tommaso's killing? What if it's on that phone?"

He held his hand up. "We never found proof Davide and Tommaso were in the same place that night. Nothing. There's just a thread that ties them together."

"It wasn't a thread." Her eyes were on the flames in the fireplace. "More like a rope between them. Between all of them, and I think it might stretch back longer than we both imagine."

"Meaning?"

"Anais Lavoisier wrote me into her will. When she died, a lawyer contacted me."

"When, Olivia? Why wouldn't you tell me that? Here you are paying me to find out what happened to your husband, and you're withholding important information? Am I wasting my time?"

She turned to him. "I didn't think it had anything to do with all of this. Her will was updated only last year and still named me, as Tommaso's wife—"

"How much?"

"I don't know yet. But I have to go to a place called La Héronnière de Haut, a small town south of Cherbourg, for the probate. The Acte de Notoriété has already been drawn up."

Her investigator was at her side. "She left you something in her will? And you thought it meant nothing? Did any of the Lavoisier family reach out to you? Ask you why this woman was leaving you money?"

She touched his arm. "I don't know that it is money. It could be anything. Nobody reached out to me but the one lawyer."

"No contact at all?"

She shook her head. "Not yet. I assume now I just need to go to this meeting. I just wonder what the connection between the two of them could be. I don't know when they met, how they knew each other. The *only* reason I knew of the connection was because I found her name and information in his phone after he died."

"I'm going to the lawyer's office to ask him a few questions."

"*Lo sento dentro di me.* Leave it alone. Please? I'll know more after the meeting."

"I'll call you later. I need to think." With that and a burst of frigid air, he was out the door.

She watched from the window, her forehead pressed against the glass as he drove away. "Give it to him in pieces, Olivia. Otherwise you're going to look bad," she whispered.

She went to the desk and pulled out the number she'd scrawled across the page when the lawyer had called.

The phone rang six times in a high-pitched short trill before someone answered. *"Allo?"* It was sleepy, distant.

"Monsieur Rotton?"

"Oui?"

"This is Olivia Lacroce. I am so sorry to call you at this hour, but it's urgent."

It was as if he suddenly sat up in his bed and put the phone to his ear. "Ah. Madame." There was rustling. "Is this about the meeting in La Héronnière de Haut? Did something happen?"

"Tell me why Anais Lavoisier left something to me."

"It's complic—"

"No. There's no time for that. I have a private investigator that may be visiting you tomorrow. I've paid him on and off for twenty years to look into my Tommaso's death. If my husband was involved in something with Anais, I need to know before he gets there."

"Fire him."

"Why?"

"You obviously don't trust him anyway. Come to Paris tomorrow. I have a letter for you that you might want to read before the meeting."

"If I fire him, he'll be suspicious. He's ex-police. He'll keep looking anyway, without pay. The timing of his release would be too interesting to him."

"I'll come to you, then. Good night." He hung up.

CHAPTER 18

RUSSELL

Haddon Township, New Jersey

He was wet, the cold rain pelting his head, his sneakers soaked through so that his feet felt like frozen logs. "Come on, Joanne. Open up." For a half minute he almost thought she was leaving him there to punish him. Again. For having sex with Bridgette. And it had taken an acquaintance at a bar, someone he only sort of knew, when he was spilling his long sad tale, to point out that Joanne's fury over his extracurricular activities was odd. Out of place. Unless she wanted more from him than an occasional cup of coffee and a shoulder to cry on.

That had never occurred to him until that minute. After her divorce, her son, Steven, now almost fifteen, had been her main focus of attention. He'd never seen her date. Or express interest in it. It had never occurred to him she had hormones. He hadn't even put her in the sister category; he'd shifted her up one notch so that she sat on a shelf next to his mother.

The door swung open. "Sorry." She moved out of the way. "I was in the bathroom. Didn't hear the bell."

She was wearing sweats. Gray sweats and a hoodie of the same color. Her hair was pulled straight back from her face, revealing a few gray strands at her temples and reminding him that she was a few years older than him. Her face was free from any hint of makeup. He wondered if his half-drunk bar mate's assessment that she had a thing for him was flawed. She didn't seem all that eager to please him—at least visually.

"You dragged me here, saying 'urgent, urgent.' So, I'm here. What's up?" He took off his coat and hung it on a hook. "It's freezing out, by the way. And wet." He noticed her living room floor was scattered with loose papers.

She nodded. "Okay, so look. Ava called me. Yeah, I know. Out of the blue."

"Don't tell me—Victor's dead?"

"Well, she implied he'd been stabbed but that she didn't do it. She was mostly concerned about how Marie knew this was going to happen."

"Have you slept, Joanne? Like in the past week? You're looking a little manic."

"No. Stop. These are all our old files. She mentioned a man, Tommaso Lacroce, and I knew that name. So, I started looking through these notes. And I found this." She waved a sheet of paper. "This is a log of Marie's comings and goings that you got from the convent up north a few months ago."

"And?"

"She said Tommaso was murdered the night her father disappeared. July twentieth, nineteen ninety-six. Guess when Marie was absent from the convent in New York. Just guess."

"July twentieth of ninety-six. And you think she was in the place where this man was being murdered?"

"Bingo. She flew to Rome, stayed at the Vatican only one night. She didn't reappear in the States until three days later."

"What else did Ava say?"

"She begged us to help her. To start with Marie. We need to do this together, Russell."

He touched her arm, but she jerked it back away from him. "Okay. I won't touch you, but you need to sit down. Two minutes. Have some coffee. Talk this through."

She eyed him warily and half sat on the arm of the sofa. "Go on."

"I don't mind digging into this. It might keep me out of the bars, give me a distraction. But are you sure you want to do this with me?"

"I have no choice. You're the only one who can help me, who's been involved since the beginning. Oh, by the way, Ava said to tell you she wants to see you." She shot him a nasty look.

He rolled his eyes, and then he focused anywhere but Joanne's face. "Good, that and a few thousand dollars will get me bailed out of jail. I've been there—"

"So what about this?" She cut him off.

He puckered his mouth in thought. This trip Marie made to Italy was ringing a bell somewhere. He hadn't remembered the tidbit Joanne had dredged up, probably because the information was ancillary to what they were looking for at the time. "Okay, I have to think about how to start on that. But Tommaso Lacroce's obituary—find everything we can about him. But maybe you need to take a break, a rest from this first?"

"No. No rest. Rest leads to nap. I've had crazy dreams lately. Tell me where to start. I couldn't find any obituary online for Tommaso—but you know, he died in Italy."

He put his hands on his knees. "I'll work on it."

She smiled. It was the first smile he'd seen on her in a long time. "Somehow I knew you'd say that. We're keeping this simple. Limited to figuring out if Tommaso can bring us closer to what happened to Ava's father. That's what we're after. Davide Tosi. Nothing else."

"Okay, boss, can I borrow a computer and a landline or are you going to send me home in the rain to do this?"

She pointed to the computer. "There. I'm going back to read some more of these notes. Don't interrupt me unless you find something good."

He watched her walk down the hall. She looked lighter, happier, energized. He watched her until she shut the bedroom door behind her. He shifted his gaze to the computer.

An hour later she hadn't emerged. He'd found Tommaso Lacroce's obituary, copied and pasted it into translating software, then printed it out. He read over it three times before rising and walking down the hallway to her bedroom door. He knocked gently, feeling uncomfortable. What had shifted? There was a time they could have shared a bed, laughed while lying next to one another, and it wouldn't even have been awkward.

He opened the door slowly when she didn't respond. She was on her side, asleep, still dressed in sweats, but the hoodie had pulled up across her stomach. He shook her gently, and she came alive.

"What? What?" She rubbed her eyes. "What are you doing in here?"

"Wake up. Check this out."

He handed her the obituary and watched her eyes go over it more than once, just as his had moments before. "What are we going to do, Russell?"

"That's up to you. Are we going to keep it simple or go for it all?"

"Can I say I hate Ava? I hate her. Fine. Let's do it."

"Ten minutes ago I saw a report on Sky News Italy that Victor DeFeo was indeed stabbed in his house a few hours ago. He's alive at the moment, barely—"

She stared blankly for a minute. "You seriously found that channel?" A second later it all came together for her. "Oh God, Marie was right. It was Ava? We need to go back and talk to Marie—"

"She has a parole hearing coming up. She probably won't be released, but just in case, we'd better do it soon."

CHAPTER 19

Ava

Geneva, Switzerland

I sat on the sagging bed, thinking about the look on my grandfather's face right before he was stabbed. He was afraid. Of the past. Of something that had happened years ago that was now catching up with him. With everyone. And he was so busy worrying about events that were figuratively behind him, he never saw the person literally behind him. That was the irony of it all, seeing his face twist with the realization.

Surprisingly, when the attack came, Victor, in confusion, had lunged at me, as if I was the cause of it all, and maybe I was. And in that second, I was drawn into something I never anticipated. Fighting off a man who was trying to hurt me, tangled up with the person who was attacking him, and then attacking me. It was a threesome of the worst sort. But for once, my size had saved me, allowing me to squeeze through the hair's breadth between Victor and the shelf and escape into the living room. Victor's keys, I knew, were in the desk, because I'd once watched him put them there. In that moment of frenzy, I was able to leave that house and everything behind.

This dump of a hotel, forty-seven euros a night in Chêne-Thônex, on the outskirts of Geneva, had been my savior. I just wanted to clean up, get a little rest, and wait for the world to come alive. The blood mostly washed off me in a public bathroom. My dark hair hid the traces that were left. I'd turned my shirt inside out, feeling Victor's blood damp against my skin. My black jeans camouflaged the blood well enough for me to check into the hotel at the crack of dawn without much notice, but I needed to be presentable at the bank to get the money from Anais's account. I needed to keep moving, keep moving. I wasn't free and clear. Victor's attacker might come for me eventually. In being there, and then fleeing, I had become an unnecessary complication. The hunter had finally become the hunted, and I didn't like the feeling.

I wandered into the bathroom, stripped down to nothing, and stepped into the worn ceramic tub. There were large spaces between the tiles where the grout had fallen out. A few tiles in the corner were missing altogether. Mold had taken up residence in dreary crooks. I didn't care. I turned on the spigot and stood under a torrent of warm water. The sliver of used soap in the holder was good enough. I scrubbed my skin and hair the best I could, rinse and repeat, until I hurt. Then I changed into a clean white shirt and jeans, a bit wrinkled but serviceable.

On postcards, Geneva looked like Swiss heaven. And some parts were quaint—the city nestled up around the Rhône with the Alps as a backdrop. But the everyday Geneva could be as stark and bleak as any other major city. And this little suburb was charmless, filled with stone-block buildings and a cluster of practical shops to meet the basic needs of people who couldn't afford to live in the city proper.

In the meantime, I was stuck in this hotel, staring at the walls. I turned on my phone. I knew that Joanne would be able to find out more than I could on my cheap international phone, but I had time to do a little research. I typed *Tommaso Lacroce* into the browser. There were hundreds of them. I had no idea what he looked like, how old he'd been—the only thing I knew was that he'd died within days of my mother. And that date was burned in my memory forever.

I added the Italian word for *obituary* and continued my search, filtering by date of death. The next page came up, and there it was—that face. It startled me, and I dropped my phone onto the bed; it slid down between the scarred wooden headboard and the mattress. I knew that face. I knew it. The nose and the chin, the light hair across his forehead.

I grabbed my hair and sat down on the bed, leaning over far enough that my head was between my knees. Why did this keep happening to me? I'd not only seen Tommaso Lacroce, I'd been in the same room with him, so to speak. Or with his photograph. In a photo album that used to sit on Anais's shelf in her cottage in Cherbourg. He was there, a boy or young teen, smiling beside Anais and her parents. In Vietnam.

CHAPTER 20

MARIE

Camden County Jail, New Jersey

She stood in the bathroom in front of the mirror. No matter how she combed her hair, it looked terrible. The gray was winning in the color war, and her natural brown seemed dull, lost within the strands of shimmering frost. It made her skin look dull and old. She pulled at her eyes, watching the loose skin move under her finger. These weeks in jail had certainly done nothing for her looks. The mirror was nothing but a slab of polished metal. No chance of breaking it and stabbing anyone, but the image reflected was blurry and distorted.

How long had it been since things had turned upside down? Her sister Claire's death followed by Anais's death only months later. Then her never-ending legal troubles. Her family, the only one she'd had, wiped out. Only Ava remained. Anais had clarified their biological connection in her letters. *Though I always had a special bond with her, I swear I never knew Ava was my grandchild.* Ava was her blood niece. Marie felt the tears coming before the overwhelming sadness overtook her.

Where was the fun in her life? The joy? The happiness? She lay back on the bed, looking at all the letters carved into the metal. There never had been any. Not really. Religion had provided the white noise to quiet her frenetic mind, nothing more. It was structure and distraction. It was order, and predictability. It was what Anais thought she needed after a rebellious teenaged past with boyfriends, lots of sex, and occasional drugs.

She rested her hand on her stomach and took a deep breath. She craved normalcy. To meet a man, settle down, maybe in a little village in France, get a job, maybe teaching. She longed to go home to a place that was actually hers, make dinner, make love, have dinner parties with friends. The things of life. But the fact that Ava was still out there with the key to any small amount of financial freedom bothered her. She had no choice but to focus on Ava first, happiness later.

Ava didn't know it, but Marie's father, Ross, had done Ava a favor by lifting her from the church massacre—an accident of sorts—and dumping her with the Lavoisiers, because her *other* family, the ones that were left of her supposed biological clan, were perhaps worse than the old woman in Cherbourg. From what Anais had told her, the DeFeos were devious, conniving, untrustworthy, murderous.

That last word made Marie laugh. Ava's DNA was a braid of psychopathy. Eventually she'd stumble upon Tommaso Lacroce. And that's when her torment would begin, because Marie was sure, almost positive, that Ava would remember something of him when she saw his face. And that would truly be worth watching.

Marie remembered the first time she'd seen the man; he was wearing white clothes. A white shirt and matching pants. When she saw him coming down the street toward their house in Philadelphia, she thought he was a baker from Kaplan's around the corner, but he wasn't. He was a young man on his way somewhere, dressed for summer, his brown hair plastered across his forehead, the sweat beaded all across his brow. He stopped short right in front of their house, propping his foot up on the first of the concrete steps.

"Your mother home?" he'd asked.

Marie had just been sitting there, barely three. He'd scared her enough that she raced up into the house, yelling for her mother. When Anais came to the door, she peered through and then shoved Marie back in behind her.

"What do you want?"

"To talk."

"No. No. No. No. Not now. Later. My husband will be home soon," she hissed.

They proceeded to have a back and forth—Marie could see the man's face through the crack in the door. Her mother's accented English rose to such a level that he had to quiet her down. His English was accented too, and occasionally her mother would lapse into this other language Marie later realized was bits of Italian. She wasn't angry with him; it seemed she was angry with whatever he was telling her.

"Anais. It's been six years. I just wanted you to know this." He took out a sheet of paper and showed it to her. "I couldn't leave it alone. I asked my father to look into it. He said it might be true. From everything he knows, it's true. Do you know what this means? She might be alive. Have you been in touch with Philomena?"

Her mother held that paper and read it over and over. "Yes. She visited once. Or twice."

"We need to stick together. The three of us. I need to trust you." He tapped the letter. "Maybe not now. In ten years, we're going to have a serious problem."

"I'll call Philomena. What are we going to do if she's alive, Tommaso? We need to find her now."

"Don't break your story, and don't turn on me or Philomena. No matter what, Anais," he said. "Do you understand? Tell me you understand." He stood there until she nodded. "Before one of us ends up dead." Then he'd walked away.

Strange words Marie mostly forgot until long after. Until the night, years later, that Anais called her. She was in the convent in Brooklyn.

Catastrophe was at her doorstep, and Claire's. Baby Ava had just been dumped with them—covered in blood—rescued from the carnage of a church in Philadelphia where the little girl had watched her mother's slaughter.

Was this not enough? Not for Anais. Anais had insisted she leave her sister and catch a flight to Rome, stay one full day at the Vatican to make it all seem logical—then she was to tear through the night driving north to Vicenza. Cresole, to be exact. To a park. To deliver some very important information to the man she remembered from her childhood—Tommaso Lacroce. He would be there waiting.

The content of the envelope was secret. Something Anais couldn't deliver herself. But the plan didn't unfold as anticipated. Tommaso Lacroce ended up dead that night. Murdered and left like a dog to die in the grass. Only a few people knew about Marie's drive through Italy that night, about what had happened when she arrived, that she had been there. Anais, Claire, and Tommaso—and all three of them were dead.

She'd found the small article about his death that Anais had cut out and stuffed in a book of photographs high on a shelf in her cottage. Marie had stumbled upon it while doing an exhaustive search through her banking information and recognized his face immediately. It was odd, and the name stuck with her. The pieces had come together slowly, and Marie wasn't sure she had it completely right yet, but if Ava was digging, it would be interesting to watch.

Marie sat up and turned on the sink, filling her plastic cup with water. She wandered to the window and looked through the grating. Camden was dark, the streetlights in the distance illuminating the occasional car that crawled down the road along the side of the courthouse.

She had this inkling, just a niggling little worry that wouldn't leave her alone, that there was someone else who'd seen her that night in Cresole. Now that things were coming to a head, it worried her more. The only safe place for her to be right now was behind these cement walls.

CHAPTER 21

Philomena

Vicenza, Italy

She stared down at Victor, bandaged, unconscious, lying so still in the bed. Her eyes were bleary from only a few hours of sleep. He was attached to a respirator, but they said they hoped he'd be weaned off as he got stronger. He had monitors above his bed; the IV tubes ran up the length of his body and attached to the bags hanging over his bed. His arms were straight by his sides; his face was swollen but tranquil. She felt a mix of fear and repulsion.

The police had left her for the moment to be with her husband in his room, but they'd circle back in a matter of minutes asking the same things. *How did the blood get on your purse? What time did you leave Olivia Lacroce's house? When is the last time you saw Victor? Who was staying in your guest room? Why was it ransacked? Was anything else stolen?* The questions circled and sometimes repeated in different form. The more Philomena tried to explain herself, the more confused she became. There was no way out.

Victor's blood was still under her fingernails, though forensics had taken implements and scraped underneath, looking for DNA. They'd told her she could wash up, but the dark stains wouldn't come out no matter how much soap she used.

She played with the phone in her left pocket. The police hadn't yet gotten a search warrant, but they would, and she needed to act fast. The old Nokia flip phone had all of Davide's last outgoing and incoming phone calls recorded. A snapshot of his last moments. In a mad panic she went to an electronics store and spent over half an hour with a clerk searching his stock for a universal charger that would fit the retro phone. Just when she'd given up hope, he came up with an odd multi-end charger and made one fit. He plugged it in, and she saw the small green charger light blink on.

Philomena handed over the twenty-seven euros and rushed from the store, her heart pounding through her ears. Victor had kept the phone stuffed under a pile of unused linens in the closet of the spare bedroom. She couldn't think of one good reason why he'd kept it all these years. And the chances were if Victor had the phone, then Davide was dead. Her mind was slipping in and out of possibilities, but one kept popping back to the top. Victor had killed him.

The handheld device seemed ridiculously simple compared to her smartphone—just a simple backlit screen, no internet capabilities. She found a café on Contrà Santa Corona and bought a cup of coffee, then plugged the phone in and waited. The thing came to life so slowly, for a minute she thought she was wasting her time. But then there it was.

She fiddled with the settings and then pressed a button, and the list of incoming calls came up. She knew because she saw her old house landline number at the top. It was the last call Davide had received, though they hadn't said a word to one another. She ran her finger down the list, almost afraid all the information would disappear. She was looking at twenty-year-old data; numbers had changed over the years. But one stuck out. Adrianna's. Philomena felt a wave of nostalgia—this was a direct link to the past. Her daughter and Davide had spoken multiple times a day, it seemed. She hadn't seen her daughter's number in twenty years. It warmed her heart and made her smile.

She closed the column and pressed another button. "Outgoing Calls." She took in a sharp breath. Davide had called their house that night. She knew it, no matter how much Victor had denied it. She stared down at the "Voicemail" button. Technology was so much better now; she wasn't certain if the information was still stored.

Her finger hovered over the button. She pressed it and put the phone to her ear. *You have ten messages.* Then the voice was there: *Davide.* It was low, breathy. She knew her daughter's voice, and her heart caught in her throat. She pulled the phone from her ear and stared at it, then started listening again. *Davide, it's happening soon, I think. I showed my father what you found, and he finally admitted what happened in Saigon—everything he knew anyway. He said Tommaso will meet with you in the Cresole park. He'll call you with details. Then you can compare information.* Then there were garbled sounds she couldn't understand. *If you're right, we can't turn against one another—no matter what. I love you.*

"What's happening?" Philomena whispered. "I don't understand."

Then that message ended and the next began. *Davide*—it was Adrianna again—*no matter what happens, we're going to be together. Don't let anyone break us up. Not my parents or yours. Giada will hold us together, I promise.*

"Signora DeFeo?"

She snapped the phone shut and put her hands over it. She recognized the bald head and blue shirt of the policeman who had been in her house. "You tracked me down . . . or followed me?"

"Your husband is being moved to another room. I thought you should know."

She pulled the cord from the wall and shoved the phone into her pocket. "I'll go be with him. Is he awake?" It was a stupid question. He wouldn't be awake for days, if at all.

"No. But we have a few more questions. Come." He motioned for her to follow him.

Victor's chest was moving up and down with the rhythm of the machine. Philomena was transfixed. She watched his eyes and saw them move slightly beneath the lids. She wanted to grab him, make him wake up. They had talking to do before the police circled around again. She had to ask him if he'd listened to the voicemail messages. She looked over her shoulder to make sure she was completely alone with him.

"Victor," she whispered, leaning down near his ear. "The message on Davide's phone? The last incoming message? You heard it? Our daughter's last words?" She wanted to shake him. "She seemed so scared. You knew what was happening that night Tommaso was killed and kept it a secret all these years? You sent Davide there? Didn't you? Victor, wake up."

CHAPTER 22

Olivia

Vicenza, Italy

She hadn't expected the knock at her door so soon, so she peered through the curtains before opening it. She hesitated slightly. The man standing on the other side had information that was going to change her life.

"Signora Lacroce?" Milo Rotton asked.

"Yes. Come in."

The attorney was short, about two inches shorter than she. His hair was completely gray, almost silver, but he had a lot of it. He was wearing a dark suit.

"I'm glad I found you at home." He spoke perfect Italian.

She wondered what he would have done if she hadn't answered the door. After she ushered him to a seat, she came right to the point. "Let's not waste time with small talk. Tell me why Anais Lavoisier has named me in her will. Why am I on the Acte de Notoriété?"

He nodded. "If anything was bequeathed to you, it'll be explained at the meeting. But it is imperative that you be there. Transportation can be arranged if that's an issue. I understand this meeting is far away from Vicenza."

"I didn't even know my husband knew this woman until after his death." She looked at the man across from her. "My husband was murdered twenty years ago not even a mile from here. Anais surely must have known this."

"I met with her exactly twice about this matter. I only know that she wanted you there this Saturday." He handed her an envelope. "All the information is in there. There is a letter for you as well. It should answer some questions." He stood up.

The legal-sized white envelope was blank save for a printed name in the upper right-hand corner. *Olivia Lacroce.*

"Wait—"

"Signora?"

"Sit for one moment. When you met with her, what did she say?"

"About?"

"Her family, my husband. Anything." Olivia was wringing her hands despite her best efforts to keep them still. "Me?"

"Hmmm, I'm not sure what information you might be looking for. She was businesslike, came prepared with documents. She said nothing directly about you. Please, don't let me keep you from reading." He gave a slight nod and sat still, waiting for her to open it.

She held the envelope in her hands for a full minute before sliding her thumb under the flap and ripping it open. *Olivia,* it began. Not Signora Lacroce or Signora Olivia Lacroce. Just Olivia. As if Anais knew her. It was written in Italian. She'd taken the time to write in a language other than her native tongue. To accommodate her.

> *I instructed my lawyer to give you this letter in the event of my death. I met your husband many years ago when he was just a child. There was not a month that went by that we were not in contact, either by phone or in person.*
>
> *When I saw him the month before he was killed, I think he somehow knew what was coming. We both*

feared it. He requested several things from me at that last meeting, and I did everything within my power to fulfill his request. My gift to you (which you will understand later) is a result of that conversation. I have watched over the years and see the police may be no closer to the truth as to what happened to Tommaso. To that end, I want this last act to bring some closure.

Your husband's murder was not a random act. I am almost certain it was an act of vengeance exacted after many years. There were witnesses to his murder that are still alive. I can't say any more because, though I may be dead, I have a daughter. A granddaughter to think of. My lawyer will have given you an address at La Héronnière de Haut, very near Cherbourg. It is important that you attend. Enjoy the time you have left, Olivia, because it's very precious.

Olivia looked up at him. "What am I supposed to do with this?"

"She did enjoy games of all sorts. But this is quite straightforward."

"A man named Victor DeFeo was attacked last night. He may not live. Is he on the list to attend this meeting?"

He looked at some notes in his file. "Pity about Victor. Victor's name was on the Acte de Notoriété. Both he and his wife, Philomena. Under the circumstances, he might not make it. Your husband's mother will be there as well."

"His mother? Why Tommaso's mother?"

"You don't see her, but you must know she's alive, living in Teramo." It chilled her that he knew so much about her family. "That she suffered the loss of her daughter when your husband was just a boy. Her husband sometime after that. And then her son's murder twenty-eight years later. She's suffered terribly. You didn't know this woman's whereabouts, to let her meet your son? Her grandson?"

"I know where she is, but my husband never wanted to . . . he said she's got dementia. She wouldn't recognize me if I visited. I don't understand why Anais would bother to include her in this."

He leaned back a little in his seat. "He told you she has dementia? Is that true?"

"I don't . . ." She stumbled. She became engrossed with the letter again. "It says Anais and Tommaso met often, were in communication up until he died. How could I not have known that? I only learned of her after she died. Why wouldn't he tell me about her?"

His brow furrowed. "I don't know what secrets were held at either end. I'm sorry. Signora, take your time and think about this. You've spent twenty years revisiting your husband's murder with the police. I'd look at this meeting as one more clue."

"You could have told me all of this on the phone. You could have mailed this letter to me. Why was it so important for you to come here?"

"Madame Lavoisier was clear about this, about the necessity of certain people attending the probate of her will. Given her interest in you, it sparked my curiosity, and I thought it merited a visit, to give you this information face-to-face. Let me know if I can be of assistance—arranging a car for you, or anything else you might need, Signora." He stood and smiled, showing small sharp teeth, before showing himself out.

After he'd left, she locked the doors and windows and reread the letter, looking for anything she might have missed. Her next step was obvious. She was going to the hospital to see Philomena—see what she knew of this meeting, and then depending on what she found out, maybe she'd go to Teramo and talk to Tommaso's mother. Maybe the old woman hadn't lost her memory; maybe there was another reason Tommaso had kept them apart.

CHAPTER 23

Ava

Geneva, Switzerland

I fished my phone out from behind the bed, finding a black sock and a used condom in my search. I didn't want to see his face again, and I wasn't completely sure why. I just knew I didn't. His face haunted me from Anais's books I'd looked through as a child. His obituary along with several other snapshots had littered pages in her albums. Not for the first time, I was grateful for my facility with languages.

> Tommaso Lacroce passed away suddenly on Saturday, July 20, in Cresole, Vicenza. He was born in and raised near Teramo. He spent over a year as a child in Saigon, Vietnam, where his father, Paolo Lacroce, was employed by the US-supported Military Assistance and Advisory Group in an advisory capacity as a retired Italian Air Force officer. Tommaso's adult years were lived in Italy, France, and the United States. He was working as an accountant for the firm of Russo, Marchiano, and Calio before his death. He is survived by his wife, Olivia (nee Rossi), and his son, Maximo. Services will be held . . .

My eyes slipped off the screen. Vietnam. He was in Saigon, at least part of the time growing up, and had to have met Anais there. That's how Anais knew him. That was the connection. I stared at his face peering back at me from the screen. His wide-set eyes, thick dark brows, large forehead. I knew those details without even studying his image. *Think, Ava, think. The albums.*

Anais had those blue photo albums up on the shelf. And when I had the opportunity to look through them, they were crammed with photos of Vietnam. I couldn't sort them all out in my brain. They were still there, at the cottage, I was sure. The place had been ransacked when Marie and I were looking for the money, but all her belongings were still there. I had to get to Cherbourg.

My phone started vibrating in my hand. It startled me. Very few people had this number.

"Ava?"

It took me a second to place the voice. "Sandrine?" My grandmother Anais's neighbor in Cherbourg. Her friend for years. The woman who lived two doors down, took care of me when I was little, arranged her funeral when Anais died, and looked after the mostly empty cottage now. "How did you get this number?"

"It wasn't easy. I've been trying to reach you. Your grandmother's will is being probated this Saturday. Your name is on the Acte de Notoriété. You need to be there—"

"Sandrine, no. I got what she left me already. The treasure map of her bank accounts and letters that's had me and Marie at each other's throats for the past month. I don't want anything from her. I'm not even supposed to be alive to collect anything else."

"No, it's important you come. It's being held—"

This was another of Anais's games. I couldn't take any more than what was on my plate. "Don't even tell me, Sandrine. I don't even want to know where it is. I'm not playing. In fact, I'm headed to her cottage now. I'm outside Geneva, but I'll be getting the train in an hour or so."

"No, listen, Ava, this is important."

"No, Sandrine. No, you listen. I'm coming there to look through Anais's old photograph albums. Are they still there?"

"Nothing's been packed up yet. You know that—you were just here for her funeral. But we need to talk about this meeting with her lawyer, Ava. I've read through her things; if you just—"

"I'm not going. I don't need to be there. I'm dead, remember? Problem solved. I don't even want her money. It helps solve basic issues, but in the long run, all it does is complicate my life. Do you know the name Tommaso Lacroce, Sandrine? Does that ring a bell?"

There was a half second too long of silence. "No. Why?"

"You must. He apparently was in Saigon with Anais and Philomena years ago. Do you remember her saying anything about him at all?"

"When are you coming here—to the cottage?"

"I'm catching the train to Paris in a couple of hours. Then to Cherbourg. You figure it out. I'll be there within the next twelve hours or so, I'd say. Why?"

"Just so I know. We'll talk more about your grandmother's—"

"I'm hanging up. See you soon."

The half pint of whiskey was there, at the top of my bag. I unscrewed the top and took a huge gulp. I felt the fire in my mouth and throat. I loved that feeling because the warmth would spread to my empty stomach and then my limbs, and eventually my brain, numbing everything. I sat cross-legged on the bed and rested my hands on my knees. I tried to breathe deeply, filling my lungs.

She wouldn't answer any questions about Tommaso but seemed hell-bent on getting me more involved in the distribution of my grandmother's financial assets. From the little I knew of French law, there was no executor assigned to the will; it was up to each beneficiary and the Notoriété to handle and distribute assets. Maybe that's why Sandrine insisted I be there. But I didn't care. Anais's money had been stowed away before she died. The cottage, or so I'd been told, was to be divided between me and Marie. What else could there be?

Marie was in jail in the States. There was no way she was going to be available to attend this meeting, so it seemed reasonable that I didn't need to attend either. Any curiosity I had, and there was some, was quickly overridden by the trail of blood from Victor's body that led directly to me. It was possible Philomena had called me back to the house to set me up to take the fall for her husband's murder, but I didn't think that was true. I doubted the answers lay in Anais's will.

I put the bottle to my lips and took a big gulp. My path was clear. I needed to get some money from an account in Paris before it disappeared, get on that train to Cherbourg, and hide out until Victor's body and the trail to me grew as cold as ice.

CHAPTER 24

PHILOMENA

Vicenza, Italy

She sat in the chair by the window watching the light and shadows make patterns across Victor's face. She had known, of course, this day would come. But it hadn't for so long she'd held out hope it never would. The years had lulled her into a safe space, where the past was gone, never to be relived again. But here she was. Ava searching for her father was like pulling a thread on a large blanket and watching it unravel.

She deserved to know what happened to him, and there wasn't a day that went by that Philomena didn't wonder the same thing. And she knew the minute she saw Ava's face sitting in that car outside her home, when she'd returned to Vicenza to let them know she was alive, this was going to happen. Yes, she had known this day would come, she just hadn't known it was going to be so soon.

She took a breath and tried to remember the first time she'd seen Tommaso after he'd moved to Vicenza. It was by accident—in town. She was eating at a café on the street, with a friend, and she saw him pass by, just the side of his face. She'd dropped her fork, hearing it clang onto the plate, her mouth gaping, staring at him as he disappeared into the crowd.

Many sleepless nights later she learned he'd settled nearby. With a young wife. With every intention of staying on in town. He'd been raised near Teramo, three hundred miles south of Vicenza. He had no family in the area that she knew of. His work as an accountant was generic; he could find a job anywhere in Italy. Maybe even Europe. He'd chosen Vicenza for a reason. He told her it was to stay close, to keep each other safe. She never saw safety in his face or felt it in his presence, just anxiety and fear.

Saigon and the years of turbulence. That's how she thought of them. She was a teenager when the French lost their battle in the north. Her parents were there on *un'avventura*, as they called it. An adventure it was, investing in the burgeoning rubber and crude oil industries. The oppressive heat, the fogginess and humidity, the bugs, the dirt made her ill for almost the first full year in the country. An odd mixture of militant Vietnamese, French military, and a smattering of civilians filled the cobbled streets every day, but the tension between the factions was growing. She could feel it.

Then it exploded. Her parents talked of returning to Italy but opted to stay in the country and huddle with other ex-pats in Saigon in hopes of recouping lost revenue. The French were leaving North Vietnam, the country was split in two, and civilians were being pushed south or crossing the borders into Cambodia. The resettling, the scrambling for resources. During that push, that's when she met Anais Lavoisier. During the most turbulent time of her life.

Tommaso came several years later. And all she thought when she met him was, another Italian family, another Italian child was there. And that's how they all came together on dirty streets filled with so many people, so many languages, so much confusion, uncertainty. American advisors, government people, were beginning to appear in the south as quickly as the French were evacuating, mostly around the embassies, but then settling in other parts of the city. Philomena started hearing so much English in the streets, where before it was

Vietnamese, Cambodian, a smattering of French, and much less of any other language.

Finding an Italian family in that mix was like being transported to a café back home in Vicenza. Delicious. Comforting. She'd latched on to Tommaso, even his younger age hadn't mattered. He understood her. She understood him, and that was the springboard for all the problems that followed later. It seemed to spiral. And if she could take only one thing back in her life and no more, she'd take back the day she'd met him.

But there were no take-backs. She'd live forever knowing that she was to blame for everything that happened from that point on. Everything, if examined properly, could be pinpointed to that moment when she met the Italian boy, and that horrible day in Dong Xoai—it had changed her, the way she saw people, the way she felt about herself. She was a hostage to guilt and remorse. That all culminated in the bizarre way she'd given birth to Adrianna in the barn, Anais's anger and hostility, Adrianna's death, Davide's disappearance, even Ava, misguided Ava, who apparently had no qualms about killing another human being—that was her fault too.

She heard the door open, and two police officers and a nurse entered the hospital room.

"Signora DeFeo, the doctor says he is getting stronger. His vital signs are stable. It's a good sign he may wake up." They seemed to be watching her face. She just nodded. "You'll be glad to know we found his car."

Her head jerked up. "Where?"

"In a car park on the outskirts of Geneva. There were some blood drops found on the seat and the door handle. They're going out for testing now. We'll have results soon. We're going to need your DNA. I'm sure you don't mind."

She shook her head. "No."

"No?"

"I mean, no I don't mind. But I can't do it now. I want to sit here in case he wakes up."

The officer put on latex gloves and took a tube out of his pocket. "It's just a cheek swab. Nothing more."

He approached her, unscrewing the cap and pulling out a swab. She hesitated. She hadn't anticipated this. He held the swab and motioned to her mouth. For a split second the world stood still. They'd trapped her. The cotton moved against the inside of her mouth before she could decide what to do.

"So, we're done with your house," he said, screwing the cap back on. "And we have a question for you."

She was so weary. "What?"

"We believe your husband was attacked in the mudroom first. That some sort of struggle occurred there. Blood-spatter evidence, and luminol—well, we're exploring the possibility that there may have been two assailants."

"Two?"

"Or more. Yes. DNA will tell us exactly, Signora."

She stared down at Victor. His eyes flickered. His lids parted slightly, and she could see a pupil. "Oh my God. Nurse! Help him!"

The two nurses who entered the room and hovered over her husband, adjusting knobs and lifting his eyelids, gave her enough time to slip out the door. His waking up had saved her and condemned her in a literal blink of an eye.

CHAPTER 25

Joanne

Haddon Township, New Jersey

The picture Russell had been able to find in an archive was grainy black and white but clear enough to identify everyone. Anais was at the center. A man and woman, presumably her parents, stood on either side, Anais's arms wrapped around them. Two other people were crouched down in front of them, smiling. One was Philomena. The other was a younger boy; he was leaning into the frame, a big smile on his face, like he'd jumped in at the last second before the shutter snapped.

"That's him?" Joanne asked. Russell had reappeared on her doorstep at the first crack of light, seemingly recharged and ready to jump-start the investigation.

Russell nodded. "I'm pretty sure."

His coloring was hard to see in shades of gray, but it looked like he had light hair, medium complexion, an eager, happy face. "He looks so average. So normal."

"What did you expect?"

Her shoulders moved upward. "For him to be remarkable in some way? He's just . . . not."

"If I had to guess, I'd say this unremarkable boy"—he flicked his fingers at Tommaso—"is connected to everything—Davide's disappearance that same night he was killed, the fact that Victor was just stabbed—"

"Seriously, Russell? How, if he's been dead for twenty years?"

He was focused on the picture. "My gut says it has to do with something that happened even longer ago than that. Some secret all these people carried with them."

"I wonder . . . is there another family, anyone that was there in Vietnam with them, that might know them? It can't be that hard to find out who was attached to the American or British embassy in the late sixties. Maybe they know something about Tommaso," Joanne said.

His eyes lit up. "That's not bad. And not hard to find."

Twenty minutes later her head was buried in her computer, and Russell was on his phone with the embassy. She glanced up at him. He'd lost weight; dark purple-black circles had made a home under his eyes, making them look sunken, harsh, angry. He looked haggard, so different from even six months ago. His hair was frizzier, his skin yellower. His nails were chewed. Everything about him was defeated. He looked up and caught her inspecting him.

"Anything?" he asked.

"In a minute. But right now I need to know, just for myself, before we go any further with this: What was it about Ava? Why'd you feel so much for her that you let her escape? What was it?"

He sighed. "Joanne, at some point, when this is all over, I'll explain it to you. I promise. I'm a screwed-up human being; that's all I can say. I've maybe always been a bit screwed up—even before I went into the navy. Maybe that's why I went into the navy. Why I became a cop." He stopped for a second. "Not that cops are all screwed up. They aren't. But it worked for me."

She was staring at him. She'd never seen him like this before. Maybe everything she thought she knew about Russell had been a front. Fake.

This was the real person underneath it all. "Okay for now. So, I have two things—a list of the American ambassadors and staff in the late sixties through seventy-two. It might be best to start there. And an article." She stopped talking as her eyes ran over the page. "Interesting. It's just talking about the difficulties faced by civilians and government officials in the south. People evacuating, disappearing altogether."

"Is there anyone we can talk to? Any names mentioned?" he asked her.

"I say we take this list of names and divide it."

He nodded and hung up his phone. "No help there. It was just a voice message."

In the end it came down to two names. All the others had either passed away or couldn't be located. Of the two possibilities, one was a James Anderson that lived near Washington, DC, still alive. Nearly eighty-five years old. The second was a woman. Eleanor Clinton. She was a bit younger at sixty-five. An assistant to an assistant, her name only appeared once. Apparently she hadn't stayed long. Her address was listed as Ridgewood, New Jersey, a city to the north, close to New York.

"Both are Americans. They may not know anything," she ventured.

He grabbed his keys. "Maybe not, but it's a start, right?"

"Are you seriously going to just show up at the woman's door without calling? Isn't it a bit early? Can we stop for breakfast on the way?"

He stopped and looked back over his shoulder. "All I have is now, Joanne. Everything else in my life is gone. Come on."

Eleanor Clinton looked a full fifteen years younger than her stated age. She'd opened her door tentatively when they first knocked. She might have been sleeping, as her gray hair looked slightly disheveled and she was off guard.

"I'm not sure what you're looking for. I was only a child really," she'd said after many minutes of letting them in, then warming up with conversation. "Well, not really a child. Eighteen, in my first real job."

"I know you were. We're just wondering if you could give some insight into what it was like in Saigon after the French left—"

Her face twisted slightly. "Most people go to the library. There are many books on the subject. How did you find me?"

"From a list of dignitaries we found online. Terrible to burst in on you like this. But it's important. I guess we should get to the point."

"Please do."

"The American embassy, it was close to the French one? They were located in the same area of the city? They intermingled?"

Her eyes narrowed slightly. "The embassies were all together in the same general area, yes. I was there only nine months. My father had some connections and got me a job as a secretary. An intern of sorts. I hated every minute of it and left when I could."

"Why?"

"It was difficult every day. Hot and dirty, filled with disease—cholera, dysentery, malaria. Everyone's life was in upheaval. Everyone. The people from Hanoi were flooding south. There wasn't enough housing, food shortages. Families broken up. Divided interests within one household. And we"—she jabbed at her chest—"were outsiders. I never belonged there."

"Did you know other people from other embassies, like if I gave you a name?"

She shrugged. "It's been so many years. I doubt it."

"Lavoisier," Russell said. He threw it out when Joanne had wanted to ease into it.

Eleanor Clinton just stared at them for a minute. "The Lavoisier family lived down the street from me. I rented a room from a friend of my father's two houses away. Lavoisier was high up in the French embassy."

"So, you knew them?"

She nodded. "Sort of. People attached to an embassy lived in the same area. Socialized together. The daughter was around my age."

"Anais?"

"Yes. That one didn't have to work. It was all one big party. Her and her friends."

Joanne leaned in. "That bothered you?"

"It did. You don't understand. There were so many poor people. The country had been occupied for so many years. Colonized. Then this huge upheaval. They were struggling to get their footing. It was so unpleasant to be in the middle of it, and there she was, like nothing was happening. Money to spare, drinking and partying. Nice clothes. Oblivious to it all, really."

"Do you remember the Fiores? They had a daughter, Philomena. She later married a man named DeFeo. Victor DeFeo?" Russell jumped in.

She shook her head. "No, it doesn't ring a bell. But there were so many families—"

"Do you remember any of Anais's friends in particular?"

Her eyes darted between Joanne and Russell. "I'm sorry. I don't. All I know is that girl got hers. People always do. I heard she got pregnant by one of the young Americans in town. It was scandalous."

Joanne and Russell glanced at each other—that was Ross Saunders—and then back to her. "The pregnancy? The marriage?"

"Yes, that."

Joanne took a breath. "Do you know the name Lacroce? An Italian family there?"

Eleanor half laughed. "How could I not? Is that why you're here? To talk about them? You should have started there. It would have saved us time."

"What do you mean?" Russell jumped in.

"The father worked as an advisor to a US committee. He was in Italian intelligence. I'm not sure if it was through the Italian government or he was a mercenary for hire, but it didn't end well for them. They lost a child. Left the country right after."

"You remember that?" Joanne blurted. This woman couldn't remember Philomena but did know the Lacroces.

"I'll never forget. People were disappearing at the time; it wasn't unusual for families to be torn apart. Crossing into Cambodia. Running from the Viet Cong. The police were not organized. It was chaos. But a white child missing? That was something different. Especially in our small ex-pat community. People all talked about it. She could have been taken, who knows? But the family made an enormous stink about it. Rightfully so, but impossible. There was nobody to help them, even if they were European, even if they did have some money. Even if the father was with the government."

"A girl? It was a little girl that disappeared?"

She nodded. "Adrianna was her name. But they'd always called her Na. Just Na. Na Lacroce was all over the posters."

Joanne sat up straight. "No, that can't be right."

A line appeared between the woman's eyes as she scowled. "Of course it's right. I'll never forget. Na Lacroce. Three or so. She was with her older brother at the time it happened. And Anais Lavoisier was there too. They went out for the afternoon and came back saying they lost her; she ran away and got lost in the crowd."

"Her brother, Tommaso Lacroce?"

The older woman nodded. "Yes, that was his name. I left Saigon a month or so later . . ."

The woman's words floated away as Joanne and Russell locked eyes. Neither of them could say a word.

CHAPTER 26

VICTOR

Vicenza, Italy

His brain was awake before anyone knew it. They were all talking around him, but he couldn't respond. He couldn't move, not even a twitch. He was forced to lie there at the mercy of everything around him, locked inside his own brain. At times he would panic, feeling trapped and claustrophobic, but then it would subside, either through sleep or excruciating pain.

It took some time for him to piece together what had happened, where he was, why he couldn't move. He didn't know, couldn't remember. His brain was so foggy that he didn't even know his own name. The past drifted to him like pieces of a jigsaw puzzle sliding into place, with vast chunks of the whole picture missing. His wife, their little house in Vicenza came to him first. The dull pain of losing his daughter long ago. Then for a split second, his granddaughter. But that alarmed him because he couldn't remember their names. His mind was failing him. But it was more than that. There was a story about her that was important.

In moments when his mind became exhausted, he dreamed of his youth, of his mother and father, of Vicenza and trips to Venice before it was overrun by tourists, and Zagreb in Croatia, and Nice. His mother's hair was chestnut brown; he saw her smiling mouth. Then it was gone. His mind would awaken to blackness, nothingness, and he was unable to move or call out a name. He felt pain. Throbbing, then sharp desperate pain, and then he would mercifully pass out.

But during moments of clarity, he knew something had happened. Something terrible that had gotten him here, and he needed to remember. It was the only way he was going to wake up. He heard a woman's voice in his ear, but he had no way of reaching her. She said she'd taken a phone, Davide's phone. She'd found a way to charge it and listened to the messages. That made his heart rate go up, though he wasn't sure why. His mind seemed to jerk, his eyes fluttered, and for the first time he saw a bit of light that blinded him.

Hands were on him, they were adjusting him, poking him. He felt his eyelids being opened; a light shined that was so intense he thought his brain might burst, but he had no strength to try to move away or close his eyes. He was at their mercy. He heard the woman's voice.

"I need to stay here. I need to be by his side. I'm not going anywhere," she said.

"Philomena, Signora DeFeo, your husband is in good hands. I would think you might want to assist in finding out what happened to him." It was a male voice.

"I know what happened to him. Someone stabbed him in the throat. Go wait for the DNA you gathered, and let me know what it says," she countered.

"Signora. There is no change. It was a reflex reaction. I'm sorry," a female voice said. "We'll continue to monitor him closely."

Victor would have yelled if he could have. His wife's name was Philomena. He'd been attacked—stabbed in the throat, that's what happened. His thoughts were random, disorganized. Blurry. The details of the house where they lived were becoming clearer. Philomena's voice was familiar, comforting, but everything else was murky.

"The DNA came back from the blood on your purse. It's your blood mixed with your husband's. And a third party's. It defies explanation. So, we may insist you come to the station to discuss it further."

Philomena had not stabbed him. That wasn't what happened. He wanted to tell them, but he was a mannequin in the room, a piece of furniture. He was part of the bed, melting into the frame like one of Dali's clocks.

He remembered a flash. Somewhere in the back of his head. A flash of movement from behind him. A surprise jolt of pain in his neck. There was someone there. In front of him, but someone else too. Someone behind him. He had looked back over his shoulder at the pain but only saw a black hood. A bit of hair. The face—a woman's face—was completely covered. The eyes were so familiar. He knew her.

"I'm not answering any more of your questions without an attorney."

Victor wanted to hear their questions. He wanted to hear his wife's answers. They were so close to giving him information. If they mentioned the people who were there when he was attacked he would remember. He knew he would.

"As you wish, Signora. The blood from his car will be back soon, and I'm sure we'll talk again."

Philomena sat down next to him. He could hear her rocking in the chair. "When is this going to end, Victor? First Tommaso, now you. Anais is dead. The only one left who was there in Saigon, who knows what happened, is me. I got a letter, by the way. It's from Anais's lawyer. He's requesting our presence at the probate of her will. He says it's very important that we attend. That Anais has something to give us. Like she hasn't given us enough. What do you think? Should I go? I have no choice. It has me really curious now."

Victor suddenly felt immense fear. Philomena was in danger too. They were coming for her next. He wanted to scream out to her not to go to this meeting. It was a setup of some sort. But he had no way of communicating with her.

CHAPTER 27

Ava

Paris, France

I felt every bump, every jolt of the bus seat against my bottom as we moved down the highway toward Paris. It was a spontaneous but necessary move. I needed to get out of Geneva, putting as much distance between me and Victor's car as possible, and the cottage was the obvious choice. It's where the past was—the answers to so many questions. I'd stop in Paris to access money if I could. Otherwise, I'd have to make do with what was in my pocket and circle back to the bank in Geneva later.

I'd been watching my phone, desperate to hear something from Philomena, Sandrine, even Russell or Joanne, but it had been silent. I had no idea if Victor was dead or alive, sitting up in bed, being physically probed by nurses and mentally probed by police officials. The one thing I knew for certain—he'd never tell them what happened. He'd never name names, or recount the events that had played out in the mudroom. I knew that—the minute I saw the knife plunge into his neck and I stared into the eyes of the person holding the blade. When I heard his words to her—*I knew you were coming. It's not over. They'll get you eventually.* He knew her, but she answered him only by cutting him deeper. By opening up that can of worms, he'd be indicting himself.

"Mademoiselle? This is the last stop."

The voice jolted me. I grabbed my bag and rushed onto the platform. It was almost three, and I wanted to catch the train so I would arrive in Cherbourg before sundown. I had all my documents associated with the account organized to cut down on time. I checked my watch. If I walked fast, I could get to the bank, just across the river, in fifteen minutes.

I bumped into people as I rushed, transferring my bag from one hand to the other. If the bank closed, I'd be forced to move on with just the money in my pocket, which wasn't the worst thing in the world, but it left me feeling wanting, insecure.

I moved with the flow of people across the bridge, but I had an odd sensation I was being watched, followed. I looked over my shoulder, but the people all seemed to be like me, in a hurry, passing me, pushing me. I was getting paranoid.

The bank was open, and I pulled at the heavy glass doors and rushed to get my place in line. I kept looking in my purse to make sure my papers were still there, still clipped together, right on top. I felt a nervous flush cross my face. If there was an alert on my name, my journey ended here. They'd call the police; I'd be detained and sent back to the United States. I was wanted for murder in Pennsylvania and New Jersey, so it was likely if I landed in Philadelphia, I'd be staying there for a long time. At least I wouldn't have to hear Marie calling my name from the cell next door, as she'd be miles away, across the Delaware River.

I stepped up to the counter and pushed all my papers forward, my identification with my real name on it. If she asked for my passport, I didn't have one. Not in the name Ava Saunders anyway. I held my breath.

"Je voudrais le montant entier dans un chèque de banque, s'il vous plait," I said. I wanted it all in a cashier's check. It might take more time, but it'd be easier. Nine hundred thousand euros was a lot of money. It could last me a lifetime if I was careful.

"You have the pass code to this account?" she asked.

"Yes. It's not a number. It's a name: Adrianna Lavoisier." I breathed heavily and looked to the side.

"Just one minute." She took all my documents and went into the back. I slapped the marble counter with the palms of my hands, realizing I was sweating from head to foot.

She returned with my papers. "The manager wants to see you in the back, if you don't mind," she said. Not what I wanted to hear. I grabbed my bag and started to follow her when I noticed someone by the entrance to the bank. Their back was turned. A smallish frame, black coat—a woman. A hood hanging down her back. A hood like the one Victor's attacker wore, and a scarf that covered most of the back of her head. She had her hand on the doorframe. As I moved around the counter, I glanced back. She flipped her hood up and turned sideways, allowing me a half-second glimpse of her profile. Only a bit of the nose and a hint of chin.

I stopped in my tracks, my papers dropping to the floor and scattering. I couldn't see her full mouth, just the corners of her lips, but I knew she was smiling. It was her. She'd been following me.

I didn't want to scream or call attention to myself. Not now. I squatted and gathered my papers, and when I glanced up again, she was gone. My heart was rattling in my chest. I sat down in the chair in front of the manager's desk and tried to pull myself together. "Can I have some water? I don't feel well."

The woman smiled and handed me a small paper cup. "They'll be with you in a minute."

The meeting was straightforward, just a few questions for verification, but while I waited for the check to be drawn, I wasn't watching the clock. I was watching the door. Which was more terrifying—the fear of getting snagged for crimes in the States, or the fact that a potential murderer was lurking behind me, watching my every move, because I had witnessed her crime? It occurred to me then that I had instilled this same sort of fear in others many times over. I felt a familiar nauseous feeling starting in the pit of my stomach, then rising into my throat. It always happened when I thought of the people I'd killed. It rendered me unable to eat for days.

"Mademoiselle Saunders?" The man in front of me was expensive from head to toe. His suit might have cost the sum total of everything in this account. He wasn't smiling, his lips pulled thin into an expression of worry. "We cannot honor your request today. It's such a large amount of money . . . we need to refer this to our main branch—"

"And where is that?"

"Rue du Colonel Driant. First arrondissement."

"And how long will this take?" My fingers clenched and unclenched the armrest of my chair while I waited for an answer.

"It's hard to say. It will not be today. It's too late. Tomorrow, perhaps. Are you staying in town?"

This could not be happening. It felt like a trap. "If I need to. Is there some problem with the account, with my paperwork?"

"It's just unusual. An amount over five hundred thousand euros needs special approval. We have your cell phone number—we will call you tomorrow with an update."

He made a motion with his hand, and I knew this conversation was over. I pulled up from my seat and scanned the bank. The woman was gone and maybe so was my money. I left the bank, sorting my options. I could head to Cherbourg and then backtrack to get my money. Or I could wait it out in Paris for one night. One night wouldn't kill me. Though the murderer might.

Money was freedom, but that freedom had come at the price of my sanity.

CHAPTER 28

JOANNE

Haddon Township, New Jersey

"What do we do, Russell? I mean what do we do?"

He glanced over at her. "You said that twice."

"I know I did. Watch the traffic." They were headed south on 295 toward south Jersey. "So, this little Adrianna that disappeared? You think Philomena named her daughter after her for some reason? Was there a reason you can think of? Because it's weird."

"It is."

She turned sideways to face him. "Why, Russell? I mean this started as just a question of what happened to Ava's father. Simple enough, right? Then it turns into this other guy that was killed that night. Tommaso, I like saying that name."

"And now it goes back even further to Tommaso's sister—things that happened in Saigon fifty or so years ago. Let me tell you"—he shot her a look—"I can't imagine trying to investigate something that happened then. Records in Vietnam would be harder to access, probably incomplete. Memories are faulty. The truth may be gone—"

"It's not. I'll tell you why. Someone just stabbed Victor in the neck. So whatever it was, it's not gone."

"Joanne, we have to do something. We have no choice. Hear me out—"

"What? Hear you out, what?"

"We need to go to Europe. And maybe even Vietnam. I don't think we're going to get anywhere here in New Jersey. Everything we're looking for is there. That call from Ava—I can't just leave it."

"Yeah, no. That's one call that should have gone unanswered. And I've never been out of the country in my life, unless you consider Canada and Mexico foreign nations."

He whipped his head toward her and then back to the road. "No better time than now. We're both free, no jobs. We'll go back, pack bags, meet at the airport tonight. Those flights usually leave at night. We have a few hours."

"Just like that? It's that easy to take a trip? No planning, no preparation? Just go to the airport and hop on a plane to a place we've never been?"

"It is. With a valid credit card and a passport, you can go anywhere."

"I want to go to the jail instead. Now. I need to see Marie before I do anything."

"You can't just walk in. There's visiting hours. You have to plan it."

"What time is it now?" she asked.

He checked his phone. "Almost noon."

"I'm calling there now and asking for an emergency meeting. I'll say somebody died."

She started to dial, but he stopped her. "I'll just drive there and let you plead your case. But after that we're going to the airport."

◆ ◆ ◆

The machine blinked on before Joanne even had time to reach for the telephone receiver. Marie was there, looking at her, her lips curled at the very edges into a slight smirk.

"My mother is dead. My sister is dead, my niece, Ava, is supposedly dead, so what's the emergency, Joanne? Please? You said there was a death. That's the purpose of the visit. Who was it now?"

Joanne watched her for a long moment without reacting. "Eleanor Clinton. Ring a bell?"

Marie shrugged. "She died? Who is she?"

"She was in Saigon briefly. Long enough to know Anais, long enough—"

"Ah. Ha. You actually went looking into the past, then? You've gotten that far already? Shocking."

Joanne was starting to feel her blood pressure rising. "This isn't a game. Victor was stabbed—"

"And I told you he would be, didn't I?"

"So cut to the ending, do you know Tommaso Lacroce?" Joanne watched her face, but it was blank, expressionless. "And what happened to Adrianna One? Na, they called her. His sister."

Marie tilted her head back and laughed. "Adrianna One, I like that."

"You know what happened, though, and why this even matters?" Joanne countered. "Tell me."

Marie seemed suddenly captivated by the camera. She folded her hands and stared straight into the lens. "I wasn't alive yet during that time, so I don't know any of this firsthand. I met Tommaso when I was little. He was just walking down the street in Philadelphia. I knew something was wrong when I saw him and my mother interact. He was upset. He'd gotten some sort of letter or report—"

Joanne slapped the table and started to stand up. "Your family never ceases to amaze me. How much more is there, Marie?"

"Do you want to know what's going to happen next? Is that why you're here? I was right about Victor, and you want to know how I knew."

"You think Ava did that?"

"I sent that card to pique your interest. When I said Ava was going to kill, it was just a lucky guess—a little game. But I'm going to tell you this much. When Ava discovered her birth family, it was only a matter of time before she asked about her father. And in asking about her father, it set some things in motion because he's connected to all of this."

Joanne couldn't find the perfect response, though she tried and several things came to mind.

"So, if you and Russell want to keep digging, keep digging," Marie continued. "Just be careful, because it might have started nearly fifty years ago, but it all still very much matters to certain people."

"I'll bite, Marie. What's going to happen next? Tell me."

She shrugged. "Am I Nostradamus now? Fine. I'm going to answer your question with a list of new questions. Answer them at your peril. Ready?" Joanne nodded but said nothing. "Okay then. One: How is Anais connected to all of this?"

"She was in Vietnam with—"

"Don't answer now. Just listen. Or write it down. Question two: How could Davide, Philomena's daughter's boyfriend—because that's who he was—be connected to something that happened almost fifty years ago in Saigon?"

"Go on. Next question."

"No, that there is the nugget, Joanne. I've said too much already."

"You know everything, don't you, Marie? The whole story, the backstory, the in-between story. All of it?"

Marie smiled. "I do. In many ways, I've lived this story. And thank God, for now, I'm in here. Because I wouldn't want to be in the middle of this for anything. So, my next prediction is that the lies sweet Philomena has told over the years will blow up in her face. Some terrible wrongs will be made right. Ava may or may not survive it. But in the end she will realize Anais and Claire protected her for many years from this. She owes us all a big thank-you."

"That's all?"

She smiled. "Oh, and you will meet the man of your dreams within the next six months and will marry—"

"Cut it out," Joanne blurted.

"You'll see."

"What happened to Na? Tommaso's sister. At least tell me that?"

"Russell's a detective. If I were you, instead of trying to figure out who killed Tommaso, find out who he was. Go find his family." She hesitated. "Not his wife, his family. His father was working for Italian military intelligence back then—that's why they were in Saigon. Figure out the story behind Na's disappearance. Victor was getting too close to the truth, or maybe he'd been sitting on it for a long time. That's why he was stabbed."

"Why do I have to go on a scavenger hunt when you can just tell me what I want to know, Marie? Where were you between July sixteenth and July twentieth, nineteen ninety-six? Were you in Rome? Is that why you're telling me to go to Italy? Did you kill Tommaso?" Marie stared blankly into the screen. "But why? Why would Tommaso be a threat to you? Unless you were just doing your mother's work—Anais was always good at keeping her hands clean. Was he threatening Anais in some way?"

"I'd say you have your work cut out for you. Because I have no idea what you're talking about." Without another word, Marie pushed up from the table and turned off the camera.

CHAPTER 29

Olivia

Vicenza, Italy

Enjoy the time you have left, Olivia, because it's very precious.

Her brain hurt from reading the words in Anais's letter too many times. Olivia steered her car into the hospital parking garage and sat there for a minute trying to figure her next steps. She needed to see Victor DeFeo before deciding if a visit to Tommaso's mother in Teramo was necessary.

The hospital corridor was brightly lit but empty save for a few unoccupied stretchers pushed against the wall. Olivia moved quietly to the room, holding her breath slightly, concern and rage building with each step. She wasn't sure what she would say to Philomena if they came face-to-face, but she didn't have the chance to figure it out. The room was blocked by two police officers. When she peered in, Philomena was backed up against the wall, watching the nurses attend to Victor. One lone officer seemed to be consuming her energy.

Philomena looked up and caught Olivia's eye. "Why are you here?" She took a step into the room and stopped. "To see Victor?"

"He's not awake."

She walked to a side table and put down a small plant and a card she'd grabbed in the shop. "I just wanted to pay my respects."

Philomena took a step toward her. "He's not dead. You pay respects when someone's died. He's not dead."

"Of course. That's not what I meant." She faltered. "I . . . Philomena, I need to ask you some questions. It's bad timing, but—"

"About?"

There were six other people in the room, between nurses and police. Olivia glanced at them, bothered she wouldn't be allowed a private word. "You came to my house that night. The night this happened. And I don't understand why. After giving it some thought, I realized you were there for another reason," she whispered, making sure no one was close enough to hear.

Philomena folded her arms. "And what reason was that?"

"Other than an alibi—"

Philomena backed away and looked at Victor. "I don't need one. I didn't do this."

"But I think there was more," Olivia continued. "Showing me Davide's phone but not letting me really see it was a tease. Why would you do that? What did you find on the phone? Or did you just want me to know it's there?"

Olivia was angry at herself that she hadn't waited for Philomena to turn back to her before she'd said that. She'd needed to see her face. Her reaction. All she caught of her expression was the side of her face. But that little bit showed surprise.

"Davide's outgoing and incoming calls. Messages from my daughter. Is there something in particular you're worried about, Olivia?" Her arms were now crossed. She was getting annoyed. "Maybe information about your husband's movements, why he went to the park that night?"

"What do you mean?"

"Olivia, your husband died twenty years ago. You were only in your forties at the time. You could have moved on, yet you've wasted all this time circling his corpse. The only reason I can see for that is overwhelming grief or guilt. Was he headed there—to the park—for a reason, and you didn't stop him when maybe you should have? Is that it?"

Olivia recoiled at the harsh words. But she knew Philomena was trying to distract her. She had to stay the course. "When is the last time you talked to Anais?" Olivia said.

This time, it was Philomena who took a step back. "It's been many years. Why?"

"I'm on her Acte de Notoriété, and I'm wondering why. What's this probate all about?"

Philomena covered her mouth with her fingertips and seemed to be thinking. "I don't know. I was invited too. I've debated going. There's nothing Anais could have left me that I want."

"I never even met her. What was her relationship to Tommaso? Other than being acquainted almost fifty years ago."

"Just that."

"She left me a letter saying she talked to him constantly. That he knew he was going to be killed—"

"Don't put too much stock in Anais's games. It's a reach from the grave to torment you. That's all."

"How would he know he was going to be killed? Philomena? What were the three of you—you, Anais, and my husband—what were you up to? What was the pull between you?"

"Olivia. Please. I know you've been through so much. If you keep digging—"

"If I keep digging, what?"

"You may be the next one stabbed. My husband was doing exactly what you're doing—pushing and digging. He had this theory—we were all so paranoid of one another by then. We would get these letters—they went on for years. He thought Anais was behind it. Then he thought it was one of Anais's children. For a while, he even thought it was me. Be careful. Sometimes ignorance is bliss."

"I was never allowed bliss. Tommaso was getting them too. The letters. I always knew when he got one. He'd be quiet for days. Really nervous, but he'd never tell me what they were about. Funny, he always thought it was Anais that was sending them too. But I never understood the threat." Philomena stared at the woman so long without saying anything, Olivia tilted her head to the side. "What?"

"I thought you never knew Anais existed before Tommaso's death. That's what you said. The widow who stumbled upon her husband's past—that was the role you were playing? Tommaso told you everything, didn't he?"

Her face reddened. "No, I—"

"Game's up, Olivia."

She glanced at Victor and then back at Philomena. "I'll tell you when the game's up, Philomena. Next time you stab someone? Don't come to my house afterward, okay? It put me in a bad spot. And if you want to show me Davide's phone, show it to me. You and Anais are two of a kind." She glanced at the bed. "Take care of your husband."

Philomena's face was suddenly in hers; she grabbed her arm and squeezed it. "Play your little act if you want. See where it gets you. Be my guest." She cast her eyes toward the officers. "But be careful, Olivia. You may not know as much as you think."

One officer glanced over at them, and Philomena let go. Olivia smoothed the sleeve on her blouse and hurried out the door.

CHAPTER 30

Victor

Vicenza, Italy

He felt the lights on his lids. They were bright, hot, shining relentlessly on his face. They were keeping him awake. Keeping him from sleeping. He wanted to sleep. Being unable to move, stuck in one position, hearing the movement around him was making him feel trapped. When he slept, he dreamed of his life, in the past, moving in front of him in slow motion, but he was the star. He could savor the good parts, and he always knew what was coming next. It was like watching a favorite movie over and over.

The lights dimmed, and he felt himself drift. He saw Philomena's face. She was smiling at him. They were on a busy, dusty street in Saigon, standing on a corner watching people move impossibly large items on bicycles and mopeds. He turned his head and poked Philomena. A man had balanced an armchair on the back of his bike, a child had taken a seat on the handlebars. He watched the worn tires tread past where they stood, expecting the rickety wheels to either fly off or deflate. Neither happened.

Families stayed together, using wooden wagons to wheel bigger children, with infants strapped to women's chests. It was upheaval. He was only visiting at Philomena's insistence, but it seemed he'd picked the most dangerous of times to accept an invitation to Saigon. She seemed unaware or indifferent to what was happening around her.

"I don't think you should go, Philomena," he said. The conversation was playing out for him in detail, complete with dust on his clothes and the feeling of oppressive humid heat bearing down on him.

"Why?" Her expression was one of innocence, but later, he wondered whether she'd known something was going to happen.

"I don't like Tommaso. I told you that before. I don't like him. I'm not sure I even like his parents."

She stopped walking and looked at him. "Why? His parents are fine to me."

"His father is deeply involved in political happenings here. It's dangerous. And he's only coddling your relationship because you're familiar. Your language, your culture. Otherwise he wouldn't care a thing about a woman five years older. And an engaged woman at that."

She laughed a high-pitch trill that annoyed him. "He's thirteen years old, Victor. He's not looking for romance. He's looking for trouble—"

"He's big for thirteen, almost as tall as I am. Restless. Is what you told me before, what he did to that animal, was it true?"

Her hair was dark, tucked back behind one ear. Her eyes were smiling, though her mouth wasn't. "I shouldn't have told you that. I shouldn't have. But yes, it was true. It was just a rat, though. So many rats here. Disgusting."

"He belongs in lockup. And you feel safe going with him—"

"And Anais, don't forget Anais."

He smirked. "I don't think I could if I wanted to." Her sharp elbow hit him hard in the ribs.

"We're going north on an errand for his father. Nothing more. We'll only be gone half a day."

"You told me. But how far north?"

"No farther than Dong Xoai. He begged us to go with him. Begged."

"If anything happens with Tommaso—if he does anything strange, I want you to leave. I want you to run—"

She took his hand. "We're going to be fine . . ." But he knew they weren't. He felt it in his gut.

Victor wanted to yell at them, to tell Philomena not to go. But the voice faded, and he felt the light on his eyes again. Glaring against his closed lids. A hand was touching his arm, a needle being inserted into the back of his hand. It hurt, but he had no way of resisting. He heard voices around him.

"I redid his IV. It seems to be working fine. Just be careful not to bump his arm," the female voice said.

"Okay." It was Philomena. She was there, by his side. "Victor, I know you're in there. I can feel it. I just wonder what you're doing with yourself. What are you thinking about? Maybe I should come here and read to you. Maybe the novel you left on the nightstand? Would you like that?"

"Mrs. DeFeo?" A male voice this time.

"Yes?"

"The blood results are back from your husband's car."

"And?" He heard his wife's voice go up, becoming reedy. He hated when she talked like that.

"There was a mix of blood in the car. Same as on your purse. Three different blood types. We ran DNA and came up with two matches. One was your husband's, which wasn't surprising. One didn't match in our system, but we're still looking. And the third was yours."

"Yes, I told you I cut my hand when I put it on the shelf. The knife was there—"

"There's no explanation for your blood being in the car. You cut your hand after the killer escaped in the car, right? Is there anything else you want to tell us?"

He couldn't see her expression; he had no idea where she was in the room and how many police officers were with her. He kept trying to put the information together. Philomena wasn't there. He would have known if his wife had done this.

He suddenly felt woozy. They'd put something in his IV that was making his thinking confused. He was trying to hold on to his thoughts, but in the flash of a second, the light was gone. It was dark outside, and Philomena was with him. They were outside her house in Saigon, near the cracked concrete steps. She was crying. Her face was so stained with tears, it was red and slightly swollen. She had deep angry scratches on the side of her neck from her collarbone to her jawbone. She'd been running, and her whole body was shimmering with sweat. Her hair was plastered to her scalp.

He took hold of her wrists. "Lolo, what happened?"

"Take me away from here," she begged. "Take me to Italy with you. Tomorrow. Promise me?"

"Why, tell me why? What happened with Tommaso and Anais? Did you go to Dong Xoai?"

Her gold-brown eyes were swimming in tears. "You were right. I never should have gone with Tommaso. People were killed, Victor. Tommaso killed people. If you don't take me to Italy, I might not get out of here alive."

CHAPTER 31

Marie

Camden County Jail, New Jersey

She heard the heavy lock click, and her door opened. "You have an hour out, Nun. Take a shower, use the phone, whatever." The officer turned and walked to the sliding doors without a glance back.

Marie was on protective-custody status, and all the inmates on the block were locked in and probably resentful that they had to concede the day room for an hour so she could lounge around in their common space. They watched her every move through the porthole cell windows, she knew. Marie went to the phone and dialed a number.

"We need to talk," she said when the other line picked up.

There was just the sound of breathing at the other end. "I told you not to call me from the jail. This phone is just for emergencies."

"I have no choice. You're the only contact I have. What's going on?"

"Things are moving along, I'd say."

"Joanne was here for the second time." She put her back against the cinder-block wall and saw a pair of eyes staring out through the window of the cell directly across from her. "I told her to contact Tommaso's family."

There was a heavy sigh from the other end of the phone. "Why? Marie, finish your time there. We'll talk when you get out."

Marie flipped around and faced the wall, lowering her voice. "Any word from her?"

"I'm keeping an eye on her, let's put it that way."

Marie bit her lip. "Watching her? She went to the cottage, didn't she?"

"She'll show up . . . she's on her way—"

"And she'll find the photograph?"

"She will, trust me. And she'll do what she's supposed to do. If not, there's going to be a complication we didn't plan on."

"How so?"

"If Ava still refuses to go to the meeting—"

"Anais wanted her there—"

"She wanted you there too. And look what happened."

"Handle it, then," Marie sputtered. She realized she'd said it too loud, and now more than six pairs of eyes were peering at her, watching her every move. "I arranged everything else, even from in here."

"I need to go. Do you have any idea how much this call is costing me?"

"Ava has the bank code. There's millions just sitting there. The fifty-something this is costing you is nothing—"

"I can get the code without you, Marie. I'm not in this for money. But I'll cut you out and leave you there if you cause me one problem. Is that clear?"

"Cut me out and I'll turn you in. It'd make a fantastic story, don't you think?" The words weren't even out of her mouth when she heard the line click off.

She hung up the receiver and stared back at the eyes staring at her.

"What are you looking at?" she muttered.

She wandered into her cell, listening to the voices coming through the walls. The acoustics caused a hollow echoing sound all the time.

Everything was amplified tenfold. She put her hands to her ears to block out the sound just as an officer came to the door.

"Nun, you got a letter."

She took the piece of mail from her hand. It had been opened and read, as all mail was that came into the facility. There was no return address on it, but the sender had known the exact address where to reach her, including her inmate number. It had been postmarked from Philadelphia. A piece of paper inside had been folded and unfolded many times by the looks of it. She opened it gently.

> *Marie,*
> *I have proof you were in the Cresole park that night. You rented a car in Rome and drove north. I tracked you all the way to Bologna. I saw you get gasoline at that old station. Did you know I was watching you, following you? Did you see me? It wouldn't take much to interest the appropriate parties. I wonder how long extradition to Italy would take?*
> *Cheers.*

The letter wasn't signed. Marie tossed it onto her bed and put her hands to her face. Someone was watching her, was searching her past, knew where she was, knew where she'd been. She suddenly felt afraid and pulled her cell door shut until the lock clanged into place.

There was banging that started from inside one cell door and multiplied from there to the entire area. "Hey, if Nun is locking in, let us out!"

That one voice sounded like a thousand. Marie put her hands over her ears and started rocking.

CHAPTER 32

Joanne

Rome, Italy

It was 3:20 a.m. Philadelphia time when the plane landed in Rome. Joanne didn't care that the clocks said it was morning, or that the sun was shining brightly through the airport windows; her body knew what time it was. And it bothered her that Russell didn't seem to feel the same way. He was moving at a fast clip, his black case rolling smoothly behind him. No sign of fatigue at having flown for over eight hours with no sleep.

"So, what's the plan?" She was scurrying along, talking to his back.

"I don't have one. Immigration. Then we'll figure it out. Rent a car. Head to Teramo—Tommaso's mother is still alive. It's a few hours away. We're close—it should be the first stop."

She picked up her pace so she was walking beside him. "To his mother's? We're going there first?"

He shot her a look. "I don't know. I'm sorting it out in my head. I want to hear more about her missing child."

"Who are you going to say we are—that we're just showing up with questions?" They'd reached the end of a long line twisting toward a row of immigration officers.

"We have two things going on here. One, it seems implausible that Marie would go to Rome, then head north to this one particular park unless she was meeting him or knew he was meeting someone else there. How else would she know he was going to be there? And then why? Why would she have any desire to get involved in any of this? She'd already been in the shitshow in New York after Ava's mother was killed in the church. It's inconceivable—"

"Andare avanti." The man was motioning them forward.

They moved up and went through immigration one after the other. "And two?" she asked.

"Two? We have the missing child, which I just feel in my gut is the string that ties this whole thing together."

"So, are we getting a hotel room first, so we can sleep a little? Sort this out?"

Sleep came later. Russell seemed unfazed by the two-hour drive from Rome to Teramo on a major highway through Italy, shifting the gears as necessary because the rental company had no automatic cars left for hire. Joanne pressed her head into the crease between the seat and the window and tried to rest.

"The only reason Marie would have made that trip is because of Anais. Marie didn't have connections with Tommaso. Or Philomena either. She was living her nunny life in New York. Claire was knee-deep in the baby-Ava drama at the time. It had to be Anais." Russell broke the silence.

"Do you know where you're going? Exactly?" Joanne asked. "The street signs aren't even in English."

"She's in Teramo. That much I got from my phone when I was waiting for the car. A nursing home from what I could make of it. But I'm not sure which one." He tossed the phone in her lap. "Try and figure it out."

He seemed to be charged now, directed, focused. Like the Russell she had known when he was with the Prosecutor's Office. On top of things. Competent. For a half second she was glad she'd agreed to come with him.

It took a half hour for her to find a tentative address. "I don't know, Russell. All these names are so complicated, but I think this is the right one. Casa di Riposo, City Residence." She sounded it out. "I had to pull it up from the address listed. Via Vincenzo Irelli, 16, 64100, Teramo, Italy. That's what it says. What do the numbers mean?" When she looked up, he had plugged it into the GPS.

He pulled into a parking lot a few minutes later and turned off the engine. "Really? You're going in?" Joanne asked.

"That's the third time you asked that. Yes. We have to do this, Joanne."

"Okay, well, maybe they're eating lunch. Should we wait? Go get a hotel room? Take a nap?" She started to unzip her purse.

"If you open that purse one more time to make sure your passport's in there, I'm taking it from you, Joanne. I mean it. Get out and come with me. You can sleep tonight."

The old woman's room was empty, but they found her in the day area, sitting by a window. Tommaso's mother was in her late eighties but was ancient by the looks of her skin. Her face had caved in on itself and lost so much flesh that had padded her bones, she looked like a walking skeleton. The jowls hung so that they shook every time she moved her head. Her gray hair was cut short and was thinning so that her pink scalp was clearly visible between strands. Her leg was in a cast up to her knee.

"Signora Lacroce?" Russell started. She moved her head toward them but didn't respond right away. They waited—Joanne was slightly annoyed that they'd driven two hours to see this woman, and she was just sitting in her seat remaining silent. "Do you have a minute?"

"It doesn't look as cold as it's been. Things have warmed a bit," she said. She probably thought they were staff.

"Mrs. Lacroce? Do you speak English?"

"Yes?" Her brow wrinkled. "A little bit." Her words were correct but very heavily accented.

Russell sat near her. "You don't know me. But I know about you. Sort of. You were in Saigon around nineteen sixty-eight—or sixty-nine?"

"Saigon? Yes. How do you know that?"

Joanne felt clumsy just standing, so she sat in the empty chair on the other side of her. "It's hard to explain, but we know Anais Lavoisier's granddaughter . . . we're trying to piece together what happened—"

"Anais Lavoisier. Her and that Philomena. I blame them for what happened to my baby. I hope the granddaughter is a better person."

Joanne thought about Ava and started to roll her eyes but caught herself. "You've had some losses—"

"Because of those two, I lost my daughter. They went out with Tommaso. On a half-day trip to Bu Non—that's where they said they were going—I'll never forget that name. I didn't want them to go—it was dangerous, but my husband kept insisting it was okay. My biggest mistake was letting them take my daughter, Na, with them. She was just three. Just three at the time."

"Tell me the story from the beginning. Please? Maybe there's something—"

"There isn't. But I'll tell you anyway. Things were horrible in Saigon in '68. The Viet Cong attacked the city during the Tet holiday—the Vietnamese New Year. I remember Tet fell at the end of January and the fighting went on for almost a month. They were blowing up the city, setting things on fire. Nonstop gunfire everywhere. There were dead bodies in the streets, just lying there and nobody could get to them. Buildings and cars in flames. We were hunkered down that February, almost didn't leave the house. They even took hold of the US embassy. Did you know that?"

Russell nodded. "Yes."

"Viet Cong held the American embassy in Saigon for hours. Five or more Americans were killed." She shook her head. "Terrible. We were so scared. The ARVN—that was the army in South Vietnam—were fighting back. It calmed down gradually in the months after that, then started back up again that spring—bam, the Viet Cong were all over the city again. All I wanted was to go home. I told my husband that very morning—the morning they took that bus trip—that I was going home. If Na hadn't disappeared that day, we would have been gone within the month. So they went out that morning and came back without my daughter. Philomena said she let go of her hand in town, and she slipped away. In Bu Non! It's not a busy city. They said they were in the marketplace. And they looked everywhere. They didn't come home until late, crying. All three of them. Anais was all dirty. I'd never seen her like that. Philomena's face was swollen from tears—she had big scratches on her neck—said it was from Tommaso. He'd hit her or something when he realized what she'd done, losing his sister. That's all I know."

"So what happened after she disappeared? Did the police search?"

She half laughed. "There were no police. Nothing. We made a report. They said they looked. My husband looked. My husband was ex-intelligence. He couldn't find her. He stayed back for over a year looking for her. It was like she vanished off the face of the earth."

Joanne watched her face as she was telling the story. It was an old worn track she'd gone over many times, but the pain hadn't subsided. "So after you left, then what?"

"Then the country was in chaos with the worst part of the American War. There was no looking for her. No talking. I called the Italian embassy every week. So much that they started expecting my calls. Nothing. By the time the war was over, and it was safe to travel, it was way too late. But the worst? My Tommaso was murdered twenty-eight years later. For no reason."

They were all quiet for a moment, letting it all settle in. "Did your husband leave any notes? Anything at all about his investigation into your daughter's disappearance?" Russell asked. "If he did, I'd like to see them, if you don't mind."

"He left some boxes. I don't have them here. They're in my house, in the basement. I'm only here because I broke my leg. I was living at home up until a few months ago. But what do you think you'll find at this point?" she asked.

"I want to find out what happened to your daughter. And who murdered your son. I have this idea that won't go away, that the two are connected. Give me access to the files, and I'll do my best for you. I promise you that."

"Anais Lavoisier is dead. I'm not sure how I learned that, but I did. The only one left is Philomena. Make her pay, and you have a deal."

CHAPTER 33

Ava

Cherbourg, France

It was dark as the train pulled into the Cherbourg station, and even darker without city lights for illumination, when my taxi dropped me off at the end of the road where Anais's cottage stood. The windows reflected a stillness, as if it had been abandoned for decades.

The night before, in Paris, I'd left the bank, sorting my options. I could leave town and give up on this particular account, though I feared it would raise concerns, red flags, investigations. And they had my identification, not that I needed it, but I didn't want to leave evidence behind that Ava Saunders was alive and breathing and sashaying into banks in Paris. No, I had no choice but to hole up for the night in Paris and try and sort it out the next day.

Paris had never particularly been my friend. I could never quite enjoy the charm and splendor, the architecture, or the history. Each time I passed through, it was either during turmoil or when my money was so scarce that finding a two-euro coin in the couch was a godsend. Days and nights on end of crummy jobs, never having enough to survive. The City of Light was a stark reminder to me of exactly how bleak life could be when you're alone and broke and undesirable. Being trapped there for the night made me feel all of those things even more so.

I weighed my options and my money and took a room in the Grand Hôtel Lévêque, a dodgy little dated tourist trap of a hotel not too far from the Eiffel Tower. The room was so small that when the door opened, it hit the bed, but the room had a Juliette balcony that opened onto Rue Cler, a charming little market street, good for people watching. A bottle of booze, a pack of cigarettes, and my phone for company, I squeezed myself onto the window ledge and watched the merchants close for the day, the sun set, and most of the lights fade away. It was in that moment that I realized, whatever the next day would bring, there was not one person in the world who would care. I was utterly alone.

The call from the bank came at exactly two twenty the next afternoon. I'd almost given up all hope and considered bolting, but instead I checked out of the hotel and took up residence at a café, whiling the hours away with wine and cigarettes. The man from the bank who finally reached out was abrupt and to the point. They were requesting my presence at the same branch I'd been to the day before, at my earliest convenience. I saw the wall of men assembled in the lobby before I even entered the building. An ambush waiting for me. I took a halting breath and stepped over the threshold.

"Ah, Ms. Saunders. Come to my office; have a seat." The man from yesterday pulled out a chair for me. The other men followed behind.

I sat and crossed my legs. My black jeans and white shirt looked out of place next to their immaculate suits.

"We have some questions for you. Regarding this request. You provided identification, but we need more. A passport? An address? Your country and place of residence? For starters."

I was stuck. I didn't have any of those things, really. "I don't have a passport with me. It's in Cherbourg. That's where I'm staying. In

Cherbourg. At my grandmother's cottage. Is it necessary to have a passport to withdraw this money?"

They looked at one another. "This entire situation is out of the ordinary. Under normal circumstances the money would be wired to another account. With a sum this large—"

"That's not possible. I don't know where I'm going to be. I can go to Cherbourg, get my passport, and come back. That's going to take some hours and make me angry."

"We want to make sure you're really ready to withdraw this money. There are so many other options. I'm not sure you're aware it can be available for withdrawal through any of our sister banks. We can assist you in any way possible, provide a list, set up another account, move the money, maybe invest it. We don't want to lose your business. Let us explore—"

I shook my head. "I'm late. I need to leave town. I'd just like the cashier's check and my paperwork and identification back. Please." All of my angst melted. They only wanted my business, not me. A half hour later, I left the bank with everything that belonged to me, with a group of men staring after me, wondering how this woman in semidirty clothes had lost them a major account.

Now, in the darkness, I took a breath and went around to the back patio of Anais's house and tried the door. The lock was broken, ripped from the wood panel; the knob turned in a circle without undoing the latch. The door was slightly ajar, moving back and forth a centimeter with each burst of air. Someone had beaten me here and broken in.

The place was cold, damp, abandoned—nothing more than a collection of stone and mortar that provided a barrier to the elements. I shut the door and latched it from the inside and flicked the light switch. Nothing. The electricity and heat had probably been turned off. Wood was still stacked to the side of the fireplace, and it only took ten minutes to get some flames going. I turned on the flashlight on my phone and looked around. At initial glance, everything was the same as the last time I'd been here. Russell had tracked me down here only weeks ago and nursed me back to health. The empty liquor bottles he'd dumped were still lined up on the counter in the kitchen.

I wandered in there and opened the cabinets. I hadn't eaten anything in a day and a half. I hadn't even had much to drink, boozewise, and I was feeling light-headed. There was nothing but some spices, an old bottle of soy sauce, and a half bag of white rice in the cupboard. Enough for a meal. I set a saucepan filled with water on the burner and turned the knob. I heard the gas hiss, but there was no flame. After lighting the burner with a match, I went into the living room.

The bookshelves were there, but it was obvious someone had been in here, had dug through Anais's things, looking for something. Books were pulled out, scattered about the floor, pages ripped out, photographs from the albums were loose and littered the shelves. I stared at the mess for a few moments. My conversation with Sandrine had been short, but she knew where I was, when I should have arrived, and that I was interested in Anais's albums. It had to be her who'd ransacked this room. What was she afraid I'd find? I headed into Anais's office. The desk was in the same condition. But oddly, her will was lying on the top.

Anais Lavoisier-Saunders Testament et Dernières Volontés. I hadn't seen an actual copy before and wondered why it was just sitting here out in the open. Then I saw the note. My name was scrawled across the top. *Ava, I knew you'd get here eventually. Please read at your leisure. When you're done, come to my house.* It wasn't signed, but I knew it was from Sandrine. I picked up the document and carried it with me to the kitchen.

The water was boiling so hard I pulled the pot from the burner and poured in the last of the rice from the bag, salted it, and added some herbs and spices and a little soy sauce, then covered it before putting it back to simmer on a diminished flame. I desperately wanted a bottle of something to lull me into tomorrow, but this cottage was far from anything that might be open. I could walk down the street to Sandrine's but opted not to. She might see the light from the fire and come to investigate anyway. But my gut told me to leave well enough alone for now.

I opened my grandmother's documents and spread them out in front of me. Anais had hidden and stashed money her whole life. It was compulsive, based in anxiety and fear, in case someone tried to come back and take it from her. The years from the start of her marriage until she left Ross five years later had scarred her, made her know what it meant to have absolutely nothing. Going from an openly extravagant lifestyle in Saigon to living on a warehouse worker's salary in Philadelphia had jarred her. Anais was flamboyant and frugal, innocent and conniving all at the same time.

Her beneficiaries were listed on the top page. It was a short list. Her daughter, Marie; granddaughter, Ava; friend, Sandrine; four cousins—two from her father's sister, two from her father's brother. Her lawyer, Milo Rotton, and one Olivia Lacroce, wife of Tommaso Lacroce. That was it. The bequests, as far as I could tell, didn't include the money she'd stashed all over Europe and Asia for Marie and me to battle over.

I stared at the name Olivia Lacroce. Anais had added her to the Acte de Notoriété, left her something in her will, probably called her to the probate. I was so transfixed, I was only roused when I smelled a strong odor coming from the kitchen—my rice. I took it from the heat to see the bottom had formed a burnt crust. I scraped it onto a plate and went back to my reading.

Olivia Lacroce bothered me. Not her personally, just her name being included in Anais's Acte de Notoriété. Anais never did anything casually. She wasn't random or reckless. Everything, down to the smallest detail, was coordinated, calculated. She wanted Olivia at this meeting for some reason, and I was sure it had nothing to do with giving her money. Anais was up to her drawn-on eyebrows in something.

I shuffled through Anais's will, page by page. Boring, and more boring. I flipped through to the end, eager to concentrate on my burnt-rice dinner, when I saw something flutter to the floor. I stared at it. The will was just left as a minor draw, a curiosity. It was the photograph lying near my foot—that was what I was meant to see.

CHAPTER 34

Olivia

Vicenza, Italy

She sat on a chair in the garden and pulled a cigarette from the pack. It wasn't a usual habit, but she found herself reaching for them more than she would have liked. She watched the smoke climb above her head in swirls. Philomena had made her so angry. Her face, the way she talked. Everything was a lie, on both their parts. Olivia *had* known who Anais was before Tommaso's death; she'd heard the name, Philomena's too. She'd known about their time together in Saigon years before.

So many things were a lie. The private investigator had been hired for a purpose, but every time he called, she held her breath. She feared he'd trip over the unimportant inconsistencies in her story, how she knew more than she was supposed to, but he never did. Either his focus was off, or he was terrible at his job. She wasn't sure which.

She put out her cigarette and went inside. The letters. They'd been safely put away, a string around them to keep them secure. Tattered from being opened so many times, some had tiny tears at the creases, or yellow faded spots from the sun. They mesmerized her.

She pulled at the knot and spread them out in front of her. Eleven of them, complete with envelopes, all posted from Geneva. She started at the beginning and pulled out the first one. It was dated 1975. April.

> *Tommaso—*
> *It's so hot here. The sun is burning up the sky. I woke up this morning and wondered why you left me here like this. I thought surely you'd come back. I thought Momma and Papa would come for me. But as the days went by and the bombs shook everything we knew and loved, I lost hope. The war is coming to a close, I think, after thirteen long years. The PAVN are getting closer. I can smell them at night.*
>
> *I think that since seven years have passed and you have not come to me, I should come to you. They are evacuating civilians in a few days. I will be on one of the flights out. Mamma and Papa will be so happy to see me! I cannot wait to tell them everything that happened to me that day in Dong Xoai. The day I got lost. Until then, Brother.*

It was unsigned. She hadn't met Tommaso yet when he'd gotten this, and she only stumbled across it much later. She often wondered what his face looked like as he read it, if he was scared. Angry? Upset. She'd never know. The way he'd shared the details about his sister had been slow and sketchy. At first it was just a name. Na. Which initially she thought was Vietnamese, but later learned was short for Adrianna. It was like the sky broke open, him just admitting she existed, saying the syllables that represented her.

When Olivia ventured to ask what had happened to her, he said she got lost. Disappeared. He didn't ever want to talk about it again. But they did. When what turned out to be the fourth letter showed up in their mailbox. She rifled through the envelopes and pulled out that one. It was the first she'd ever seen.

"Do you know this section of Geneva?" he'd asked, pointing to the postmark.

She'd taken the envelope and studied it. "It's near the university, right downtown."

He pulled out the sheet of paper and laid it flat on the table. Olivia now ran her hand over the sheet.

> *Tommaso—*
>
> *I'm so unhappy I haven't seen you yet when I promised you in my first letter I would. Plans changed. You're still on my list. Not first, though. That spot should go to Philomena, I think. She deserves to see me first. So I am moving to Italy! Don't worry, you are second, and Anais is third. My hair is darker now, you might not recognize me. I grew too! I look nothing like that three-year-old you last saw. Which gives me an advantage. I know what you look like, and I'll be watching.*
>
> *Na*

Olivia put the letter aside and moved to the last one. It was the one that disturbed her the most, made her the most desperate. After Tommaso was murdered, she would sometimes sleep with it in her arms and cry. It was the letter that led to his death.

> *I might have waited too long, distracted by my family, underestimated by everyone. I missed my chance, and it might be too late. I survived everything, Tommaso. You can't even imagine my struggles. But I might not survive this. I got a letter from one of you just two days ago. One of you has found me, and I'm guessing it was you. Now*

is the time to strike. I need to get to you before you get to me, or it's all been for nothing.
Na

Tommaso died in the park two days later. Olivia doubted Tommaso had sent this woman a letter. In fact, she knew he hadn't. He would have told Olivia. Somehow she would have known. It wasn't her husband that had contacted this woman. His death was for nothing.

She folded the letters and put them back in the envelopes, bundling them together with string. She heard the faint sound of her phone ringing from the garden where she'd left it. She saw the number and held her breath for a second.

"Hello?"

"Everything is set."

"Set for what? No."

"The meeting is in two days—on Saturday. In La Héronnière de Haut. The probate of Anais Lavoisier's will."

"No. No. Were you invited? I don't think you can go unless you were invited. I don't want you to be there," Olivia said.

"Why not? And what makes you think I didn't get an invite? You got one. And you didn't know her any better than I did."

"My husband did—"

"Don't talk about your husband. Please? I've got the address. There's nothing that's going to keep me away."

Olivia dropped her head. "What's this about anyway?"

"Look. Maybe I'll show up and maybe I won't. I haven't made up my mind yet, but I wanted to see what you'd say. Since you're so dead set against it, it's making me look up the train schedule."

"I'm not saying another word. Do what you want."

"I will. But if I do show up? At least one person is going to die. Tell me the guest list, and I'll tell you who it should be."

"I don't know the entire guest list. I don't. I only know I was invited."

"It'll be a game, then. When I get there, I'll decide. The only question is how to kill them. I hate guns. Maybe a knife, but that's messy. Or a bomb. Are they serving refreshments at this thing? Because if they are, poison might be the way to go—kind of slow but very dramatic. Don't you think?"

"No. I don't. How'd you find out about this anyway? Were you invited? Tell me."

"Not answering that. So, maybe I'll see you Saturday, then. Maybe I won't."

"*Won't* is better."

She clicked off and stared down at the letters, knowing she was already doomed.

CHAPTER 35

VICTOR

Vicenza, Italy

The city didn't change. But the small group of ex-pats did after Na Lacroce went missing. They'd been housed in an area of the city near the embassies; the dignitaries that had been located in Hanoi were now pushed into housing in Saigon. Housing was scarce, but they'd banded together, waiting to see what was to become of the country. Lives were being torn apart all around them, but this part of the community went on alert the day that Anais, Tommaso, and Philomena returned without the three-year-old little girl in tow.

The turmoil hadn't died down, it had only escalated as each day passed without new information. From his hospital bed, Victor watched it all play out in front of him. His life in review, of sorts, forced to relive events he would much rather forget. Standing in the cramped living room of Philomena's house. Her parents were seated on the divan, eyes wide, hands pressed together in their laps. Philomena sat across the room. Her head was down. She wouldn't raise her eyes to look at them, and he knew it was because they'd see the scratches on her neck and face. She'd carefully arranged her dark hair to cover them, but as the minutes passed, her parents' questions took on a new urgency.

"I don't understand, Lolo. You just lost sight of her? How did that happen?" It was hard for Victor to see the pain in this woman's face again. The first time had been horrible enough.

"*Mamma. Non lo so. Non lo so.* There were so many people. It was crowded. And I let go of her hand for a minute. She was just gone."

"In Bu Non? Really. It's not a crowded city. Not so many people there now. Why were you there anyway? That's the part I don't understand. Tell me again and look at me when I'm speaking to you," her father jumped in.

Philomena looked up into her father's eyes. He saw the scratches. "We went on an errand for Tommaso's father. He needed something delivered to someone there and asked us to take him."

"He sent his thirteen-year-old son on an errand miles north of Saigon. At a time like this? And he took a three-year-old child with him? Why? What were you delivering? What happened to your face?"

Philomena shrugged. "I only went along with Anais because she asked me to. It was an afternoon outing. Something to do in this godforsaken place. I want to go home, Papa. I want to go back to Italy. I'm leaving with Victor tomorrow."

He gave a long sigh. "You can't. The police may need to question you. They may need your help."

She shook her head. "Tommaso and Anais are here. They don't need me. I'm old enough to go back to Vicenza by myself. I'll stay with Aunt Rosa for now."

"Your face?" he asked.

She bit her lip and brought forth a new bout of tears. "Tommaso. He gets so angry. After Adrianna was gone, we were frantic. I was crying and screaming. He hit me. I guess in frustration or anger. I was the last to see her. He blamed me, Papa. But I don't care that he hit me. Let it alone, and let me go back to Italy with Victor."

Her father slowly nodded. Victor watched his wife-to-be worm her way through it, play the victim, fragile and hysterical. He saw her in a new light that day and married her anyway. The truth about what had happened came out in stages only when they were thousands of miles from Vietnam. When they were safely back in Italy, she started talking about it. Not all of it. All of it came from Anais. Years later on a trip to Philadelphia, when he and she were lying in bed.

Anais was on her back, a cigarette poised between her index and middle finger. "Tommaso is here, somewhere. I saw him yesterday," she said.

Victor sat up and stared at her. "He's here? You saw him? Are you kidding?"

She drew on the cigarette and blew the smoke up to the ceiling. "I just said that. Yes. He came to the house. Knocking on the door, like it was nothing. It's the first I'd seen him since I left Saigon. I was hoping I'd never see him again."

"Does Philomena know?"

Anais laughed. "Philomena doesn't know anything. I didn't tell her about Tommaso, and I didn't tell her about us. Do you think she suspects?"

"I can't believe you think this is funny. We were talking about Tommaso. Not about us. What'd he want? What'd he say?"

"He said the situation with his sister, Na, isn't over yet. That Saigon might be a different place now, but his sister may not be dead. He said someone knew what happened to her. They were sending him documents."

"What documents?"

"I don't know. Some hospital papers. That's all."

"Were they blackmailing him? Asking for money?"

She laughed again. "No, not now anyway. And if they're looking for money from me, they'll be sorry. If I had any, I'd be in France. Not stuck here. Packing my husband's sandwich and coffee in his lunch bag every day."

He shot her a look. "Then you shouldn't have gotten pregnant by him. What else did he say? Did he have any idea who they were from?"

"He thought it was me. He actually thought that was my idea of a joke. It wasn't."

Victor sat up. "Did he mention me? Does he know about us?"

Anais shook her head. "No, Victor. He doesn't know about this. And if you're so concerned, why do you meet me like this? Why travel all this way? Philomena's pregnant. Again." She swung her legs over the side of the bed and sat up. "You really should be a better husband to her. Maybe she'd carry to term." She ground her cigarette into the ashtray and wandered into the bathroom.

Victor was behind her and slammed her back against the bathroom door. "What's wrong with you, Annie? You're so mean. If Tommaso is being blackmailed, they're coming to Philomena next. And me. So, tell me what happened that day. The whole story. I need to know now."

She pushed him back and closed the bathroom door behind her. When she came out, she was dressed, her hair was combed, her lipstick just right. She sat on the edge of the bed and lit another cigarette.

"You want to know what happened? I'll tell you. But promise you won't think anything worse of your wife?" He gave a slight nod of his head. "We left that morning. The four of us. I didn't know this at the time, but Tommaso was supposed to meet an associate of his father's. My guess is he was Viet Cong. I guess Lacroce didn't want to be seen with him, so he sent his thirteen-year-old son—less conspicuous that way. I don't know why. The only way to get there was by bus. All other major transportation was cut. The bus was crowded. We had to stand for hours across a bumpy road. Na should never have been with us. The only reason she was, was because her mother needed to go out at the last minute and didn't have a babysitter. One of us—me or Lolo—should have stayed back with her. But there we were. She was hot, miserable. Crying the whole way. We didn't have any water with us." She turned to look at Victor. He was putting his pants on, buckling his belt. "Are you listening?"

"Every word," he muttered. "Philomena told me most of this. Move ahead to the important part."

"Girl was a brat. Spoiled. With her little blonde curls. I wanted to rip every one of them out. All of us did. Two hours of stop and start on a bus crammed so tight with people we were sweating all over each other. Putrid. And the kid didn't stop crying. Not for a minute. We got off three stops ahead because we couldn't take the heat anymore. Barren except for a few houses, if you could call them that. Squat little houses on stilts. Dirt farms. Poor. We started walking. But, oh my God, the humidity. We needed water. So Tommaso led us to this little house. But that was his plan all along. He knew exactly where he was."

"What plan?" Victor took a cigarette and put it to his lips, lit it, then pulled on the end. He blew the smoke into Anais's face.

She waved it away. "If I tell you, will you give me the money to leave Ross?"

"No. We've been over this before. So, you killed the kid? Is that the end of this story? You and Philomena? Or all three of you? You choked her? Or smothered her and left her in the rice paddy? She scratched Philomena?"

Anais took a puff of her cigarette and blew the smoke back at him. "No. So much worse. And those scratches on Philomena were from Tommaso. Not the kid. I told you that before."

He stopped and looked at her. "What's worse than killing the girl?"

She shook her head, and he saw a bit of what looked like moisture in her eyes, but he couldn't believe it. Anais was hardened, a slab of granite. Pretty but unyielding. He'd never seen her cry. Ever. Not unless it was part of some manipulation.

"What?" he asked. "Do you want me to guess?"

She started talking, and he listened without moving. "We went to the house. It was a family. A woman, a man, and a baby. They spoke some French and a bit of English. Tommaso had a knife—"

"What for?"

"I'm telling you, it was part of his plan."

He kept listening as she spoke, and when she got to the crux of it, he was so stunned he put his cigarette out and missed the ashtray, marring the end table with a perfectly round circle burned in the wood. When she was done, there were tears in her eyes. "I don't know which one of them hurt Na. I couldn't see. All I saw was her shoe . . . it was lying in the dirt, on its side."

The lights came back against Victor's eyelids, and he knew he was back in the hospital, with the footsteps of staff coming in and out. He knew that Philomena was sitting next to him. He could feel her presence. He felt revolted. Forty years or so had passed since that day he and Anais had sat in that hotel room, having their affair, talking, being perfectly horrible human beings. And he'd never been the same since.

CHAPTER 36

RUSSELL

Teramo, Italy

Nghia Trang Dong Xoai. He stared at the words written on the sheet. *Ngoc is the key.*

"N-g-o-c." He spelled it out. "If it's the key, we should start there," he muttered. "If only I knew what that meant."

Joanne wasn't too far away, sitting on a folding chair in the old Lacroce woman's damp basement, looking at her husband's files. Her purse was in her lap. She fiddled with the buttons on her phone. "*Ngoc* means *jade* in English according to the Internet. Take the box and let's go. This woman's niece is just sitting upstairs. Give her our information, and tell her we'll bring everything back."

"*Nghia Trang Dong Xoai.* Put that in and see what comes up," he said. "I'll spell each word for you." He turned around. Joanne had her head against the clammy cement wall. Her eyes were shut. He took the phone from her lap and plugged the words in himself. It took several attempts because the system needed to correct the sentence by adding accents over certain letters. In the end it gave him *Dong Xoai cemetery.* He pulled up a map and entered the location. Someone was pointing at an obscure cemetery in the southern part of Vietnam.

"Damn." He was supposed to go there with Juliette on their honeymoon. Da Nang. China Beach. The over-the-water huts. The boat tours. A train ride north for a cruise on Halong Bay. Commercialism. Sunshine. A cool vacation that was forty years away from bloodshed and upheaval.

Trying to pick at the bones of something that had happened in that country between when the French evacuated and when the American involvement in the Vietnam War started full force, that murky period where the country was ostensibly cut in two, with people moving back and forth, rebellion against colonialism, the wealthy noncommunist Europeans huddled in Saigon, licking their wounds from displacement and financial loss, would prove to be impossible. The memories that lingered on in the people who had lived there, that was all that was left.

The cemetery wasn't necessarily important. It was what had happened to the people that had ended up there. Who had died? He Googled some maps and started searching. *Dong Xoai* was about two and a half hours outside of Saigon proper. Now, it could probably be easily driven to, but back then, there was no way of knowing. It was probably at least a half day's trip.

He rubbed his temples. He had little time to figure this out, and none of it was making sense. Pieces of different puzzles that didn't fit together. The Saigon puzzle, the Tommaso-murder puzzle, and Ava's father, the Davide Tosi puzzle.

He picked up another paper and studied it again. The note was short. An address of sorts. Not an address like one you might find in the United States, but after looking at it, he realized that's exactly what it was. The name of a road and a description of a house that when translated meant *Ho Xuan Huong Street, first farmhouse from center of town*. The only other thing written on the paper were a few short phrases that he'd translated to *witnesses* and a list of Vietnamese names. Russell felt like he was so close to some important truth. The tug was building that he needed to go there. It was so far away, so expensive and time consuming, but there was only so much he could do from here.

There was a light rap on the basement door, and it opened, the niece coming down the steps slowly. Her English was minimal, and his Italian even more so. He'd communicated by plugging sentences into a translation app and then letting her read them.

"Devi andartene adesso. Devo andare a casa," she said.

He handed her the phone, and she typed it in. He read it. "Okay. I'll leave," he wrote. "Can we take these boxes to a hotel? And bring them back tomorrow?"

She read it but went upstairs without another word. Russell gathered the papers and notebooks he wanted and stuffed them into a box. He hit Joanne's knee. "Hurry. Come on."

They climbed the steps and went out through the back door to the car. Russell shoved the box into his trunk and locked it.

He started to get into the front seat when the woman came out. She spoke in broken, heavily accented English, but he understood every word. "You can't take that. I called Signora Lacroce. She said no. Her daughter-in-law—Olivia Lacroce. I should keep it for her."

Russell smiled, got into the car, and shut the door, locking it. She came to the window and repeated it again. He waved and put the car into gear and pulled out onto the street. He saw her in the rearview mirror, running after them. She even managed to slap the trunk with her hand.

"Did you understand any of that, Joanne? What's wrong? You're whiter than the paint on my living room wall."

"You're going to make me go to Vietnam, aren't you?"

His eyes narrowed. "Not today, I'm not. I'm going to get out of this town, head toward the coast, I think, and we'll find a hotel. You can relax. Sleep."

"What was in the notes?"

"The writing is Vietnamese. Something about a cemetery. North of Ho Chi Minh City. In Dong Xoai." His lips and tongue struggled to wrap themselves around the words. "The rest of this case is in Vietnam." He sighed. "There was also an address. A place. A house on that street. The street is not too far from Dong Xoai. Whatever is there, we need to see it."

"And something happened in this house?"

"Something happened in this house that followed Anais, Philomena, and Tommaso, their spouses and children, for the past forty-something years. I think it was a shadow. It killed Tommaso, maybe Davide, attacked Victor—"

"Why Marie and Claire? Or Davide? They weren't even born yet."

"Who knows. Maybe they found out—Anais told them whatever happened in Saigon, or they figured it out on their own. Maybe Tommaso showed up unexpectedly. Or was blackmailing them."

"I don't know, Russell. It sounds a little farfetched to me."

"It explains why Philomena never called the police after Anais attacked her in the barn when she went into labor the same night Anais gave birth to Adrianna. It just fits. They have a bigger secret between them. What I think is that we need to go there to figure it out. Not today." He reached over and touched Joanne's arm. "Not today. But there's only so much we can do from here. Are you in?"

"Seriously? Russell, I don't travel well. And I hate Vietnamese food. Hate it."

"We'll get a box or two of cereal to bring with you, then. That'll hold you. We can start the visa application here and then pick them up when we land in Ho Chi Minh City."

Her eyes were large. "And what exactly is the weather like? Is it steaming hot? Cold?"

"Look it up." He pulled out and found a highway headed east. "Superstrada Teramo-Mare," he said pulling onto a highway. "Heading toward the ocean. That should make you happy."

"It's a balmy ninety-one degrees today in Saigon. But on the bright side, it's the dry season. Hardly any rain. So I won't need my rain jacket," Joanne quipped.

There was silence for a few moments.

"It's a bit ironic you were supposed to be in Vietnam anyway. Just for a different reason—on your honeymoon with Juliette. Maybe this is destiny."

He motioned to her phone. "Call American Airlines and see if they'll honor the tickets I bought with Juliette. I mean, since she died, it's worth a shot." He saw her visibly bristle at his words. "I mean, no sense wasting the money, Joanne."

She threw the phone back into his lap and physically moved away from him toward the car door. "Now why did you have to go and say that, Russell? Just when I was starting to like you again. Be quiet and drive. And I want my own hotel room."

CHAPTER 37

PHILOMENA

Vicenza, Italy

Victor hadn't moved, not a flick of an eyelid for over a day and a half. A horrible thought crept into her mind. If he was going to die, he needed to just do it. This interminable waiting, sitting under fluorescent lights, was making her head hurt. It was also making her heart thump. If he died, she'd suffer; if he lived, she might suffer more. She stared down at his pale skin, his eyebrows losing their color, white hairs among the dark ones, giving him an unruly look. When had she first laid eyes on him? She tried to think. The summer she turned seventeen. When her parents returned to Italy for a few months.

The whirlwind of visiting friends and neighbors had brought her face-to-face with her future husband. He was taller than most boys she knew, more mature, funny. But their lives were ten thousand miles apart. She returned to Saigon feeling she'd never see him again, but they found a way. Through endless letters, exchanged photographs, and the very occasional visit, the relationship grew.

"We never should have gotten on the bus, you know," Philomena said out loud. "You were right. If we'd just stayed in Saigon, no matter how Tommaso begged. No matter how much Anais begged, we wouldn't be in this position now."

His face remained slack.

"I'd do anything to take it all back. I am so stupid. So weak, to just follow along like a little mouse behind Anais. You warned me it was dangerous. What I should've done was stay back at the house with Na. So, what do you do, Victor, when the people around you do horrible things and you happen to be there? Do you speak up for yourself? Or do what I did? Not only followed along, but actually participated. Maybe more than participated. I cleaned it up. Hmmm, Victor?"

"Ma'am, the sergeant wants to speak with you." The officer's voice broke her train of thought. He was motioning for her to leave the room with him. She was exhausted by these police. They never left her in peace.

"Go get him. He can say whatever he needs to say here. Nobody's listening. Not even him." She patted Victor's arm.

The officer looked annoyed but didn't say anything. He left the room and came back trailing a short man in a sergeant's uniform. The short man said, "We have some more curious details from the blood samples taken from your husband's car. The unknown sample—the one that has no match in our system—is actually a match to your husband in a familial way. It's someone related to him. Would you have any idea who that might be? Child—"

"Our only child was killed twenty years ago."

He looked down at his papers. "I see. I was thinking of maybe a child or grandchild from his previous marriage? The blood wasn't a match to you. Just him. A close match. I'm going to ask again if there was any family visiting. Protecting someone won't help you. We'll find out in the end."

Philomena's mind was frozen. How could Ava's blood not match her own, but match Victor's? Victor was her grandfather, she was her grandmother—she'd given birth to her mother in that barn in Tuscany.

She stood up and started pacing. "We didn't have anybody visiting us. Perhaps you can ask Victor if he ever wakes up."

She pushed up off the chair and kept walking without looking back. The information the officer had given her didn't make any sense. It couldn't make sense. Her mind swam back to the night Adrianna was born. Anais had kept Philomena in that barn, forcing her to give birth on the floor, in the dirt. Anais had been pregnant too but lost her baby later that night. The only way any of this could make sense was . . . was if the child she'd raised all that time wasn't really hers. She'd passed out at one point and woken up with the baby in her arms. Was it possible? But the implications of Victor being the father of Anais's child were far too painful to think about now.

She kept moving faster and faster, until she dropped in a heap on a bench outside the hospital. She picked her phone out of her bag and dialed a number.

"Who is your grandfather?" she asked when the connection was made.

There was no sound on the other end of the phone save for breathing. "Victor is my grandfather," Ava said when she found her voice.

"And who is your grandmother?" Her voice rose higher. No matter how hard she was trying to maintain her emotions, the anger was coming through.

"Philomena—"

"Is that why you refused to call me Nonna? Because I'm not your grandmother at all? Should I go back to Tuscany where your mother was born and find out the truth?"

"How—"

"They ran the blood you left all over his car. It matched him but not me. Not me. But I bet you anything if Marie was here, and I could get her DNA, it would match yours. Is that right? Am I finally getting it, Ava? Anais gave birth to my husband's child?" She lost control and could no longer speak.

"Nonna—"

"Don't!"

"Philomena. I don't know how any of this is going to help either of us right now. It just muddies the picture. I'm at Anais's cottage—"

"Anais was a very dangerous person, Ava." She barked a laugh. "Even more so than I thought I knew. Whatever quest you're on? Every step you take has been anticipated. She's way ahead of you, leading you toward some end—"

"You're talking about her as if she were alive."

"I've reason to question her timely demise. Let's leave it at that."

"Why didn't you say anything when she did that to you? Why would you not go to the police? She forced you to give birth in the dirt. You could have died—"

"Because of something that happened years ago in Vietnam. That's why. She'd held it over my head for the longest time. I couldn't risk it."

"Something happened involving Tommaso?"

"He was there too," Philomena answered.

"Is that why he was killed? Because of that? What happened? You need to tell me now."

"Listen, they know the blood was someone close to Victor. Watch yourself. I have to go—I have something I really need to do. I need to go to Victor."

"Do they have ideas about who did it yet? Who stabbed him?"

"No. But I'm pretty sure they'll think it was you, if they ever find you."

"How did his body get up in the hallway, Nonna? When I left, he was in the back room—"

"I have to go, Ava." The line went dead.

CHAPTER 38

VICTOR

Vicenza, Italy

He wasn't dreaming; he wasn't awake. He was somewhere in between. This was the first time this had happened. He knew when he was awake—the hospital noises told him, and the fact that he couldn't move. When he was dreaming, reliving his past, he could move. He'd hear the sounds of birds, or people moving on the streets. He could smell it all too. The vendors on the street cooking crab soup. The tonal language of Vietnamese all around him. It was real.

But now he was feeling both worlds at the same time, and it startled him. He could see the dusty street in Saigon, an American soldier walking in front of him in full uniform, his keys jangling from his fingertips. He could also see the searing hospital lights against his eyelids, hear the nurse's shoes shuffling against the linoleum floor.

"His father still has some connections in the north, business dealings—maybe not all legal, depending on what *legal* means on any given day in this place—" It was Philomena's father talking to him. The dark-haired man had a sturdy build, only slightly taller than he was wide. Brusque. Determined. Matter-of-fact. Victor had always liked him. "So I can see him sending his son in his place. Less conspicuous. You have no idea what was in the envelope Tommaso was to deliver to this person?"

"I don't know, but I am worried about Lolo. She was up all night. Worried, sad, crying. A nervous wreck. She's never been like that before."

"Ah, yes," the older man answered. "I put in an inquiry with the Italian embassy to look further into the little girl's disappearance. Something has to come of it."

"I offered to go back to Dong Xoai to just walk, maybe look? See if we can find anything. I said I would even try and get a car so she didn't have to take the bus. She refused."

His eyes became larger. "They aren't going to look too much into this, you know that. Maybe you and I should take a ride up there. Talk to some locals. They know everything happening around them, even if they pretend otherwise."

Victor nodded. "We need one of them to come with us to walk us through where they went, what they did. Philomena won't go, so should it be Tommaso or Anais—"

Philomena's father held his palm up to him. "Tommaso. Definitely. I don't want the Lavoisiers getting into the middle of this. Tomorrow. The three of us."

They shook hands and parted ways. The sidewalk faded, the businesses and the people walking disappeared, and all Victor could feel was his own heartbeat. He didn't see lights against his lids. He didn't hear the whooshing of the respirator pushing the air in and out of his lungs. He was in blackness, and for the first time he thought maybe he was dying. There was nothing. Then a tiny pinpoint of light appeared in the distance.

The light grew and moved toward him until he saw the town of Dong Xoai taking form. It wasn't from memory. It was there. The dirt road that parted the dense tropical foliage. The sun blazing down, creating dizzying heat. The humidity that was almost visible in the air, making it hard to breathe. His shirt was soaked through. He looked down to see sheets of sweat falling from his shins. Philomena's father was in front of him. The man was almost twenty years older than he, but was moving twice as fast, trying to keep up with Tommaso.

A house appeared on the left side of the road, more of a hut on stilts, surrounded by fronds. There was no gate, only more weeds and mud to navigate to the stairs to the front door. It was cracked open; flies were everywhere.

"What is this place, boy?" the man asked.

Tommaso turned to him, out of breath, his face bright red. "We were here. This is where we came to ask for water."

"You didn't tell me you stopped for water. Why would you stop for water in a place like this? You'd get dysentery. Parasites."

"We were so thirsty. All of us. It was Philomena's idea."

There was a smell coming from within. The smell of death left to bake in the heat. The older man surveyed the flies for a minute before stepping back. "Was anyone home?"

He shook his head. "No. We yelled and then kept going. Philomena thought she saw the family out in the field."

"Come on, Victor, let's take a look inside." He motioned toward him. "We'll just put our heads in."

They covered their faces with their shirts to block the odor and took two pushes at the door. A Vietnamese man was in the front room on the floor. His neck had been sliced open straight across. He was on his back, flies nesting in the open wound, in the blood that pooled by his head, and in his open eyes. A woman wasn't far away from him. Her sandals were still on her feet. She was on her stomach, her face against the floor. It was clear she'd been stabbed in the back. The back of her shirt was torn open; the wounds had seeped through, saturating her clothes and the floor around her.

"No more," Victor said. "No more. Let's get out of here." He gathered his shirt around his nose and mouth and rushed outside, where he vomited into the mud.

But Philomena's father wasn't swayed. "Tommaso. What happened here? What happened? Tell me."

The boy shook his head. "We came to the door, nobody answered. Nobody was here. Maybe they were dead already. We didn't see anything. There was no smell. We just left."

"Might have been the damned Viet Cong. God only knows. Let's go on. We'll tell the police—or the military or whoever is in charge these days—when we get to a town. We need to keep moving before we get killed ourselves. Show us where your sister disappeared."

They walked back to the car and piled in. The engine started, and they eased down the street, past the house. Victor looked back over his shoulder. Something was fluttering in the grass, some bit of white.

"Stop the car," he yelled. He jumped out and ran back, his eyes searching to find a meaning in what he was seeing. As he moved closer, the white fabric started flapping again. Though it wasn't really white, it was more of a dirty cream color. A baby was partially wrapped in the cloth; the face and upper torso were exposed to the elements. The skin was a bluish-purple color, the eyes closed.

Victor took three steps back, away from the horror, and fell backward onto the ground, then scrambled to his feet and ran to the car. "Go, go, go, go," he yelled.

Philomena's father obeyed and never asked what Victor had seen. Tommaso looked straight ahead, his eyes never wandering with curiosity toward the field or the house. Maybe he already knew what was there.

The image faded to black, and Victor hung in nothingness, conscious of it, aware, just waiting. Another image took shape, of his house in Vicenza. He was in the mudroom looking at a pretty girl in front of him. He didn't know her name, but he knew she was related to him.

Her presence angered him. She stood by the door and seemed terrified. The attack came from behind him. He saw a bit of the metal blade after it had punctured his neck. He turned to his attacker and saw the face.

He blinked twice to make sure he wasn't dreaming. The image disappeared.

He heard a click, and his respirator went off. Then he felt something clasp over his nose. He couldn't breathe. And in that moment, he opened his eyes. He was in the hospital, and someone was looking down on him. A firm hand was on his face. He struggled against the glove.

"You need to go, Victor," the voice said. "Time's up."

CHAPTER 39

Ava

Cherbourg, France

The photograph was facedown near my foot. The off-white backing of the picture made me nervous. I knew before I had even picked it up, it was of something that was going to upset me, change my life, or at least my perception. The photograph had been placed inside the copy of Anais's will for a reason. For my eyes only.

In the glow of the moonlight coming in through the window, and what was brought to life under the beam from my cell phone, I saw my father's face for the second time—this time in color. His features were unmistakable: the chiseled cheekbones, dark hair, bright eyes. The smile. I was lost in it for a minute, so I didn't put the pieces together. It came to me slowly. He was looking off to the side, like he'd been caught unexpectedly. I pulled out the photograph I'd gotten at Philomena's and compared them. It was absolutely the same person. But there was more. The color photograph had been taken in this cottage. The distinct fireplace stones could be seen in the background. He'd been here, not even twenty feet from where I was sitting.

I dropped both photos to the desk and rushed to the bathroom. The contents of my stomach spewed into the bowl. I leaned over farther and retched again. The ins, the outs, the twists, the turns, the machinations of this family had finally crossed a line. Not only had Anais kept her involvement with my mother a secret, she'd also had some knowledge of my father. Enough that he'd visited her at least once.

I ran some toilet tissue across my mouth and rushed back into the office, grabbing the photographs again and comparing them. Davide Tosi, in this picture, was not a nineteen-year-old boy. He wasn't even twenty. He looked closer to twenty-five or even thirty. He'd survived the night Tommaso had been stabbed in the park. He was alive. Somewhere.

My phone rang, and I saw it was Philomena. I hesitated to answer and was sorry I did when I heard the anger in her voice. She finally knew the secret of Victor's infidelity, Adrianna's maternity, and all it took was a savage stabbing and some misplaced blood drops to clue her in. I hung up knowing she'd survive this. She'd survived nearly sixty years with this man. The depths of his depravity could hardly be a surprise.

I took the photograph of my father and put it in the side pocket of my purse. My head was pounding, and I felt light-headed. I knew it was from lack of alcohol. But I was out of luck—there was nothing nearby. Only Sandrine, Anais's friend and neighbor, two cottages away. I was half surprised she hadn't knocked yet, eager to see who was here.

Two thoughts invaded my brain at the same time. Sandrine might have a bottle of wine or some whiskey, but she also might have gotten to the cottage and rummaged through the photographs before me. She was the busiest busybody I had ever met. I slid on my jacket and exited through the back patio doors. The sidewalk lamps were illuminating enough for me to make it to her door without any trouble. She was either asleep or in bed. All of the times she'd shown up at Anais's, banging at the door uninvited and unwanted, the time I needed her she was conspicuously absent. I rapped on a windowpane and then hit the door knocker twice. Nothing.

I walked around to the garage and peered through the window. Her car was there. It was late, and the air was too brisk for her to be taking a random walk. Her back door was open, so I helped myself to her home as she'd done so many times at my grandmother's, just popping in without notice or introduction.

Her living room was bright enough without the lights on. I headed for the dining room cabinet, hoping there'd be something there. Luck was with me. I pulled out half a bottle of bourbon and poured some into a glass. I wandered about the room sipping and then gulping until there was only an inch left at the bottom. I felt warm and buzzy, so lost in my own thoughts I almost forgot why I was there until I saw the note. It was sitting on the kitchen counter near the old landline telephone complete with rotary dial.

La Héronnière de Haut. Rue Le Ferrage was printed at the top—the meeting Sandrine had spoken of. I'd passed through the area, a little north of Valognes, but didn't know it well. It was farmland. Some businesses, warehouses, granaries. Nothing much. There was a crossroads there with a bus stop, some stores, a few cafés. But it was a nothing spot for a gathering.

Then there was a list of names—some of them had a tick mark next to them. Ava—no tick, Marie—no tick, Olivia Lacroce—tick, Philomena—tick, Victor—no tick, Francesca Tosi—tick, Mrs. Paolo Lacroce—tick. Proof that Sandrine had lied at least once during our call: she certainly knew the name Lacroce.

There were a few scribbled notes underneath that I couldn't decipher. Then the name Milo Rotton with his number next to it. I recognized the name immediately. Anais's lawyer. Anais said she picked him because they were alike—of similar minds—devious, skilled, and had no problem blurring the lines a little when necessary. Under Rotton's number was Olivia Lacroce's number. Multiple numbers. Home, mobile phone, then a third one that had an asterisk, with the word *emergency* next to it.

I sat on the couch and flipped through the notepad. This was the meeting Sandrine kept talking about, even when I said I wasn't going. The cast of characters was interesting. Gathering Tommaso's widow, his mother, and Davide's mother under one roof. And then there was Marie. No way she was coming, not unless she had a huge metal file and a spoon in her cell. And I'd been there—neither of those would get her out. Marie was definitely going to be a no-show.

Anais had something up her sleeve. I stood and was walking the perimeter of Sandrine's living room when she appeared in front of me.

"Ava? What are you doing here? In my house?"

I turned to face her. She had her dog on a leash. I'd forgotten about the dog. "I helped myself. I figured you wouldn't mind, as you've done the same with Anais many times." I held the bottle up in the air for her to see.

"You startled me. How long have you been in town?" She shut the door behind her and flicked on the light.

"Not long enough to find my own booze—I got here a few hours ago. The cottage door was open when I got there. Things were a bit of a mess. Did you see anyone? I know you're keeping an eye on it."

Her back was to me. "I didn't see anything unusual. Was anything taken?"

"Sandrine?" She turned to me. "There's nothing really left to take. But you always keep an eye out. You see everything."

"It might have been at night. I do sleep. Why are you back here—in Cherbourg, Ava? Are you in trouble?"

I laughed. "Aren't I always?"

"What is it now?"

"Ah, a little stabbing incident in Vicenza." I held my hands up, the bottle still clutched between my fingers. "It wasn't me. This shit finds me, I swear. Do you have a cigarette?"

She shook her head. "No. I don't." The disgust on her face made me smile.

"I found your little list here." I lifted the papers for her to see. "This is the meeting about Anais's will? She's holding it where? A feed store? I don't understand."

"No." Her mouth twisted to the side. "Not in a feed store. In a building there. Near her lawyer's house. It was his idea—"

"Nah. His office is in Paris. Anais would catch the train there—"

"So, maybe he has a summerhouse—"

"In La Héronnière de Haut? A summerhouse? Not at the beach, or maybe in Spain? Portugal? But in this sad little crossroads to nowhere."

She looked disturbed. "Don't be so snobby, Ava. It's what your grandmother wanted. Have you changed your mind yet? About going?"

"No." I pulled the photograph from my pocket and showed it to her. "It was taken in front of the fireplace. That's my father. Can you explain it?"

She took it from me and held it but said nothing.

"Anais must have known him. I don't know how or why she'd be involved with Philomena's daughter's boyfriend. But she apparently was," I continued.

"It does seem to be taken at her cottage."

"It had to be. Look at the fireplace behind him. And it was sitting there, with her will. You left it for me? He's at least twenty-five. He disappeared when he was nineteen. Never heard from again. Why can't you just tell me what this is all about? Why just leave the photograph?"

I could see her wheels turning. She had always protected Anais when she was alive, acting as a buffer or go-between, hiding information or passing it on, whatever the situation called for at the moment. I could tell she didn't know which way to turn with this one. Was admitting to seeing this man betraying her old friend or helping her memory?

"I did leave it for you—in case I didn't see you. He was here," she said.

Her words stunned me. "Really? You remember him, then?"

"I remember him at her house once. It was in the spring, I don't know, maybe ten years ago now. Might be more. He stayed overnight, so I knew it wasn't a workman or hired help. So I asked her about it."

"And?" My heart was beating fast. This was about my father. Not about some man that was killed the night he disappeared. My father was alive.

"She said it was one of her brother's children. A nephew. I never talked to him myself, so I had no reason not to believe her. It didn't seem odd to me."

"And you never saw him again?" I desperately wanted a cigarette—something to do with my nervous energy. I chewed my lips instead.

"I don't think so, Ava. I don't believe I did, but I can't be sure—"

"Sandrine, you've known my grandmother since you moved in on the street, like thirty years ago. You were with her all that time. You know everything about her. Everything. So, I don't believe you, that you don't know if or when my father was here. And I don't believe you never met him—"

"Believe what you want, Ava. I'm telling you what I know. But consider you might be looking for someone who doesn't want to be found. And you of all people know what that feels like, don't you?"

"And why wouldn't he want to be found? Why wouldn't he even want his mother to know he's alive?"

She got suddenly restless and went to her desk and opened the drawer. She pulled out a small velvet box and handed it to me.

"Since you won't be there Saturday, here's something for you. From Anais." I flipped it open. A brooch. Her favorite one, made of one center sapphire stone surrounded by small diamonds. Probably worth a fortune. "She insisted you have it. Wear it. Don't let it sit around. The clasp is a little loose, you might look at it before you put it on."

I slipped the box into my bag. "Thank you."

She went to her liquor cabinet and pulled out two more bottles, one of wine, one of vodka, and handed them to me. "You need to get out of here. It's not safe. Take these for your journey. I'll make you a sandwich?"

"No. I don't need a sandwich. This is fine." I held up the bottles.

"I mean it. Get out of here now, Ava. Get a taxi, whatever you need to do to get to downtown Cherbourg tonight. Just make sure you don't—what is that expression in English?—go on a wild-goose chase to find your father only to find the goose is dead. Or maybe the goose you chase will turn around and kill you?"

She was making me uneasy. I had everything that mattered with me. My purse, my bag, money, the photographs, my liquor. I was too spooked to even venture back to Anais's cottage. The look in Sandrine's eyes told me to take her advice.

I grabbed the bottles and looked back at her as I reached the door. "They never say that in English. Or in any other language that I know of."

CHAPTER 40

JOANNE

Giulianova, Italy

The hotel was pretty, right on the ocean, very rustic, Mediterranean. That's all she could really think before she dropped her suitcase and fell onto the bed. The town of Giulianova was quiet. It was around fifty degrees outside; beach season hadn't even started, but it was easy to see how nice it would be when it warmed up. Blue water, Italian architecture, palm trees. Joanne barely had a glimpse; her eyes felt gritty, and everything looked blurry. Russell had only gotten one room, but it had two beds. She didn't have the energy to complain.

"You should try and stay awake until around nine o'clock tonight. Otherwise you're going to get your sleep patterns all screwed up," Russell said. "Trust me."

That was the last thing she heard before she closed her eyes. They popped open and everything was dark. She pushed herself up and rubbed her face. Russell was in the corner in a chair, his feet propped up, a beer in his hand. He had pulled all the papers from the boxes he'd taken out of the Lacroce basement and spread them all over the floor.

"Are you having a one-man party?" she asked.

"Something like that. You slept for a few hours. Now you might be up all night," he responded.

"What'd you get from all that?" She got up and headed to the bathroom. She studied herself in the mirror. She was a mess. Her skin looked gray. Her eyes were red and sunken. Her hair looked greasy. She looked like she'd aged ten years in the time it took to cross the Atlantic.

"I'm working on two things at once. I could use your help."

Joanne shut the bathroom door on his words and rested her head against the window. People were moving about the street below. She could see the ocean—just a hint of inky watery movement in the distance. When she opened the door, he was in the same position, engrossed in something in his lap.

"We should take a walk, get something to eat."

He patted the chair next to him. "Sit. We can eat later. I think we might check out in an hour or so."

She was still standing. "What? To go where? I wanted to shower, change clothes, relax, sit in the piazza, and—"

"This isn't a vacation, Joanne. We're working. Tommaso's father compiled all these notes—he went back to Dong Xoai several times. He was looking for his missing daughter. If he was Italian intelligence—and I know he was—he'd know exactly where to go to get information. He outlines all his steps and then stops. It all just stops. Either he gave up, or something prevented him from finishing this." He held up a paper.

"What's the last thing he documented?" She was interested now.

"An address in Geneva. A street name and that's it. He'd been to the house; there are interviews, some in Vietnamese, some in Italian. A few in English."

"So, did you look up the address? What's it to?"

"It's a street near the University of Geneva. A private home."

"Who lived there?"

"Someone named Rossi."

"Rossi? That's an Italian name. I recognize it. It just popped up recently. We need to go through our notes, but I'm so hungry I can't think."

"All Lacroce's notes ended there. Done. He went as far as to find the house, and nothing more. I wonder if they still live there?" He pounded his forehead with the palm of his hand. "I know that name too. I know it. We need to do a property search for this address, but everything is in French, or German. Call Ava."

"For what?"

"Translating skills. Let her do this for us."

She dialed the number and waited. The line picked up after four rings. "Hello, Ava?"

"Yes?" She seemed breathless. "Joanne?"

Russell took the phone from her hand. "Ava, we're in some seaside town in Italy."

"Giulianova," Joanne interrupted.

"I have an important question for you—does the name Rossi mean anything to you? Think hard," he continued.

Joanne pulled the phone back from him and put it on speaker. "Does it, Ava?"

"I don't know. I don't think so. Listen, I think my father is alive. I was at Anais's cottage and found a picture of him. He was older than nineteen. Way older. He looks like he's twenty-five or so—"

"That makes no sense," Russell interrupted. "We were just there, together, a few weeks ago. The cottage was almost empty. Now all of a sudden a picture appears?"

"Sandrine left it for me—I have so much to tell you."

"But why would Anais have a picture of your father?"

"I don't know, Russell."

"Are you still in Cherbourg now? Where are you going from there?" Joanne asked.

"I can't stay here anymore. I'm going downtown to a hotel for the night. I'll figure it out from there."

"I need you to do something for me. It'd be so much easier for you. A phone call or Internet search. I need the name of the owner of a property in Geneva. I started a search online, but it's too hard—an assortment of foreign languages. Can you do it for me? Or call the town offices in the morning and get the name for me?"

"You came all this way? For me? To help me?" she asked.

"We went where the information was. It was too interesting to leave alone," Joanne responded.

"Give me the address. If I can't find it online, I'll make some calls tomorrow and text you the info."

"Okay, here it is." Joanne rattled off what they knew. "Be careful. We'll wait to hear from you as soon as you get anything." She clicked off the phone. "But tonight, we eat. We get a few drinks. We sleep," she said to Russell.

He nodded. He was engrossed in his papers again. "I know where I saw that name. Rossi. Tommaso's obituary. It was his wife's maiden name."

"Wait . . . what?"

"I have it somewhere, saved. Hold on. Here it is." He held it up for Joanne to see. Her eyes ran over it and landed on the line *He is survived by his wife, Olivia (nee Rossi), and his son, Maximo.*

She glanced up at him. "What do we know about Olivia Lacroce?"

"I don't know anything more about her than her name. She's younger than Tommaso by ten years or so." He flipped some pages. "It never occurred to me to look up anything more. How are the things that happened in Saigon in the sixties connected to Tommaso's wife? Her parents?"

"I can't imagine. Were they in Saigon too? Was the whole world in Saigon then? Were you in Saigon too, Russell?"

"Wasn't born yet, or I might have been." He jumped up and started throwing the papers back into the box. "Change your clothes, wash up. Don't just sit there."

"Where are we going?"

He'd moved to the bed. "It's your one chance to see Italy before we fly out tomorrow."

"Fly where? Where are we going?"

"Depends on Ava's info. Geneva or Vietnam. Flip a coin."

Russell's phone dinged with a text. *That was easy. That address is owned by a man named Schroeder. German. He's owned it for nine years, rents it out. It's a big rental district because of the university. Does that help?* "Crap," Russell said. "Vietnam it is. Let's go, Joanne. I want to be in Rome tonight at the airport so we can catch a flight out as soon as possible."

"Are you serious?"

An hour later they were on the interstate headed to Rome. Joanne had a bag of McDonald's in her lap. "The best food in the world and I'm eating this. I hate you, Russell."

CHAPTER 41

Philomena

Vicenza, Italy

She couldn't see him. The view was blocked by no less than seven people standing around his bed.

"The respirator went off? How is that possible? For how long?" the senior nurse asked.

"I'm not sure. It just looks, from what the computer is reading, like there was a malfunction of some sort. For about six minutes."

The respirator was back on, forcing air into her husband's lungs. They applied paddles to his heart, and she watched his body rise and fall with each shock. After several attempts, they turned and seemed to notice for the first time that she was standing there.

"I'm sorry, Signora DeFeo, please wait outside," a tall woman with dark hair said, coming to her side.

Philomena didn't move. "He's dead? His respirator malfunctioned, or someone turned it off?"

The charge nurse jumped in. "We have our eyes on him at all times whether we are in the room with him or not. There are monitors. Nobody did this to him."

"But he's dead?" Philomena could see the commotion continuing only a few feet away. They were applying paddles again; he was arching off the bed. She could smell burned hair.

"We haven't called it yet. Please wait. Outside."

"Stop!" she screamed. "Let him go in peace. He wouldn't want this."

Hands grabbed her and pulled her back into the hallway, sat her down. She didn't look at who it was until they let her go. "Please sit, Signora DeFeo." It was one of the police officers. Why couldn't they leave her alone? "We don't want to have to arrest you when your husband is like this. I can't imagine anything worse."

"Someone turned his respirator off just now. That's what happened. You're sitting here bothering me about blood in his car, how my blood got there, when someone just came back to finish the job. Apparently you don't care about that!"

"We're not here about blood, Signora. It's something more. Something we found in your house after a complete search. We need to know when your husband last had contact with Anais Lavoisier."

Philomena stared at the officer. He loomed over her, at least a foot taller. "I have no idea. She died about a month ago."

"We got his telephone records—home and cell. Trying to see if anything interesting popped up. And it seems there were a few things. So, when is the last time you spoke to her?"

"No, I haven't. Not in years. Not since my daughter, Adrianna, was born."

"That would be how long?"

"Almost forty years now."

"And in forty years you've had no contact, but your husband has?"

"What is this about? My husband is dying in the other room. I need to go." She started to stand up.

"Well, it's interesting because there have been a series of calls between two numbers, which lasted at least ten minutes each. This goes back as far as we were able to look. You have no idea who that might have been?"

Philomena felt the bile rise in her throat. "If Anais was alive, obviously that's who he was speaking with. After she died? I have no idea."

"Okay, so someone texted him before he was attacked, the unknown number. Let me read it to you again." He shuffled a few pages in a notebook. "'How long will you live, Victor?'—that's what it said."

"Yes, but they said there was no number attached to it. There was no way of knowing who was sending it—"

The officer shifted slightly. "We found that information. The phone company was very helpful."

"So, who was it?"

"One number." He held out a notepad to show her.

She stared at the number until she felt her eyeballs burning into her skull. Things blurred and then came back together. "What are you saying?"

The officer nodded. "Stop playing games, Philomena. You bought the phone at the electronic store downtown. You paid cash. The clerk remembers it was a woman who purchased this particular phone. He remembered your name. Philomena. Do you think he'd recognize you now? Pick you out of a lineup, maybe?"

"No—"

"You were threatening your husband with this text, not even an hour before he was attacked. You didn't know we could retrieve it? Technology these days."

Philomena shook her head. "I never texted him. If I wanted to get a new phone and threaten him, why would I mention my name? Think about it."

His head tilted to the side. "Okay. Can you tell me where you were when your husband's respirator went off about a half hour ago?"

Her body started shaking, buzzing. "I was on my way here."

He flipped the notepad to another page. "No, according to the surveillance cameras you entered the hospital at approximately 8:30. Does that sound right?"

"That's not right."

"It is. And his respirator went off at 8:40 p.m. Plenty of time to get to his room—"

"Signora DeFeo? You can come with me?" The charge nurse was back, touching her shoulder lightly. Philomena turned abruptly and followed her back into the room.

Victor was there. His eyes were open and darting around the room. He'd come back to life.

"He's not able to speak or move anything but his eyes at this point. But this is a hopeful sign, I think," the doctor said.

Her hands went to her mouth. "What happened? I thought he'd died. I thought he was gone. How is he awake?"

"Stranger things have happened. We almost lost him—thought we did, actually. Sometimes the spirit wants to keep going. We got his heart beating, and a few minutes later he opened his eyes. Neurology is coming to do some testing. We'll know more after that."

Victor's eyes landed on Philomena and locked on her, not moving. His eyebrows went up, his eyes widened. He looked like he was struggling to move but couldn't. His face was turning a bright red. Philomena stood where she was, held his gaze until she couldn't look anymore, then turned and looked up at the waiting police officer.

"I think he's done my job for me, Signora. He can tell us himself what happened. I'm putting an officer at the door. Don't go anywhere without notifying him."

CHAPTER 42

MARIE

Camden County Jail, New Jersey

They kept talking about updating everything—giving the inmates iPads, about how all the mail would be scanned into a system, you could open your account and read your mail, access your inmate account to see if you really could afford the ramen soup priced at a dollar fifty-seven, even schedule visits, store phone numbers, watch movies. But everything evolved so slowly in this place, she was sure she'd never see an iPad within these concrete walls while she was here. So she was forced to wait for the mail trolley to come along to deliver her letters the old-fashioned way.

Not that she had much mail. But she was waiting for one letter in particular that she knew was coming. Every day she would wait by the sliding door for the mail cart to go by, half in expectation, half in dread of her name being called. The letter she'd received before had haunted her. Who could have known about her trip to Italy at the time Tommaso was killed? Who would have known her whereabouts to find the address and send a letter to her? For what purpose? To blackmail her? She had no money. Ava had it all.

A moonless night on unfamiliar roads, in a rented manual-shift car. The loneliness and the fear had taken over, driving north through inky blackness. Twists, turns. At the time, Marie had cursed the decision to make the trip, having only agreed after significant pressure from Anais. Nobody knew about the trip except Anais. Anais and the person in the park, the person who made eye contact, who knew her face.

Since that first letter, one more had come. It was much shorter than the first, containing only a few sentences. *Did your mother tell you what happened at Dong Xoai? What happened to Na Lacroce? Did she suffer the same fate as Ngoc Le, smothered by her blanket, the breath sucked from her lungs? Why were you at the park looking for Tommaso Lacroce? Someday you will answer these questions. You can't hide in jail forever.*

Marie had picked it up and read it again and dropped it because the date printed after the note was staring her in the face. It was the date she was to appear before the parole board. Her potential release date. It had caused her to scream out loud. *It wasn't my fault. I wasn't even born yet. How can any of that be my fault? Leave me alone. Leave me alone, or I will kill you.*

Someone had heard her crying out alone in her cell and brought the man from the mental health department to her doorway. He shifted back and forth from one foot to the other, a clipboard in his hands, while she sat on her bed with her hands folded in her lap. She couldn't remember his name, but it was the same person who had done her initial intake. Middle-aged white guy, overweight and glistening in a thin coating of sweat.

He'd eyed her bed, her few belongings, then her, his glasses slipping down his fat nose. "So, they said you were screaming about killing someone. Who are you going to kill, Marie?"

She stared defiantly at him. "I'm not going to kill anyone. I got some bad news. That's all."

"Bad news from where? They said you didn't make any phone calls."

So *they* were watching her. Of course they were watching her. "I got a letter, okay. No big secret, they read them all before they're delivered to us."

"Okay," he responded, completely uninterested in her bad news. "How about yourself? Are you going to kill yourself?"

It had made her angry, this man asking her that question. If she wanted to kill herself, she would, and none of his ridiculous questions would make any difference. "Not today. No. I'm absolutely fine." She saw an officer push a cart filled with Styrofoam containers onto the unit. Dinner was about to be served. She looked at the clock on the wall. Two forty-seven in the afternoon. Almost time for dinner. Breakfast was twelve hours later—in the middle of the night. Her stomach had never adjusted to the timing or the food, and her digestive tract was rebelling. It was good she was housed alone. "I was upset for a moment, but now I'm fine."

He didn't move. "Huh. Well, officers are concerned because you're screaming in here, and it's not the first time."

"And it might not be the last either. Jail is a painful experience for most of us. But I'm not going to hurt myself or anyone else."

He nodded. She was speaking his language. "If they call me again, I might have to put you on close watch, take all your clothes. Okay?"

His eyes had lit up like he might like that option. She nodded and watched him move from the doorway while they shut the solid metal door on her, leaving her alone again. When she wanted to scream, which was often, she'd have to bite her lips or the inside of her cheek.

Now she paced, waiting for the mail delivery, racking her brain as to who could be behind this. Who could have followed her the night she drove north from Rome? They made mention of the place where she'd stopped for coffee and gas. No one could possibly know that unless they were there. At that particular moment she hated Anais. The woman had forced her and Claire into terrible situations with her machinations and labyrinth of secrets and lies, going so far as to pull in things from a past best forgotten.

Marie saw the officer with the mail cart standing at the sliding door of her unit. Another officer was sorting through it and then entered the cell block. Marie held her breath. She desperately wanted to know who was behind these notes, but at the same time she was petrified of what the next letter might say. She heard the key in her door and the heavy clicking of the lock opening.

"Nun, a letter came for you." She handed the envelope to Marie and then shut and locked the door again.

Marie held it in her hands but refused to open it. It was the same kind of envelope as the others—plain white, legal sized, no return address. She put it on her bed and paced in circles, but the cell was small and she couldn't get too far away from it. It was calling to her.

She picked it up and pulled out the one sheet of copy paper, typed, just like the others. A small photograph fluttered to the floor. *Here's a riddle for you to ponder until we meet, Sister: What do you and Tommaso Lacroce have in common? Don't think too hard. XO.* The photograph was of a girl. No older than two or three, with blonde hair hanging in waves around her round face. She was smiling, and there was a gap where one of her baby teeth had fallen out. Marie had never seen a picture of her before, but she knew without knowing that this was Na Lacroce—the little girl that had disappeared nearly fifty years before.

Her parole hearing was tomorrow. She'd be facing the judge in the morning. The sender was someone she knew, or used to know. Someone who'd been close at one time. Claire was the one who always called her *sister*. It was their joke. Nun sister and sister sister. But Claire was dead. It was someone else tormenting her. Marie clasped the letter in her hand and lay back on her bed, staring at the metal bunk above her.

What did she and Tommaso have in common? Other than that they'd both gotten dragged through life by Anais Lavoisier. Marie got up and rattled her door to make sure it was secure—that no one could get to her. Only then did she feel safe behind the heavy metal doors with enormous locks.

CHAPTER 43

Ava

Cherbourg, France

I ended the call and shifted my bag on my shoulder. It was heavy with bottles of booze and my belongings. Anais's cottage was dark, but I didn't want to go back there. There was something in Sandrine's eyes that disturbed me. Concern, fear, anxiety? Before I even reached the street, I saw the car pull up. A white Fiat. The driver rolled down the window. "I'm Sandrine's son. I don't know if you remember me—"

I studied his face. I did. A little bit. "Maybe."

"She called, said you needed a ride into Cherbourg." He leaned over and opened the passenger's-side door. "I don't mind taking you. Better this than walking." He was wearing a dark-colored jacket and a baseball cap. I jumped in, immediately relaxing into the seat. I wanted to get as far away from this as I could. "I used to take you swimming up the road when you were little. Do you remember that?"

"Umm. Vaguely. I just need to get close enough to Cherbourg so I can walk to a hotel. That's all."

"Any hotel in particular?"

"It doesn't matter. Do you live around here?"

"Paris for a while. But I rented a flat in Hainneville about eight months ago to be closer to Mum." His eyes shifted sideways, and he seemed to be looking me up and down.

I saw street signs and knew we were about a mile from town. Maybe less. This man was making me nervous. It didn't matter if he was Sandrine's son. I wanted out. "This is good enough. You can pull over here. Thank you."

He didn't acknowledge my words for a few moments. Then the car slowed down and pulled to the curb. "Listen, Ava, I'm going to tell you what to do from here. When you get out, find a hotel. Get yourself together. Don't do anything until Saturday morning. Stay in the hotel. Stay in and get some sleep, get some food. Do you hear me?"

"Why?"

"Don't ask questions. My mother didn't want to get any further into this . . . On Saturday morning, go to the train station at Cherbourg and buy a ticket to Paris. Get a ticket on the ten o'clock train."

"I don't understand."

"If you think your father's alive, this is your one chance to find out. Ten o'clock train to Paris. Last car. Saturday morning."

I stumbled for words. "Fine. I got it."

"I can give you a ride to the hotel. You don't have to walk in the dark."

I shook my head. "No. I need to walk to clear my head. I have a lot to think about. Why are you doing this?"

He shrugged. "I can't answer that."

"So that's it, then?" He just nodded, and I got out. The car sped away so that all I saw was the exhaust spewing from the tailpipe as it rounded the corner.

I barely remembered Sandrine's son. He was so much older; I hadn't seen him in years. He was vague, a backdrop in some of her conversations. I walked the fifteen minutes to the nearest hotel. La Maison Duchevreuil—an old farm reconstructed into a three-room hotel. Just three spectacular rooms that I knew well after visiting many times with Grand-Mère in the summer. A minivacation within a vacation, she called it. Only ten minutes from her house, it was a few blocks from the beach and served the best croissants and marmalade I'd ever had. The rooms were large, rustic, with beams crisscrossing the ceiling, rough-hewn walnut floors, and a separate sitting area. One had a private courtyard.

The owner smiled at me, though I doubted he remembered the young girl that had been here years earlier with her grandmother. He said I was in luck that they had two rooms open. I didn't consider it luck. It was winter. The tourists that would flock to see the northern coast of Normandy were tucked safely in their beds for the winter. I chose the courtyard room and paid in cash. The man cocked his head a bit at the fact that I didn't have a credit card, but let it go. He wasn't getting another customer tonight.

If there had been a camera in the room to capture what happened after I closed the door behind me, it would entertain many. The smell of lavender and citrus transported me back years. I dropped my bags, stripped off my clothes, and wrapped myself in the bulky cotton robe in the closet. Then I proceeded to jump on the beds, eat the cakes smeared with butter and jam they'd left on the coffee counter. I nibbled on chocolates, and opened a bottle of merlot, pouring it nicely into the wineglass instead of putting the bottle to my lips. The room was heaven but short-lived.

I knew I only had a day and a half to enjoy it before a train was going to haul me from Cherbourg on a journey I wasn't sure I wanted to take. I was going to enjoy it while it lasted. My phone dinged, and I stared down at the numbers. Russell.

We're heading to Vietnam. Don't know when we'll see you; stay in touch.

Vietnam? I laughed out loud at the thought of Joanne in Asia.

When the time finally came to go to the station, the line to the ticket kiosk was short. I kept my head down, my eyes to the floor. I let my hair down and pulled part of it to cover some of my face. I had sunglasses to complete the look, though I was sure they looked odd because the sky was gray, not a hint of sun anywhere. I pushed the button and paid my thirty-two euros for a one-way ticket to Paris. Then I waited.

The shop selling coffee was crowded, so I walked out onto the platform and wandered to the end, planting my back against the wall. The train was there, doors open, but I chose not to board yet. People began filing out of the doors of the station, onto the waiting cars. When the attendant made a last call for passengers for train number 675 heading to Paris, I hopped onto the car and took the very last seat so no one could surprise me from behind.

I eyed the station through the window, wondering, waiting. It occurred to me that there were five stops between Cherbourg and Paris. I was only told to be on this train, on this car. It didn't mean anything was going to happen now. But I was still so on edge, I kept my bag in my lap, my feet firmly planted on the floor.

I looked out the window, peering down onto the platform both ways. People were still coming from the station, entering the train cars farther down the track. I held my breath. I had the option of getting off. Taking a random bus to Paris and then on to Geneva.

That's when I saw her. Or thought I saw her. My sunglasses were on, and it was cloudy, coloring everything a deep smoky gray. She moved slowly, boarding the train at least three cars up, short, wearing a trench coat and dark slacks. I saw the glitter of the bracelet on her wrist even from where I stood. Diamonds and sapphires. The little something she always wore, and said went with everything, including the brooch that was in my bag.

That bracelet that wasn't in her jewelry box when her items were inventoried. Sandrine told me it was on her when she was buried. But then said she'd been cremated. I never questioned why someone would burn an expensive bracelet; at the time, I didn't care. It made no difference if Marie or Sandrine had pilfered it, or if they had burned it with her body. But that was Anais's bracelet, and it looked like it was hanging from Anais's wrist just now as she entered a train car a few hundred feet from where I stood.

I raced through to the next car, scanning every seat for the familiar gray head. There were only ten people on it—none of them were Anais. I continued as fast as I could, my bag slapping the seats as I moved. I pushed the button and pulled the handle and jumped onto the next car. At least twenty pairs of eyes were watching me. There were only two more cars to go. The train jerked and started to move away from the platform.

"Mademoiselle, please sit down. You can't move between cars when the train is in motion." The conductor placed a hand on my shoulder and pushed me down into an empty seat.

"Did you see a woman? An older woman—sixties, gray hair, black trench coat. Bracelet? Sparkly bracelet?"

He shrugged. "No, and if she is on this train, you need to wait until the next stop to look for her."

I tried to stand up. I had seen her. The very slight stoop of her shoulders as she reached for the railing to climb onto the train. Her gray hair combed back from her face. The bracelet. Black leather satchel in her hand. Maybe it was her. And if I saw her, it meant she was alive. It meant she hadn't died last month, that she'd faked the whole thing. That she was here on this train with a purpose. She'd managed to get me here too, wanting me to be in the last car of the train for some reason.

The attendant kept his hand lightly on my shoulder. "I can stand here for the next fifteen minutes until the next stop if you make me. You cannot walk between the cars."

"Let me go back to the last car, then? I need to be in the last car. You can come with me? Make sure I'm safe?"

"No. Stay where you are," he said. He tapped my shoulder, smiled, and moved away.

I was going to get up, but stopped myself when I saw Sandrine's son coming down the aisle. He hesitated near my seat and then motioned for me to move over.

"What is this?" I asked.

"You were supposed to be in the last car. Much easier to find. You're going to come with me, Ava. We're getting off at the next stop—Valognes."

I studied him for a second. In the light of the train car, I could see he was tall, light-brown hair, maybe thirty. I did remember him now that I was seeing him in the light. He would take me to the ocean sometimes when Anais was busy. "Why would I do that?" I hissed. "I think I just saw Anais. Is she alive? She's on this train."

He shook his head. "I very much doubt you saw your grandmother. She died last month. And you will come with me because if you don't, I will call the police, Interpol, and tell them Ava Saunders is alive. I will tell them everything. And they will take you to prison."

I turned sideways to face him. "Why would you do that? Why?"

"Because my mother asked me to. I am—well, just call me your escort. I need to bring you somewhere, and you *will* come with me, Ava."

I looked out the window at the farmland whizzing by. "Let me guess. La Héronnière de Haut?"

CHAPTER 44

Olivia

Vicenza, Italy

Her eyes were heavy, though she was fighting it. Tommaso was in the bathroom with the door shut, but he was taking too long. She'd wanted to take a shower, change into her pajamas, brush her teeth, but she was so tired. They'd been out on a friend's boat on Lake Como, against her better judgment. She hated boats and always seemed to be the only one that got sick. Today was no different.

The door opened, and he came out, a phone to his ear. Her eyes were only half closed, and he didn't look in her direction. He sat on the end of the bed, continuing his conversation.

"Why can't you just give it to me. Really? Why do I have to meet you? And if you found something out, just tell me now. I'm not up for games."

More silence.

"Look, this should have been over long ago. The day we left Saigon, it was over. The day I came to Italy with family and you married that American, it should have been over."

Then there was nothing for a few minutes.

"No, no, no. It *was* her. Those photographs of that town near Dong Xoai. My sister's hair ribbon or one that looked just like it, with blood on it." He stood up and went to the dresser. "I've had enough, Anais. This is going to stop. Give me the information, and I'll take care of it. You don't even need to be involved."

He slammed the dresser drawer. The phone still at his ear. Olivia rolled over but didn't completely close her eyes.

"There's no way Na is still alive. You weren't there when it happened. I was; Philomena was. She's not alive. Someone's just pretending she is. If you know something different—" He slipped off his pants and hung them on the back of the door. "No, the last little note had my mother's address and phone number on it. If this person starts sending things to my mother? My life is over. My mother won't survive it. There's no going back to sort this all out."

He went back into the bathroom, and his voice became muffled. But he came out again in pajama bottoms.

"If I had known this was going to happen, of course I would have done things differently. I wouldn't have let either of you come with me. That was my father's idea. He said it was good cover. And I don't think he thought it was going to end like that."

He sat down again, this time on a chair on the other side of the room.

"You know if my father found out the truth about what I did to Na—and I don't know how he could not have. He knew everything and everyone; it would have taken him a day to piece it together. Tops. He knew, and he lived with it. He probably blamed himself."

He sighed deeply and went to Olivia's side. Olivia was half asleep, feeling his words roll over her like waves.

"Fine, Anais, I'll meet you tomorrow. This is the only time. Eleven o'clock at night. At the Cresole park. I'm meeting Davide Tosi there, anyway—what's one more." Silence. "The kid said he has something to tell me. Something supposedly important. Urgent." A hesitation. "Who knows. I've never met him before. Victor asked me to meet him. But listen, after I see you tomorrow, I'll do what I have to do—don't ask me any questions, and don't call me ever again."

He flipped his phone shut and got into bed. He shook her shoulder. "Olivia, are you going to take a shower? Change for bed? Go check on Max?"

She slowly opened her eyes and looked at him. "Who was calling so late?"

"Just work. It's fine."

Olivia opened her eyes now, half expecting Tommaso to still be beside her. That dream was twenty years away, in another time, but the words he'd spoken into the phone seemed so real. She remembered it. That conversation was so exact. He'd been talking to Anais. He'd been receiving threatening letters, hiding them from her, whispering into the phone at night. Each letter making him more stricken. She'd noticed but tried not to. Any answers he gave her would force her hand. And she liked her hands where they were.

Olivia got up and pulled on her clothes, stumbling to get her legs into her slacks. Philomena's house was empty when she pulled into the driveway. She sat in her car, undecided about what her next move might be. She didn't want to leave. If she left, she didn't know when she'd get another opportunity. She closed her eyes and tried to picture Tommaso's face that last night at the dinner table. He had seemed distracted, not paying attention to what she was saying.

She hadn't known it would be the last conversation they would have or she wouldn't have wasted it talking about flowers in the garden and whether it was going to rain. She would have spent hours thinking about how she'd approached him at his office, so bold, so confident. He'd latched on to her as if they were already acquainted. There was something comfortable in his face, in his eyes, that drew her in, let her guard down.

Letting her guard down had never been an easy thing. She knew from an early age her family had money. They vacationed in Switzerland, where her father owned a house in Saint Moritz. She was the only one in her school that had visited Disney World in Florida. As boys, then men, approached her, she'd become aware her money was more attractive than she was. At the Université de Genève, in Switzerland, she'd spent years dodging undesirables.

But Tommaso broke through all of that. Twelve years they spent together day in and day out. They had one son, Maximo. They ate dinner together most nights, had friends over, knew most of the same people, yet in all of that he never discussed his past. His life started when he'd met her, that's what he kept telling her.

She saw a silver car pull into the driveway. Philomena was at the wheel. She got out slowly, gathering her things, not paying attention to the fact that Olivia was parked only fifty feet away. She waited until Philomena was in the house with the door shut to walk up and ring the bell. The last time they'd met, things hadn't gone so well. Philomena had semithreatened her.

The door opened quickly, and Philomena filled the open space. Her face shifted in half a second from unpleasant-resting-face to livid. "Why are you here?"

Olivia pushed her way past her. "I know you don't want me here, but I need you."

Philomena watched her almost as if she didn't believe what she was seeing. "Things went badly last time we met. You keep circling, Olivia. Tommaso is as dead today as he was twenty years ago. Why don't you leave me alone, get on with your life?"

"Anais talked to my husband the night before he died."

Philomena picked up her grocery bags and carried them to the kitchen. "You just came up with this now?"

"Yes and no. But she did. She talked to my husband. He was meeting her the next day. In the Cresole park where they found his body."

Philomena's hand stopped moving. She hesitated a bit. "So, you've paid a detective, and all this time you had this juicy tidbit and kept it to yourself?"

"She didn't show up."

Philomena's hands were pressed against the counters. "How can you know that? How? He died in that park."

Olivia was quiet. "I think she sent someone else in her place."

"Who? And again, Olivia. It doesn't make sense. How do you know this, and why haven't you said anything before?"

Olivia stared her straight in the eye. "I'm still figuring it out. I've only had pieces of it up until now. But I'm pretty certain that's what happened."

"Very weirdly convenient. Look, there were things Anais and Tommaso knew about each other. Me too. Things that only the three of us knew. And Tommaso thought someone was threatening him with it—trying to destroy his life."

"The three of you and your secrets. Someone was sending him letters. He was quite upset about it but wouldn't give me any details. He wanted to believe it was Anais, nasty as always. Was it? Or was it really his sister writing, threatening him?"

Philomena's head shot up. "What sister? His sister died—"

"Died or disappeared? I thought she just disappeared."

Philomena's face blanched. Her lips twitched like she was trying to find words that wouldn't come. Olivia tapped the granite counter twice with her hand. "Ah. The crux of the secret, right there. Isn't it? One of you hurt the girl. Maybe in the heat of the moment, maybe it was a mistake. Maybe it was out of fear—Tommaso said those were dangerous times. But whatever the reason, someone hurt her. Was it you, Philomena?"

Philomena didn't answer. She had the refrigerator door open, and she stood with her back to Olivia, refusing to turn around.

"It doesn't matter, Philomena. If Na is alive, it would explain a lot. She'll show up eventually." Olivia left the kitchen without looking back.

CHAPTER 45

VICTOR

Vicenza, Italy

He heard the beating of his own heart in his ears. That was the first sound he was really aware of. It came slowly to him, like he was stuck deep underground, struggling to make sense of the darkness and occasional noises around him. That rhythm lulled him from one moment to the next. It wasn't unpleasant. It wasn't anything at all. It was just being.

That changed gradually as the whooshing became louder, more defined. And then he was back, the light against his lids, the noises of people moving around him. And he had more control, like the darkness had reset his brain. A computer shut down and rebooted, he *felt* more, sensed more. And then he felt an involuntary movement of his eyelids. And his eyes opened without him even thinking about it. There was a light so bright he had to close them again and rest. But gradually, he could tolerate more.

The room was bigger than he expected. Just filled with the equipment used to keep him alive. His throat hurt, burned deep down all the way to his lungs, and he felt the pressure of air being forced in and out. It was uncomfortable, but any attempts to put his hand to his mouth to pull the tube out were clumsily ineffective. His fingers weren't working in coordination with his brain. He lay still, in frustration.

His memory was better, more exact. He knew her name but was struggling for the syllables to put it all together. He knew her face intimately, including the light-colored mole on her neck. He knew it all. And he remembered their last fight. The fight they'd had shortly before he was attacked. It was over the girl with the long dark hair and green eyes. The girl who was in his doorway when he was stabbed. Thin but pretty. Her prettiness was in her eyes, not so much the rest of her. Intelligent, curious, all-knowing. Bright, in all aspects of the word. Clear and present. Those eyes would draw you in and kill you.

He wanted to talk to the nurse but couldn't move his lips. Even if the tube was ripped from his throat, he wouldn't have been able to get his vocal cords to cooperate. Someone needed to find his wife. There was so much he wanted to tell her. Important things. He felt the nurse's hands adjusting his blankets and then checking the monitors near his bed.

"It's so nice to see you back with us, Signor DeFeo," she said. "We were worried. Your wife was just here. I'm sure she'll be back soon. They're going to take you for some testing later today. We want you to get a little stronger so you can breathe on your own. Can you move your hand for me? Any finger at all?" She put his hand against her palm. He was able to flop his hand off hers, but had limited control. "That's good."

She put his hand back down by his side. "You have some mail here." She held up some envelopes. "I don't know if your wife left them. Do you want me to read them to you?" He couldn't move his head to nod so he just looked at her. "Okay, then. Here we go."

She ripped the envelope open and pulled out a card. "It looks like a get-well card, from some people you work with." She held it up for him to read the signatures. "I don't know if you can read the names or not, but there's probably fifteen signatures. Very nice. I'm going to put this by your bed. You can look at it when you're a little stronger."

She propped the card open on the end table and opened the next envelope. "Well, let's see here. It's a letter. Do you want me to read it, or would you rather I leave it and you can read it another time? Move your hand for me if you want me to read it?"

He flicked his finger for her. He was looking at the sheet of white lined paper she held in her hand.

"Okay, here goes. It's a poem, sort of. Or a riddle? I'll just read it, and if you want me to read it again, flick your finger.

> *"I remember the heat. I remember the rain. The mosquitos seemed to swim through liquid air. The flies, sensing a hint of death, hovered, lingering in blood splattered over reason gone wrong. Whiteness in a place of misunderstood incivility. The lingering past squashed under heavy tread. Some pasts die a thousand deaths and live through, like the memory of a knife against the most pliant of skins, sinking deep to find meaning within the bone beneath. A glove against the innocence of breath. An eye for an eye. A tongue for a tongue—until the sharpest of steel meets gristle again, Victor. Thinking of you always.*

"And there's a picture. Here, look." She held it up. "What is it?"

Victor focused the best he could without his glasses. A photograph of Vietnam. He knew it just by the mountain in the background. The fronds of palm trees. It was of an empty dirt road leading into the jungle. There was a large mud puddle filled with something darker than water. A dark liquid he knew without knowing was blood.

This had to have been sent by his attacker. They were watching. They knew everything. They'd put that glove against the innocence of his breath and attempted to stop him from breathing altogether. His heart rate shot up, and the nurse jumped up, responding to the beeping on the monitor.

"Victor, what's gotten you so bothered? What does this photograph mean? Do you know who wrote this? Blink for me. Twice for yes, once for no." He blinked once. "Is it related to your attack?" He blinked twice. "Did you see who dropped it off?" His eyes fluttered once and stayed shut. He was so exhausted by all of this. If they were going to kill him, they needed to get it over with. "I'm getting the police officer."

She rushed from the room and left him alone. In her haste, the photograph had been dropped on the bed near him. He looked closer. The dark mud puddle maybe was just muddy water. Maybe it wasn't meant to be anything else. But the shoe just visible at the edge of the photograph certainly wasn't an accident. A little girl's shoe unbuckled, on its side. An afterthought. It summed up everything. He thought he might throw up, but the tube was in his throat. He'd choke to death.

He pushed the "Call" button on his bed, flicked the photograph onto the floor, and waited to die.

CHAPTER 46

JOANNE

Ho Chi Minh City, Vietnam

She would rather live a thousand lifetimes in poverty than climb back into a narrow airplane again. She had no idea how Ava managed to cross the Atlantic so many times to Europe without a thought. Thirteen hours in the air had left her feeling bloated, antsy. Her legs were permanently cramped, and she thought if she were offered another little snacky plate of crackers and cheese she might jump out the window.

The changeover in Tokyo had given her a break, but not really. It was all so bizarre and foreign, she clung to Russell, afraid to let go of his arm because she'd literally be stranded. She hadn't even known how to use the kiosk in the Philadelphia airport to get her boarding pass and luggage tags. Finding her gate in Tokyo was out of the question. All the signs were in Japanese.

"Did Ava say where she was going from Cherbourg?" he asked.

Joanne nodded. "You asked me at least six times. She was on speaker. You heard her just like I did. She said she couldn't stay at the cottage, that she was going to downtown Cherbourg."

"I hope she's not in more trouble."

"She's a big girl. She has our numbers too. She can call us."

"Yeah, okay. Anyway, this flight to Saigon is only a few hours long—"

"Six hours, Russell. Another six hours. I don't even know if it's day or night. I'm so confused—"

"After we go through immigration in Saigon and get our visas, we'll go to the hotel and just rest. I'll give you the rest of the day to just relax. Room service. We'll find western food. Whatever you want."

"We're not going to one of those over-the-water things you and Juliette were going to, are we? The thought of sleeping over moving water right now is making me sick."

"No. I cancelled that and got us a nice hotel in Saigon. The Reverie Saigon. Deluxe twin room. One room but separate beds. I think you'll like it."

She had no idea how much until they arrived through the palatial front doors. Joanne was so exhausted she felt someone might have sucked out her brain midflight without her knowing. She could barely put two words together and had fallen asleep in the cab. She couldn't help but notice Russell seemed unaffected. Like over twenty-three hours of travel in a foreign land was nothing.

The lobby was so enormous and ornate she stopped after making it through the front door and just stared. The ceiling was several stories high, decorated with enormous chandeliers and marble. She only started moving again when Russell pulled her arm. Twenty minutes later, she was pressed against the floor-to-ceiling glass window of their hotel room, staring out at the lights that glittered as far as the eye could see.

"This whole room is glass. It's so beautiful it's making me dizzy." She flipped off her shoes, fell into her bed, stretching her legs out, clothes on, and pulled the cover up over her.

She'd intended just to close her eyes, but when she woke up, it was light outside, the sun just visible through clouds and smog. She sat up, disoriented, and looked over at Russell. He was sitting up, his laptop on his legs, sipping on a cup of tea.

"So, I went down to the lobby and hired a driver that will take us to Dong Xoai," he said. "Make yourself some tea." He pointed to the coffee station across the room. It was filled with an assortment of teas and coffees and a machine that approximated a Keurig.

She opted for a bottle of sparkling water from the minibar. She held it up. "Is this safe to drink?"

He smiled. "It's sealed. And I think it was bottled in France, so I'm pretty sure it's safe."

She snapped off the lid and took a swallow. "What time is it? I'm so confused. The sun's up. It's day? Have you slept?" She wandered away from him and into the bathroom. When she turned on the light, she screamed. "Have you seen this bathroom? Oh my God. It's marble. The whole thing. Windows everywhere. The tub, Russell, come and look at the tub."

He leaned up far enough to see her. "It's about six o'clock. Your sleep cycle has sorted itself out. The dining room is open for breakfast if you're hungry."

She shut the bathroom door behind her and just stood by the window watching the city below. Coming here was crazy. It wasn't her kind of vacation. She usually just rented a house in Ocean City, New Jersey, for a week with a friend in the summer. That was living. This was scary. She wanted a shower, clean clothes. Maybe order room service. Take some Tylenol PM and try to sleep a little more to take the edge off her exhaustion and forget she was chasing Ava's nightmares in an Asian city half across the world. She opened the door and heard Russell's voice.

"Nine o'clock is fine. In the lobby, yes." He hung up and looked at her, stretching back, his arms behind his head. "We have a guide. Born in Saigon in nineteen forty-one. Lived here through French occupation. His father worked for the British embassy." He stood up. "Low-level groundskeeper and janitor. But it's a start, I'd say. He speaks English. He'd know of rumors—"

"So, he's like seventy-five?"

"Probably a really good seventy-five. He's going to meet us in the lobby. Gives us a bit of time before we have to get ready."

"Did you ask him anything?" she asked.

"I did, just to confirm he was what I wanted. He seems perfect. He didn't live in the same part of town as Anais or Philomena, but he knew of them. He knew most of the families that participated in embassy affairs. I asked if he remembered the Lacroces. He got quiet. So I don't know if that means anything or not. We'll see."

Joanne gathered her things and went toward the bathroom. "I'm going to soak for a bit, so I'll be ready when the old guy comes to take us to Dong whatever."

"It's pronounced Dome Soo-aye. Dong Xoai. Say it three times."

She shut the door and ran the water into the enormous platform tub by the window, turned off the lights, lit the handy candles nestled along the shelf, and slid down into the water. All of Saigon might be able to see her naked, but she didn't care. Her gut told her she needed to relax as much as possible. Something terrible was going to happen today.

He was in a separate bed, and things were sort of back to normal between them. She was still fuming about the way he'd treated Juliette, but he'd paid a hefty price for it. She'd slept much less than she thought she would, but the breakfast food was familiar—more than she would have anticipated. The buffet was filled with bacon, eggs, pancakes, but she opted for dry Rice Krispies and orange juice.

"What?" she asked when Russell eyed the bowl in front of her. "You can't go wrong with a sealed box of cereal and oranges. I don't think. I'm sticking with what I know."

Her bones ached when they climbed in the back of the waiting car. The older man peered into his rearview mirror at them and smiled. One of his teeth was missing.

"Are you here to study the American War?" he asked. His English was better than some that lived in the United States. He pulled out into busy traffic. "A battle in Dong Xoai. I can tell you about it."

"No," Russell said. "We're interested in the time before the American War. After World War Two but before the Americans' escalation."

"Ah. French imperialism. My parents spoke French, sometimes even in our house. It was seen as a better language. Look at the streets." He pointed out the window. "French architecture. Look at the post office." The ornate yellow building looked so European it could have easily been plopped down in Paris. "It was different here then."

"You knew most of the Europeans here in the late sixties?"

"No, I wouldn't say that. There were many Europeans here. I helped to take care of the grounds at the British embassy with my father, but I was young. I was a teenager when your war started."

"But you remember the Lavoisiers?"

He nodded. "You asked me, and I remembered the name. They were a big family, important. They had a daughter."

"Yes, yes," Russell said.

"It was a violent time. Proud but not proud in our history."

"Meaning?"

"We wanted out from under French rule but not the communism of Ho Chi Minh. So we were stuck in the middle with no choice but more war. The French, they were leaving around the time you're talking about. Americans were coming in more and more. So many people killed. Death was everywhere. For nothing."

"Do you remember a little Italian girl that disappeared? Three years old. Adrianna Lacroce? A woman who worked in the embassy said everyone was talking about it," Joanne said. "If you were at the British embassy, maybe you heard about it?"

The car slowed slightly. "I remember. The day the girl disappeared, a whole family died in Dong Xoai. Mother, father, baby. Is that why you're going there? My father said that the two things were connected."

"How so?"

He looked like he was going to say something but changed his mind. "This drive is about two hours. If you want anything on the way, tell me."

"Tell me the rumors about the missing girl," Joanne said. "Were there any?"

"The family, they were killed because they were Viet Cong supporting the communists—that's what my father said. That farm was a stop-off point. Filled with ammunition, provisions. People say the little girl was there when it happened—when they were killed."

"What does that mean? She watched? She was killed too? She ran away?" Joanne asked.

The driver shrugged. "Nobody knows what happened—it's what you call an urban legend. After that, people said she was living in the hills. People say they see her sometimes. I don't know if it's true."

"They see her now? But how could they know it's the same girl? There have to be other Europeans or Americans here," Russell asked.

He nodded. "This woman has a big scar across her neck where her throat was cut."

CHAPTER 47

MARIE

Camden County Jail, New Jersey

The dark green mat underneath her was thin, pounded flat by the many inmate backs against it. It was like sleeping on a metal slab covered in foam. Her stomach felt sick, and the smell of breakfast they'd delivered at exactly 3:12 a.m. wasn't helping. She lifted the Styrofoam lid and dropped it again at least six times without taking a bite. Two pieces of toast. Some oatmeal in a cup. A carton of milk. Some eggs. And one orange. It had arrived lukewarm and had become congealed and cold hours ago.

She stared out the window, feeling as if she were waiting for the executioner to arrive. It was only a parole hearing. Her lawyer, the parole officer, the prosecutor, the judge would be there. Some members of the parole board would probably be there as well. The judge needed a recommendation as to how to resolve the charge: reinstate parole or send her to prison. In their many meetings, her parole officer, Bridgette, refused to give her any information as to how they were leaning. This was her first violation, but it was a huge one. She'd left the country without permission—Ava had turned her in.

The thought of prison didn't bother her. She was only worried at the moment about who was going to show up in the courtroom. She read the note again: *Here's a riddle for you to ponder until we meet: What do you and Tommaso Lacroce have in common?*

That sentence had kept her up at night. Tommaso was stabbed in the park near Vicenza, Italy. Whoever wrote this knew she'd been in the same area. Were they saying they thought she'd killed Tommaso? Or that her life was going to end in the same way?

Her door lock clicked, and an officer stood there. "Give me your tray, Nun, if you're not going to eat it. We don't want gnats in here. Damn hard to get rid of." She took the Styrofoam carton and started to shut the door.

"Do you know when they're going to come for me for court?" Marie asked.

The officer shrugged. Her hair was pulled back so tight from her face, her skin was reddish all along her hairline. "Not until eight-thirty or so. Why? You want to get a shower, clean up?"

Marie shook her head. "No, I want to make a quick phone call, if I can."

The officer opened her door wider. "Quick. You got ten minutes."

Marie hurried to the phone and dialed a number. The extension picked up after two rings. "I told you before not to call me from there. I'm going to get rid of this jail collect-call thing on my phone. They can trace this, you know."

"Just listen," Marie whispered. "I got a letter here. Who knew about my trip to Italy when Tommaso was killed?"

There was silence. "How can I know that?"

"Because you have to know it. It's important. Whoever this is sent a follow-up letter. Not much, just that Tommaso and I have a lot in common."

"What else did this letter say?"

"Nothing. That was it. Threatening enough. Who's doing this?"

"Tell me about the trip again."

"Seriously?" Marie hissed. "Now?"

"Give me the short version. Yes. Now."

"Okay. I flew into Rome, went to the Vatican. Had a short stay there overnight to legitimize the trip. Rented a car the next evening and drove north. The letter said they'd tracked me as far as Bologna."

"Think, Marie. What happened in Bologna? That means something."

She closed her eyes. "I did stop in Bologna. I got off the exit to get gas. It wasn't a chain gas station. It was just this place, kind of old. This man came out and helped me put gas in the car. I was wearing my habit. I remember because I ripped it off and tossed it into the back seat of the car—"

"Did anyone pull in after you, or pull over on the side of the road? Think, Marie."

Her breath started coming fast, like she was there again, that night, alone, trying to negotiate tiny Italian roads through pitch-blackness. Her gas light blinked on, and she took the first exit off E35 at Bologna. The blinding lights from the car behind her hitting her mirrors. It was a fluke that gas station was there. It had been empty when she pulled in. Nobody but her. She'd scrounged through her bag to come up with enough lire to pay the man. "No, but I had a cell phone on me. I got a call while I was in the gas station." She stopped, trying to think. "This is a game. It's all a game. Oh my God. I think I know who sent me the letter. I have to go."

"You know your mother is dead, if that's what you're thinking."

Marie hung up the phone and scurried back to her cell, pulling the door shut after her until she heard the lock click into place. Her stomach was churning, and she threw up three times into the metal toilet bowl, so thankful that she was housed alone. No one could see her in her most desperate moments. If what she suspected was true, she was in trouble. The only person who knew about that trip was the person who planned it. And if Anais were alive, she was playing very nasty little games again.

Marie's body was clammy with sweat when she heard the key in her lock. She could refuse to go to court. That was within her rights. The parole board wouldn't look too highly upon it, and the judge wouldn't either, but it was an option. She felt her insides bubbling, and she ran to the toilet as the door swung open.

"Nun, you doing your business? Sorry. Get yourself together. Big court in ten minutes."

The door was open, and she could see the day area clearly. If she was right, she needed to reach out to Ava. But she wasn't sure if Ava had her American sim card in. It was worth a shot.

She jotted down a number on a piece of paper and called to the officer. "Listen, do me a huge favor—"

"Can't do any favors, Nun. You know that."

"No, this is life and death. Call this number. I know, I know. I need to ask the social worker, but I don't have time. This is urgent. Just call it or have someone call it and leave a message on the voicemail. Tell her to watch out for Anais. Tell her things are not what she thinks. And I will call her as soon as I can." The officer was looking at her like she was crazy. Marie pressed the paper into her palm. "Please? It's all on there."

She stuffed it into her pocket like Marie hadn't spoken. "Clean up. I'll be back in two minutes to get you for court."

Marie stood where she was, realizing that Anais was the only person that could move her from wanting to rip Ava's lungs out through her mouth to feeling a desperate need to protect her from what was about to happen. There was no explanation except that family was family, and Ava was all she had left.

CHAPTER 48

VICTOR

Vicenza, Italy

His body seemed to come awake slowly, each part tingling, slightly burning, as if the nerves were regenerating. Then he felt the sudden ability to move. His fingers, his toes, then his legs, arms. It wasn't complete control, but it was more than he'd had in days. The respirator was still assisting with his breathing, and he felt like a blowtorch had been shoved down his throat. But he was back in the land of the living, having escaped two attempts on his life. That meant something.

He was able to pick up the photograph and look at it closer, each time noticing details he hadn't seen before. The shoe, the mud puddle, the mountain in the background. He knew this place. He'd been on this road. It wasn't a random photograph of this country. It was probably only miles from the house of atrocities. And he wondered why there was this sudden desire to torment and kill him. He'd held a secret for twenty years, telling no one. He decided he never would. Violence now made no sense.

The day he'd been attacked, he'd had a fight with Philomena. A nasty fight. She'd found Davide's phone. Poor kid. She knew he'd seen Davide that night at the Cresole park. Adrianna had been with him, he was sure of it. If Philomena was able to charge the phone, then she heard the messages from Adrianna. Her last message begging Davide to be careful.

None of it had been Davide's fault. He'd just stumbled onto the truth—eavesdropping on a conversation that led to curiosity, that led to questions—that's what tormented Victor. All of this could have been prevented. In another lifetime, everyone would be alive. Giada would have grown up with her parents. She would have known only Philomena as a grandmother. They might all be happy. But his daughter and her boyfriend had dug into the past, pulling up the roots of trouble.

What bothered Victor most was that his affair with Anais had never really ended. Not even after his daughter's birth in Tuscany. Not even after he and Philomena had returned home, back to normalcy, to raise their daughter. Even after he found out what Anais had done to his wife that day in the barn, he still couldn't end it.

She would call him, take the train to Verona, and expect him to meet her. And he did. She was toxic and intoxicating at the same time. He could never get enough. But when he still wouldn't leave Philomena, she began to weave her web of persuasive influence to change his mind. Nothing was off limits. Even things that happened thirty years before in Southeast Asia.

It was the oddest sort of blackmail because he hadn't even been with them that day in Dong Xoai. She had nothing over him, but plenty over Philomena. Philomena had killed someone that day, maybe out of self-preservation or panic, he'd never know which. The baby lying in the blanket, the face and lips gray-blue. Tiny eyelashes curled upward, resting below the eyebrows. That had been Philomena's doing, and when he relived that day, the dead bodies, it was the baby that sickened him the most.

Tommaso had grown up. Physically and emotionally. He wasn't the same freckle-faced boy doing his father's bidding. He'd married a younger woman and dragged another soul into his swamp of misdeeds.

And then a child, Maximo. The stakes in the game for him increased—he had more to lose.

Anais wanted Victor at all costs, but also wanted to protect her two daughters, Marie and Claire, from harm while she went along destroying lives around her. Victor wanted to continue his life with his wife and enjoy his mistress as his right, without threats and repercussions from either of them. Tommaso wanted to quiet Anais and protect his now-vulnerable family, especially his aging mother, and bury any horrible misdeeds from childhood, no matter what the cost. They all wanted to end the threats that were coming from the outside. Someone with information about what had happened that day.

And in all of this, he could never answer the one question that kept him up at night: What did Philomena want in all of this? She was one of the original triad. A charter member of the Dong Xoai assassination team, yet seemingly on the sidelines, refusing to engage completely in any of it. But with Anais dead, it seemed instead of quieting down, Philomena was gearing up, provoking, digging, setting Ava loose on all of them.

He yanked the tape holding the respirator in place and pulled out the tube, burning, coughing, hoping his lungs had recuperated enough to keep him alive and that his life wouldn't end on the floor by the side of this hospital bed. His breaths were shallow, and his head swimming. His legs trembling. It was too soon for him to escape, but it would be soon. He lay back down and pulled the blanket up around him.

"Signore, what did you do to your tube? You're certainly getting stronger," the nurse said. "Let me talk to the doctor." She clipped a pulse oximeter to his finger. "If your breathing is good, we'll keep it out. Let you start taking fluids by mouth. They're coming to do an MRI on your throat in an hour."

He saw Philomena enter the room. She looked exhausted. After the nurse left, she sat by him on the bed, her eyes landing on the photograph. She picked it up and studied it, more interested in it than in him.

"This is the road to Dong Xoai. I know the mountain. Where'd you get this, Victor?"

He handed her the envelope and collapsed back onto his pillow. He watched her read the words, *until the sharpest of steel meets gristle again, Victor. Thinking of you always.* He knew them by heart.

Her eyes grew wider. "When did this come?"

He shrugged.

"It's a threat. Victor. Whoever wrote this attacked you at the house. Didn't they? You need to tell the policeman it wasn't me so they'll let me go."

He was silent, refusing to reach for the pen and paper on the side table.

"Why is this happening now, Victor? Why now?"

He watched her face, not telling her he had just been wondering the same thing. He grabbed the tablet and scribbled a note and passed it to her.

She read it. *I can't tell the police anything.*

"Someone is setting me up, Victor. From the beginning. My blood in your car that was ditched in Geneva. I was never there. The phone registered to me with the threatening text. I didn't do that. But someone wants the police to believe I did. Who stabbed you, Victor? Do you know?"

He took the paper. *Ava showed up at the back door. I asked her why she was there. She said you told her to come. Then I was stabbed from behind. The person who stabbed me was wearing a hood covering their face. Did you set Ava up? Tell her to come?*

Her head moved back and forth when she read the words. "No, you have to believe me. No. Who stabbed you? What color hair? Male? Female? Tall, short?"

He shook his head hard and then coughed. His throat was burning. Then he wrote, *Female. It was a woman. It could even have been you. You know the truth about our daughter, don't you?*

Philomena's head was down, studying his words. "Which truth? That she was never mine? That she never belonged to me in any way at all? I might have been able to reconcile that my baby died that night, in the barn, and I was given the chance to raise Anais's child. I loved our daughter and would have, even if I knew the truth back then." She bit her bottom lip, and he knew she was crying. "But the fact that she was yours? Yours and Anais's?" She shook her head. "It's been a horrible few days for me, Victor. All my miscarriages? All the misery and tears. To bring a child into this world, and the whole time, you were with Anais. It was her you loved." She looked up at him, her eyes red. "Not me. Never me." Her head tilted slightly. "Was it because I killed that baby back in Saigon, and you saw it? Was that why you couldn't love me? Why did you marry me, then? If I'm unlovable?"

He was looking at the door to the hospital room, the blue of the police uniform just visible, then his eyes lifted to meet his wife's. He took the paper and pencil and scribbled across the page.

> *I will tell the police officer you had nothing to do with my attack. That I am certain someone set you up. I owe you that much.*

She nodded.

He took the paper back. *Though I am not certain that that is the truth, Philomena. Not certain at all.*

CHAPTER 49

RUSSELL

Dong Xoai, Vietnam

The cemetery was there. Just as it had appeared on Google Maps, though actually standing on the ground looking at the gravestones was different from looking at it through a computer screen. Their guide had dropped them at the entrance and then respectfully kept his distance.

Joanne whirled around in circles, taking in the hundred-foot-square space. Big, but not too big. "Is this cemetery significant in some way? I mean other than just a burial place—"

"Here." Their guide started walking and then abruptly stopped. "I think this is what you want. No stone. But I said before. Legend. Binh Le and his wife, Boa, were killed that day. And their baby girl smothered."

Joanne hit Russell so hard he stumbled and had to regain his footing. "Oh my God," she hissed at him. "The baby was killed?"

"Yes. Baby girl. Two months old." The guide stared down at the ground, his face hard. Bitter. "A country is lost when they are comfortable killing infants."

"So, what happened that day? The details. Do you know?"

"This family, like I said, were part of Viet Cong. Forces in the south fighting Diem—" He stopped when he saw Joanne's confusion. "Okay. Vietnam was split in two after the French were defeated in 1954. Two countries. Ho Chi Minh, communist, in the north, Diem in the south."

"Okay," Joanne said.

"Some people, like this family, lived in the south but wanted unified Vietnam. They opposed Diem. They opposed the Americans. Americans, European civilians were sometimes killed just because they were here. They set off car bombs. Bombed out bridges. Anyway, what happened—some people went to the house of this family and killed them. They say the people who did this were Europeans. Not Vietnamese. Young Europeans. Killing Binh Le during this time might have been acceptable. It was war. But his wife? No. And not the baby."

"But—"

"It may have been payback for a bombing that killed six people two weeks before in Bu Non. That's what my father said."

"These were young Europeans? Or Americans? That went to the house?"

"Europeans. One French. Two Italians. Two were women. One was a boy. How could a woman kill a child? I ask you."

"And these Europeans that killed this family had this other little girl with them? Na? Three years old?"

"This is what I heard."

"So this little girl is the one supposedly living in the hills?"

"Yes. They said someone in the house cut her throat and left her to die. Which one, I don't know. It could have been Binh or his wife. Or it could have been one of the Europeans. Her body was not there when the police came. Nobody found her."

"So wait. How could anyone know her throat was cut if they weren't there?"

"The farm straight across the way." He pointed across the field to a dot on the horizon. "The man was coming up the road. He saw them."

"Saw what?"

"He saw them in the road, heard the girl crying. Then he heard her stop."

"And he reported it?" Russell asked.

The man shook his head. "Oh, no. Not like you mean. He was afraid of the Europeans. He only told the people in town."

"Can we see the house? Is it still there?"

"Not much to see, but yes."

Five minutes later they were standing in front of a patch of grass. Two hundred feet from the road was a dilapidated stilt house. The roof constructed of straw. It was camouflaged so well a passing car might easily miss it. They got out and walked slowly, as if it still held something horrible.

"Has anyone lived here since then?"

The guide laughed. "Oh yes. On and off. Houses don't just go unoccupied here. But it's empty now if you want to look?"

Russell scanned up and down the street. "This is sort of an out-of-the-way place. Any chance these Europeans ended up here by accident that day?"

"I don't see how. Those two women and boy came here on purpose. Clever."

"What is?" Joanne asked, starting to walk through the grass toward the front of the house.

"Using their tactics. Using women and children to kill. Westerners always send armies. They don't use civilians. I'm sure this family was caught off guard. It's how they were killed so cleanly."

Joanne peered under the house. There were remnants of animal pens there. She moved around to the back and stared at the expanse of rice bogs, fields. The only other dwelling was a half mile away. She put her hand on a tree and stared off into the distance.

Russell tried to picture Anais, Philomena, and Tommaso coming here with the purpose of killing a family. It didn't make sense. They weren't that big or strong. This family was stabbed, not shot—that took more strength and coordination. His mind was working like he was a homicide detective again, casing the scene of the crime.

"Is it possible it wasn't the Europeans that killed them? That they just happened to come by maybe before or after?"

Their guide shook his head adamantly. "Not likely."

"Maybe the farmer was part of it? Maybe he was supporting Diem. Made the whole thing up so there'd be no retribution against him? You said nobody officially questioned him?" Russell asked.

"No. But he's still alive. If you want to talk to him, I'll translate."

Joanne was still standing with her hand on the tree. "The mother's name was Boa. The father was Binh," she said. "What was the baby's name? I'm just curious."

"Ngoc," he shouted back to her. "That means *jade* in English."

Joanne pushed off the tree and was at Russell's side. "*Ngoc is the key. Ngoc is the key.* It's what was written in the notes in Lacroce's father's box. Oh my God. Oh my God, Russell. After the war, he kept coming back here. He investigated this far, knew the story of Na being killed—Tommaso's involvement."

Russell stared out into the distance at the speck of a farmhouse not more than half a mile away. He looked at the guide. "Yes, if the farmer is willing to speak with us. And please, tell me more about this baby."

CHAPTER 50

Marie

Camden County Jail, New Jersey

Every sound in the cell block was amplified tenfold. The sound waves seemed to bounce off the concrete and settle in her eardrums. Marie waited for the final word that the hearing board was ready for her. Twenty minutes had passed, and all she could think about was a night drive from Rome to Bologna. She was on that road again. A highway that split, that twisted through Italy, heading north.

She'd taken the back roads. In retrospect she would have been better off on the highway. The roads were incredibly empty and winding between towns, then they'd straighten out where streetlamps lit the shops closed up for the night, and she'd feel an incredible sense of loneliness every time she passed through.

She'd been dispatched by Anais. It had felt like the bottom was falling out of the world and everything was askew at that time. A child had just been dumped on her and Claire by their father in what would end up being a nightmare that would take years to untangle. But now she understood why their mother wouldn't let them come to France to live, why she'd forced them to stay in the States.

It wasn't that she was being completely blind and vindictive. It was because Anais had a whole other drama unfolding in Europe that might have been worse than what she and Claire were facing. Her only source of comfort during the ordeal had been money. So, when Anais needed help, she felt justified in calling for Marie to jump in, going first to Rome and the Vatican as a cover, to make the trip seem normal.

The past that Anais had dragged from Vietnam was now catching up with her, it seemed. There had been so many dizzying lines all entwined, it was hard to know what was true and what wasn't. She'd told Marie that Philomena DeFeo had killed a baby in that country, in the years before things burst into war. That she and Philomena and Tommaso Lacroce had gotten mixed up in some political affair, skimming over the what and the actual how of it all. But that her life was now in danger.

Every moment during that stretch of drive, Marie had felt her heart pounding, sweat beading up on her forehead. She feared it was all a trap, some sort of a setup whereby she'd take the fall for whatever Anais had been planning. But she went stupidly forward anyway. The writer of the note had been right; she had been to Vicenza that night. To the exact spot where Tommaso had been stabbed.

She'd pulled onto the street slightly north of Vicenza and waited for a sign, just as she'd been told to do. It was a small park one block square, some grass and a smattering of trees, lit only by a few lamps at the corners. The good daughter was doing exactly what her mother told her to do, arriving at exactly eleven o'clock, waiting and watching. Anais told her she'd know what to do next. To watch for Tommaso. To give him a message in an envelope. It had to be in person. A phone call wouldn't do.

Marie had been exhausted from everything that had happened over the past two weeks. The five-hour drive north from Rome had her confused, dizzy, yearning for sleep. When Tommaso bolted out of the shadows toward her car, she hadn't been prepared. She was off guard.

She started to roll down the window but then saw someone was with him. The other person saw her. Saw her face. They stared at one another. She didn't know what to do other than jam in the clutch and put the car in gear. Tommaso banged on the back of her car to get her to stop, but she shifted and turned the corner out of sight.

She couldn't drive and dial a phone number at the same time, so she slowed and pulled out the flip phone, plugging in Anais's number, circling the block—it went unanswered. She would never forget what she saw when she came back around to where she'd started. Tommaso, in the park, partially blocked by a tree, being stabbed by a woman. She hadn't known her then, but she knew her now. If the police had questioned Marie, she could have not only given the name of the perpetrator but the address and maybe a phone number too. Marie put the car into gear and kept going, refusing to stop and get involved. She drove around to the other side of the park and pulled over. Her breaths were coming fast; her hands were trembling.

Her phone rang at that moment. "Marie, where are you?"

"What did you do to me, Maman? Why did you want me here? He came after my car. He was beating on the back of my car, trying to get in."

"What happened?" Anais whispered like she was surrounded by people.

"He's dead. Or if he's not, he's halfway there. He was stabbed—"

"Get out of there then, Marie. Drive to Cherbourg."

"That's fifteen hours away, Maman. I can't drive fifteen hours—"

"Marie, you cannot get on a bus or train. You can't have your name anywhere near this. Do you understand? You can't even stop for gas unless you have cash in your pocket. No cash machines, no banks."

"I got gas in Bologna. My tank is almost full. Maman, what am I to do? I didn't even have a chance to give him the envelope."

"It doesn't matter anymore. He can't use the information in the envelope now anyway. If you have a full tank, get driving. All night. If you have to stop, stop and sleep, but don't go into a store, get coffee, nothing. No one can see your face. Is that clear?"

"I rented the car. My name is on those papers."

"It doesn't matter. Did anyone see him being killed?"

Marie rubbed her face and felt tears on her fingers. She should have stayed in New York with Claire, cleaning up the problems her father had created. It was better than this. "Other than me, I don't know."

She hung up, put the car in gear, and drove away. She saw Victor pulling up. She saw him circling around the park. Whatever he was there for, it was too late.

The envelope was sitting on the seat next to her, her eyes bouncing off it as she tried to keep track of the road in front of her. When she'd put enough miles between her and Tommaso's dead body, she pulled over and parked. Her fingers lingered on the flap; she was afraid to lift it. Three sheets of paper fell out onto the seat. They were from a private investigation firm in Paris. They'd been searching for one Adrianna Lacroce.

Marie's eyes ran down the page. They'd found some partial records from a hospital in Ho Chi Minh City, some eyewitness accounts. The search was incomplete; the trail had gone cold. There were numerous papers from Catholic Charities and the Catholic Church, with parts redacted. The bottom paragraph outlined movement of a particular person through Switzerland and France. At the bottom was a note from Anais: *Read carefully. Contact me if you need to. Geneva is the best hope?*

There was a photograph enclosed. A four-by-four snapshot of a woman, taken from a distance. They'd been searching for someone. The person in the photograph was almost unrecognizable. Marie wouldn't understand any of it for years to come. But in that moment she knew for certain she'd stepped right into the middle of one of Anais's piles of shit.

She opened her eyes to the slat of the bunk bed above her. The time. She had a parole hearing. She no longer feared court; whoever had mailed the notes to her was no longer important.

She finally heard the clanging of the key in the lock. The officer pulled open the door. "Nun, court was postponed until after lunch. And I called that number from the social worker's phone. I left a message."

Marie nodded. "Thank you."

"I saw your parole officer. Bridgette. She was downstairs, and I heard a rumor."

Marie sat up. "What? What did you hear?"

"If you can get through the hearing without going psycho, I think they may let you go today. Or tomorrow."

Marie's face fell. Jail right now was her only safety.

CHAPTER 51

RUSSELL

Dong Xoai, Vietnam

The farmhouse was closer than it had seemed when he looked across the fields. It was mostly hidden in the trees, only bits of bamboo and straw peeking out among the leaves. Joanne and he followed along behind the guide, walking carefully to avoid mud and animal waste. It surprised him that this man and possibly his family had survived the war and upheaval and maintained the same property fifty years later.

The house was built on stilts like all the other houses in the area. There were two sets of stairs, one on each side of the house, leading to the platform above. They had started to climb when they heard a noise behind them. An elderly man came around the corner; he had a walking stick in one hand and was speaking rapidly.

Their guide jumped in, and the two engaged in a conversation. Russell was watching carefully; though he didn't understand a word of Vietnamese, body language and expressions sometimes told the real story. Their guide stepped back and motioned for them to come.

"He's willing to answer some questions," he said. "But if he doesn't like the question, he'll tell you to move on. He's a bit touchy."

Russell nodded. "We are wondering about an incident that happened in nineteen sixty-eight or thereabouts, a family in that house was killed." He pointed across the field. "I was told you lived here. You saw it?"

"He said he was here that day, right there." The guide pointed to a spot halfway between the houses. "The land was different then. But he saw them."

"What happened when the four Europeans arrived?" Russell asked.

"They stood outside the house. Binh Le was yelling at him. They start to argue," the guide translated. "And it got . . . it got louder, the boy chased him up the stairs."

"And then?"

"He says he went back in his own house. He heard more yelling. He didn't want to see the trouble or be questioned about it."

"So, he's saying he saw nothing of what happened? How'd the baby end up dead in the grass? He didn't see that? What happened to the little three-year-old girl? He hasn't told us anything we didn't already know," Joanne said.

Russell slid her a look. She was going to chase this man away. "No, it's fine, we're just trying to find out what happened exactly. If you know more than that, it would be helpful."

The older man listened to the words and seemed to be considering them. Then he spoke, and the guide translated. "He says he never talked about what happened for a long time because he was afraid. He is still afraid. He said the European woman, the one with the lighter hair of the two, has come back since that day, once before the American War and once after. He knows her father has influence—"

"Tell him she's dead. Her father is long dead. The boy that was there that day is dead. The little girl, she disappeared, probably dead. There's nothing to be afraid of. It was so long ago. He can tell us," Russell said.

The old man turned when he heard these words and went back up his steps. Russell and Joanne looked at one another. "Is that it? He's done speaking with us?" Joanne asked.

Their guide shrugged. "Give him a minute. He still seems like there is something so wrong. This was probably not a good idea."

The farmer came down the steps a few minutes later with a woman behind him. She had gray hair, parted down the middle, kept her head down, and seemed ambivalent about being involved in this. The man introduced his wife and talked to the guide for a few minutes.

"She said the boy that came that day had been here before with an older man; maybe it was his father. Many times they were here. Binh Le supported Viet Cong. Everybody knew it. He supported the north, so it was strange seeing him with Europeans. But she says the boy came many times. Never alone. Always with his father. And sometimes his sister was with them."

"So, it wouldn't seem odd for him to come again, alone with his sister? That makes sense. They welcomed them into their home," Russell said. "That explains a few things."

The guide nodded. "Yes. Then the boy pulled a knife and cut the man's throat."

"But how could they know that if they were just tending to their yard a half mile away? How could they know what was happening inside?" Joanne looked at the old man. "You were inside with them."

"He says everybody knows it's true."

Everyone was silent. Russell moved in front of Joanne, shielding her, but he wasn't sure why. "It might be enough for today," he said.

"No, we came thousands of miles for this. It's not enough, Russell. I want to know what happened to the baby. And I really want to know what happened to Na. That's why we're here. I can't actually believe this is still a secret."

They all seemed caught up in an awkward moment. The older man stared at Joanne and began speaking directly to her. The guide jumped in, translating. "It matters because it is not over. You might think it is, but it is not. This woman. The lighter-haired French woman is not dead. She may be old now, but she's not dead. She had someone contact us, come here, just like you're here, and warn us that you were coming, that we may be coming to the end of our lives, but it can be made shorter. Our children—"

"I don't know when that was, but Anais Lavoisier *is* dead. She died about a month ago. Maybe you didn't hear," Joanne jumped in.

He shook his head. "She is alive. I know it. So, I cannot talk about what happened to the baby except to say the baby was found dead in the grass. And the little girl, the little girl was cut too. Her throat was cut."

"How did she end up getting cut, did she get in the way or something?" Joanne asked.

He shook his head. "No, it was done on purpose."

"Is she alive too? Maybe she's living with Anais." Joanne was trying to be funny, but nobody laughed.

"She is alive. I know she is. I have talked to her," the guide translated.

Joanne and Russell looked at one another. "Wait, you're serious. Where is she?" Russell asked.

"He says she was taken to Dong Xoai hospital after the incident. Left as an orphan. She was adopted by a French family through Catholic Charities in sixty—"

"But her parents were looking for her. The Lacroces. They've been looking for her for years," Joanne said. "How's it possible she was in a hospital just miles from here, and they never knew?"

"It was war. People were scattered, missing."

"People say they used to see her. That she came back and spent time in town sometimes. Does she know who she is? Remember any of what happened?" Russell asked.

"She hasn't been here in a long time. But he thinks she remembered," the guide said.

"Has she tried to contact her mother? Her mother—" Joanne started.

The old man turned without another word and went up the stairs with his wife.

The guide looked at them. "This conversation is done for now. He says give him a few hours. He knows someone who worked for Catholic Charities. He'll take you to them."

CHAPTER 52

PHILOMENA

Vicenza, Italy

She sat at her kitchen table, drinking coffee from one of her hand-painted poppy cups, the broken pieces of the matching cup Ava had dropped still visible in the trash can. They were so expensive. A guilty pleasure Victor never would have allowed her. So she took some of Ava's money to buy them. Forty pieces. Almost five thousand euros. Her little shopping spree had riled Victor. He insisted on taking the rest of the money under the pretense that it was going to draw the authorities to them. But Philomena knew he'd never give it to the girl; he was going to keep it for himself. She could have fought him. She could have made him give it back. But she chose not to.

Philomena thought of Victor's face in the hospital, the words on the paper. He really wasn't certain she hadn't cut his neck. If she had attacked him. The way he looked at her had changed; he no longer trusted her.

The night of Victor's attack, she'd gone to Olivia's house. The police knew that. But she never told them she'd also paid a visit to Davide's mother. She didn't feel the need to bring it up. That was why she'd fudged the timeline to the police.

Since the day Philomena had met Francesca Tosi, the woman was always in some state of crisis or panic. The remnants of her beauty were still there, on her face, her willowy frame, the way she carried herself, the way she automatically expected things from people, even at her age, as if her beauty currency was still good. Despite this, she always seemed at a disadvantage.

Maybe it was nonstop smoking, the smoke billowing up over her head forming an ever-present cloud, the very slight yellowing of her teeth and edges of her fingernails. The nervousness. That was it, the nervousness. She was like a pretty little yellow finch ready to fly away at the slightest provocation. As if she'd suppressed a boiling anger that simmered close to the surface for so long it had taken a toll.

When Philomena showed up at Francesca's door that night, the night Victor had been stabbed, Francesca didn't seem surprised. She just stepped back out of the way and let her in. She was wearing black slacks that Philomena noticed hung off her hip bones; her black blouse was buttoned properly to the top, but it was faded, drab. Her hair was in disarray. Time had made a home on her face, creating small grooves around her eyes and above her lips from years of puckering them around a cigarette. She led Philomena immediately to the back garden and lit another one.

"Adrianna's daughter, Giada—whatever she calls herself now—was just here an hour ago, asking about Davide. I don't need this. Why'd you give her that picture of my son?"

Philomena had taken a seat beside her. "She wanted to see her father. What are you afraid of?"

Philomena saw tears in the woman's eyes. "You just appear and decide what needs to be done about my son? Maybe I don't want this girl in my life. Did that occur to you? Maybe I don't want her looking for him. Maybe I don't want him found. Alive or dead. Maybe he ripped my heart out already."

"It's not all about you. Why would you not want to know what happened to him, Francesca? I lived that nightmare for so long. I'd rather know Adrianna is dead than have that edge of hope saw me in half. Besides, she is your granddaughter. Have you thought about that? Ava, Giada, whatever name she takes, she's your flesh and blood."

The cigarette balanced between her fingers; she seemed to be thinking. "A granddaughter I never wanted. I barely knew her then. She's a stranger now."

"She's not a potential obligation like she was when she was born. She doesn't need anything from you. She may be a stranger now, but you can get to know her. You're blind if you don't see Davide in her. Maybe she's all you have left of him."

The woman's head was shaking back and forth. "I don't want to see my son in her—"

"You never wanted Davide with my daughter, I know. From the beginning you didn't like her—"

"Pffft. It's too late to lament my son's choice in girlfriends, isn't it? But of all the girls in town. Of all the girls he could have chosen, he picked the one that would give him the most trouble. Give me the most trouble." She clenched the cigaretteless hand into a fist. "She destroyed my life in so many ways. You DeFeos with your money, everything is so easy, isn't it? Your little tart gets pregnant, has a baby, then runs away, and my son follows her. Both get killed. You go on living in your fancy house, and I'm left with nothing."

Philomena stared at her. "This isn't about money."

Francesca jumped to her feet. "I should have packed the family and moved after the first time he brought her here." Her anger seemed so out of place. In the times they'd met, the woman was so odd, her moods unpredictable. She had a visceral distaste for the DeFeos. That much was clear.

"I wish that too, Francesca, you have no idea—"

"Did you put that money in his account? The twenty-five thousand euros in his account? Was it you?"

"No."

"So what are you here for?" she asked.

"To let you know our granddaughter is back. She's going to be turning over stones, looking for Davide. From the little I know of my granddaughter, she's going to be turning over every stone along the way to find her truth."

"Why are you telling me this?"

Philomena looked off into the brown dirt of the garden, the dead branches blowing in the wind. "Because. I didn't have a chance to let you know before—"

"To warn me, you mean?" Francesca abruptly got up and went into the kitchen, then reappeared a few minutes later with a glass of wine. She didn't offer any to Philomena. "This warning should have come before she showed up."

Philomena let her eyes travel down the woman's body, taking her all in. The stress of losing her son had killed her by inches. "I don't know why you think of it that way. I was hoping you might help her. You have a common goal. We all do. Finding out what happened to Davide—"

Francesca swallowed a gulp of wine. "Cut the crap, Philomena—we have no common goal. Having your granddaughter come here, unexpected, was like pulling off a scab, and you know it. Why would you do that? Seeing her, hearing this all again about that last night. It's all too much for me—"

Philomena leaned toward her. "Francesca—"

"When she was here, sitting right there, it reminded me of how glad I was when her mother took off with her when she was a baby. I felt like something heavy had been lifted back then. And now that boulder is on me again. The only good thing that came from the conversation was that she said Anais is dead—"

"You didn't say those words to her, did you?"

She shook her head. "No. I didn't. I played nice."

"Good. I'll leave you to your wine and cigarettes, then. Should I let you know if Ava calls?"

"No, no, and no. Keep that girl to yourself. Can you lock the front door on your way out?"

"I just wanted to say, Francesca, that we both lost our children. My daughter is dead. Your son is gone. I'm sorry for that." She put her hand to her chest. "I am so sorry for that. I was hoping that having their child back here with us could maybe help us both heal?"

Philomena waited for a response, but it took almost a minute. Francesca looked her in the eye. "Like I said, lock the door on your way out."

Philomena nodded and went through the living room to the front door. She hesitated. There was a pad of paper on the table by the door. The pad was empty, a pen sitting next to it, but the top sheet had indentations across it. Someone had written a number on the sheet above it. Nothing a little pencil couldn't bring back to life. She ripped the sheet off and stuffed it in her pocket. She didn't have time to look at it right away. Not that night anyway, because after she'd visited Olivia to show her Davide's phone—Philomena had been half tempted to show Francesca too but thought better of it—she'd returned home to find Victor on the floor in the upstairs hallway, his neck cut open with a jagged knife.

Philomena sat now in her own kitchen, reliving it all. She pulled the paper from her purse and flattened it out. The indentations were there. Staring her in the face. She grabbed a pencil from the desk and ran it heavily across a blank paper until one side of the lead was flat. Then she put it to the stolen paper and moved it back and forth across the sheet. The number was there. An Italian exchange. Not surprising. When the whole number was readable, she plugged it into a reverse phone number look-up webpage and waited until the name popped up on her screen. *Olivia Lacroce.*

The two had never met that Philomena knew of. Her eyes were stuck on the computer screen. If anyone was looking for a connection between Tommaso Lacroce and Davide Tosi, there it was, in smeared pencil on an old notepad. There was no way of knowing when the number had been jotted on the pad. It could have been months before, or it could have been just the other day. But it was interesting. Interesting enough that it had Philomena's mind spinning.

She stood up and rinsed her cup, drying it carefully and putting it back on the shelf. Her bag was packed, though she only needed one change of clothes. Victor had told the police just enough to let them loosen her leash, though they'd admonished her not to leave town. But that was exactly what she was going to do. She had a meeting to attend in France. Her driver would be there in ten minutes. She had one stop to make before she went to the airport.

CHAPTER 53

OLIVIA

Vicenza, Italy

Her private investigator had been there, waiting, when she arrived back home. She was exhausted and desperately wanted a few minutes alone, but he seemed charged up, eager to go over notes with her. Rehash.

"So, I've been working on this connection between Tommaso and Davide, and it occurred to me we've been missing something. Maybe not focusing in the right place." He flipped through his pages. "Of all the principal players in this, the ones who've taken the back seat are Davide's parents. I met with them at least four times, just to review things years ago. But still—" He continued flipping.

"It's interesting I know more about Philomena and Victor than I do about Davide's parents," Olivia said. "Why is that?"

"Don't know," he answered. "Father: Benito Tosi. Would be sixty-six years old, died five years ago—heart disease. Actually, he was born in Asia—Taiwan during some military tour his father was doing with NATO. He lived all over Europe until the age of fifteen, then settled in Verona."

"You interviewed him, then?"

"Yes, years ago, right after this happened. Solid man. Worked in some low-level government post. He never went to university. Seemed to get along okay. When I talked to him, he just seemed so devastated that his son was gone. Adamant that Davide was alive and would come back. He had the kind of hope that wore him down, roughed him up."

"And the mother?"

"Francesca Tosi. Born in a town, Monza, just north of Milan. Two parents, both professors at Université de Genève. She did attend university. She works as a clerk in a bank. I interviewed her too, smokes about four packs of cigarettes a day. Absolutely destroyed over her son's disappearance. She blamed the girlfriend for it. She said after they met, everything fell apart in his life. She has an angry edge, though you can't blame her. It was her only child—"

"Are you trying to say you think you need to go interview her again? Retread this?"

"Why not? It can't hurt."

"If you really think it's necessary, I want to go with you this time."

They'd only traveled ten minutes by car, and they were in a completely different world. There were plastic toys scattered in the yards and a broken window covered in plastic. Olivia sat and stared.

"It's unfortunate Francesca Tosi didn't spend her money better."

"What?" her private investigator asked.

"That things have gotten this bad."

His head tilted to the side. "She isn't exactly destitute, Liv. Her house is probably one of the better ones here. Come."

They walked through a maze of row homes and came to a door. He was right, it was nicely painted. No broken windows. It even had a few plants in brightly painted pots out front.

"This was the way it was when you were here before?" she asked.

"More or less." He knocked on the door. The two looked at each other and waited. "There's a car in her spot. She should be home." They knocked again. Nothing.

"She's either not here, or she's hurt inside."

She shook the door handle. "That's an odd assumption. Maybe she just went for a walk."

"Something's not right," he said.

"Is this your detective side kicking in? Why do you say that?"

"Mail in the mailbox. The plant in the window"—he pointed—"looks wilted. I say we go in. The question is how. I'm not one for picking locks or smashing windows."

They walked the length of the block of houses and went around to the back. "No access here. What do we do?" she asked.

They strolled around the front and knocked again. "Live or die by your choices." He slid a hard plastic card in between the door and the jamb and wiggled it. Two minutes later the door popped open. "Crappy lock," he added.

They stood at the threshold and looked in. Nothing looked amiss. "Well?" she asked.

He went in first and left her on the doorstep, holding her breath. He came back a minute later. "Nothing. Come on in."

She hesitated and then walked through. The entryway was dark, drab, but when she went through into the living room, it was brighter, painted in a pale color. Nothing was out of place. There was an ashtray with two cigarette butts in it and a half-full pack of MS cigarettes lying next to it.

"Francesca Tosi left half a pack of cigarettes behind," he commented. "And her phone." He picked it up and then put it back down. "Like she left in a hurry. Or knew we were coming."

The two went from room to room, then climbed the stairs to the bedrooms. "Beds are made up. Bathroom is straightened up too." They walked down the steps and lingered in the living room.

"What happened here?" the investigator asked. "The kitchen is clean, but it looks like she was going to make herself a sandwich." He picked up the loaf of bread, the end of the bag undone. An empty plate was nearby. Then he grabbed her phone and sat on the couch, playing with the lock screen, putting in various passwords.

"You're going to lock that phone permanently. How can you possibly guess that password?" She sat down next to him.

"Some good guesses and maybe a bit of luck. She lost her only son. I'm going to focus on that."

"Not likely. I'm going out to the garden."

He ignored her and kept working. She got up and wandered through the downstairs of the house again, going out into the back garden. The table was empty except for an ashtray. She picked it up and looked at it. Three different brands of cigarettes were littered among the ashes. She reached in and pulled out a butt when the private investigator appeared behind her.

"What are you doing?" he asked. "Why are you pulling that Gauloises butt out of the tray? Are you going to light it up and smoke the end?"

She turned around. "I'm not that desperate for a smoke yet. I just haven't seen one of these in a long time," she said.

He folded his arms, the phone still in one hand. "I saw a pack at your house just a couple of days ago. By the way, I got into the phone."

"Oh, you did?" Her eyebrows went up. "That's impossible."

"Not really. I focused on the fact that Davide was her only child. I just put in *D* and his date of birth. Bingo."

"Let me see." She reached for it, but he pulled away.

"Three questions—well, now four. Why would you want to hide that cigarette? When is the last time you were here, at this house? Why is your number in Francesca Tosi's phone? And lastly, why have you been lying to me about everything for the past twenty years?" She stared at him for a second and then headed for the door without a word. "Wait, where are you going?"

"There's something I need to do," she answered, shutting the door on him on her way out.

CHAPTER 54

Marie

Haddonfield, New Jersey

The information in the envelope was the first lead, the proof that the girl that had disappeared in Vietnam was not dead. That Anais, Tommaso, and Philomena hadn't in fact turned on one another. But Anais kept the information to herself, never sharing, choosing instead to let the paranoia of the other two grow and spread. Really, after Anais realized what happened to Tommaso, she wasn't taking any chances in trying to give the information to anyone else.

Marie had driven all night through Italy and then France to Cherbourg that night. She stopped only twice to close her eyes but found she was too paranoid that someone was following her. When she finally arrived at the cottage, Anais was there, unaffected. She took the envelope from her daughter's hand, oblivious to the fact that Marie looked like she was on her way to another nervous breakdown.

"Maman, he was killed. Right in front of me. What was in that envelope? What's going on?" she'd asked. "I left him there to die."

"Do you need another stay in the psychiatric ward, Marie? You don't look well." Then she'd grabbed Marie's face. "If you read those papers, forget what was in them. If you saw who stabbed him, forget that too. Don't even tell me. Don't tell anyone, ever. I mean it."

So, she hadn't. She'd almost forgotten the faces herself. A random man stabbed in a park in Italy was none of her concern.

But now that she was free, she needed to protect herself, maybe even protect Ava, because those long-forgotten faces were still out there, maybe waiting for the right time to make a move.

The house in Haddonfield was like a long-lost, tossed-aside, neglected child's toy. Bridgette had called her a cab from the parole office, told the driver to bring her straight there, don't stop anywhere along the way. Marie was instructed to wait at the house, that Bridgette would be around in the afternoon to check on her. That she needed to be at this exact address, no excuses, and open the door herself.

She had tried to jump in and object, but her voice wasn't heard. Bridgette felt she'd bestowed the greatest gift upon Marie. There was no room for "buts" in this conversation. She'd been allowed to dress in her clothes, the ones she'd worn when she'd been arrested in Italy. She'd had on this blouse and gray slacks while standing on the balcony of her hotel room at Lake Como. It felt strange putting them back on in the shower room at the jail.

The house, her sister Claire's house to be exact, hadn't been foreclosed on, and it hadn't been condemned, so Marie was forced to return and climb the steps again to the front porch and open the front door. She'd only been gone a few weeks, but it felt like months. The door closing behind her, the locks in place, didn't provide as much of a sense of security as the bolts and locks of jail.

She had no sooner set down her bags than the phone rang. The sound of the landline startled her. Nobody had paid the bills on the house in many months. She picked it up and held the receiver to her ear.

"Ah, I see you're home. Good. Just to catch you up to speed—Ava's in France. Her friends are somewhere in Vietnam right now, I think."

She sighed. "Can I get just one hour of peace? You didn't want to speak to me when I was behind bars, but now it's okay?"

"Something like that. I need you to do something for me."

"No. Ava has access to at least twelve million euros—but she's too stupid to just take it and disappear. No, she's got the sentimental I-need-someplace-to-belong-let-me-find-my-daddy gene. And I'm the stupid idiot stuck in Camden fucking County for the next five years in this house until the mortgage goes into foreclosure—"

"The mortgage has been paid. All up to date."

"By whom? I didn't think it had been paid since Claire died."

"Anais's last will and testament took care of it—well, her attorney did. The house is paid off completely, and the taxes are prepaid for a year. The utilities too. Including that phone you're talking on. Happy homecoming, Marie."

She was stunned. She hated this house. "What do you want?"

"I need you to fly to France."

"Wait, no. I just got paroled. Two hours ago. I'm stuck here. I can't even leave the county. Can't go to Philly for a cheesesteak. If I'm in violation again, I'm going to prison. For five years. So, the answer is no. I'm going to get in Ava's car that's still in the driveway and grab some groceries and a few bottles of booze. Cigarettes too. And I'm holing up here for the next month until things cool off a bit."

"You'll only be gone a few days. Wait until they check on you, and hopefully that will be very soon, and then leave. You'll be back before they know you're missing."

"Not going to happen. What is it you need in France? You're there. Get it yourself."

"I will be there too."

"Where am I going in France?"

"You know where—La Héronnière de Haut."

"How can I?"

"Stop playing dumb, Marie. I have an address. You're to attend the probate, then hop on the plane back."

"Ugh. Can I not just have one day of rest? Just one day of normal?"

"This is normal. I bought your ticket already. Under M. Saunders. Less suspicious. Coach. Less suspicious. Leaves out of Newark eight thirty tonight, arrives in Paris at nine thirty the next morning. Getting through Paris is easy. They don't even look at the passports. Get the bus—"

"The bus, is it?"

"Yes. Less—"

"Less suspicious, I know."

"There's a stop at La Héronnière de Haut. Get off and walk. It'll be a mile or so walk, maybe a bit more, so wear appropriate shoes. You're looking for a house with a red roof. Rue Le Ferrage. Ask, if you get lost."

"And what am I going to do there, at this red-roofed house? I don't absolutely need to be at this probate—"

"Ava will be there sometime tomorrow morning."

"I won't get there until noon tomorrow at the earliest. That's without delays—"

"If the plane is late arriving or you're pressed for time in Paris, get a car. Not a first choice, but do what you have to do to get there."

"So, if I get caught, if I end up violating parole, what are you going to do to help me?"

"Such negative thinking. You should ask what I'm going to do for you when you're successful."

"What's that?"

"I'm going to set you free from everything you've done."

Marie closed her eyes. She didn't even know what that meant. "How so?"

"No obligations. Free. Yes, you're stuck in Haddonfield for the time, but it's a nice house. A really nice house—all paid up and will continue to be paid. And you'll have money, do renovations, put in a new kitchen. Reinvent yourself. Take a lover. You're not too old. Go back to school—culinary arts maybe. Eat out at those little cafés in town. Make friends. Have dinner parties. Enjoy your life. Five years of parole will fly by."

"And if I say no?"

"If you say no, five years will drag on for a very, very long time and might be quite miserable for you. Newark. Eight thirty p.m. American Airlines flight 733, direct to Paris."

"Wait. What if parole doesn't come in time for me to make the flight?"

"Pray that doesn't happen. You used to be good at prayer." The line clicked off.

CHAPTER 55

VICTOR

Vicenza, Italy

He was feeling somewhat better, though he was stiff and his thoughts were slowed. Uneven. Sometimes words came easily, and other times, even minutes later, they wouldn't come at all; he'd pound his head in frustration.

The door opened, and Philomena walked in. "I'm leaving now. I've hired a car to take me to the airport, but I wanted to stop by to say good-bye and ask you about a few things. Things that have been bothering me. The police said Anais's landline number was on your phone recently. Calls back and forth. Is she alive? Is Anais alive still? Hiding somewhere?"

He shook his head. "No."

"Because I think she might be. Otherwise, who were you calling at that cottage? I just need to know, now, for my own protection. Is she out there waiting, ready to attack?"

He didn't answer right away, as if he was debating the answer. "She died a month ago."

"The truth. When did it start? The thing with her?"

"Lolo—"

"Now or never, Victor."

He was staring at the photograph of Vietnam. The mud puddle. The mountain. "One night, the first time I came to visit you in Saigon. It started then."

She laughed and sat on the end of the bed. "I was so stupid. So in love with you, I never noticed."

"The night of the dance, when I met your parents, your friends. The night of the huge storm, remember? That night. You left to take your mother home."

Philomena did remember. It had been so much fun. She hadn't yet cemented things with Victor, but he was visiting her thousands of miles from his home. She'd thought it meant something. "At the community center? You had sex with her there?"

"Why is this so important?"

"I need to know."

"No, I didn't have sex with her that night. You asked when it started. That was it. I just kissed her. We talked and laughed."

"You'd come to see me, though, Victor. It was so early on, why didn't you just break it off with me? Let me get on with my life?"

"You were the marrying type. She wasn't."

Philomena stood up. "No. When did you first have sex with her, then?"

He hesitated. "When we went to Philadelphia to visit them. The first time. Okay? You want to know if we had sex in her and Ross's bed? We did. We had sex all over their house while her child slept. We had sex once when you were in the hotel room asleep. Anais was so afraid you'd wake up, she made me cover her mouth with my hand. Does this make anything better?"

"Ross and I were perfect idiots. At least Anais had the sense to leave him. And Adrianna? Adrianna was your love child. Your child with Anais. And I was stupid enough to not know. To know nothing and raise her in ignorance. How many times did you and Anais laugh about that?"

"It wasn't like that."

"It was. Oh, it absolutely was. Anais couldn't bring another child home with no husband. How could she explain it? Her father would have pulled everything from her, and she knew it. I'm guessing she wanted you to leave me. To go with her. To raise your child together. So what happened? Why didn't you?"

"I just couldn't." He looked so weary. He'd given up all pretenses. "We were a family. My parents, your parents, our hardware store. I wasn't going to give it all up."

"So, it was the fear of anyone knowing. The shame of it all that kept you with me in a loveless marriage?"

He was getting angry. "It wasn't all bad, Philomena." Now she was Philomena, not Lolo. "You loved Adrianna. You raised her. She made you happy. Anais gave you that."

She took two steps toward him, her legs against the side of the bed. "What did you say? She gave me that? Let me give you a two-second recap of what happened the day I gave birth, Victor. Anais held me captive in that barn. I went into labor and gave birth in the dirt, alone. I could have died; my baby did die. And she handed off her baby to me—"

"She didn't make that choice. She didn't hand off anything. She didn't know. She was beaten and left on the side of the road later that night. When she woke up she believed she'd lost her child—"

"Are you defending her?"

"No, but someone else switched the babies, gave you hers."

"I've been the stupidest person on earth, to live like this. To put up with this."

"Go to the probate, Lo. You're late."

"No, one more thing—Adrianna was never in the park that night Tommaso was killed. You saw her because you wanted to see her. She was dead already in Philadelphia. She was never there with Ava. Dead for almost a week by then. The pining for your daughter came too late. But it's nice to see you grieved for her. Surprising but nice. But a little too late."

"No, the toy . . ."

"It was just a dog toy. Nothing to do with her."

He closed his eyes and felt tears.

"I'm not coming back to you, Victor. If Anais is still alive, and I think she might be, she's yours. See if it's just as good when you're not hurting someone. When you can enjoy it out in the open. And if Anais is dead, then good riddance. There's nothing holding you and me together."

He heard the door open and shut.

Two minutes later the door opened again. He couldn't bear to deal with one of the nurses right now. He kept his eyes shut, hoping she would assume he was asleep.

"Victor." A hand was on his arm. He opened his eyes, and when he saw who it was, he tried to push up off the bed but couldn't. "Are you afraid? Are you?"

"No." It was a whisper and the only word that came to mind. "No. No. No."

"Yes. Yes. Yes. The stabbing wasn't enough. Trying to smother you wasn't enough. How many lives do you have? What's it going to take?"

"I'll scream." He reached for the nurse's button, and she pulled it away.

"Scream? We're just having a chat." She picked up the photograph and the letter. "It was a nice poem, don't you think? I liked it when I wrote it."

She pressed the pillow over his face. He tried to fight, but he had no strength. Seventy-eight years had sapped it all. Her age didn't seem to affect her persistence. In those moments in between life and death, the darkness not quite black yet, he saw Adrianna. She was standing in the distance, but she wasn't welcoming him. Her arms were folded in front of her, and she was just staring, a strange frown on her face. Then everything faded away.

CHAPTER 56

Ava

La Héronnière de Haut, France

Valognes was a pretty town. Once filled with historic buildings, much of it had been reduced to rubble during the last war and had been rebuilt. I debarked from the train, Sandrine's son holding tightly to my arm, though he didn't need to. I had no choice but to go with him to this meeting. My life swung in the balance. If I were arrested, the quest for my father ended. I'd never see the light of day or freedom again. I'd never know the truth, and the check for hundreds of thousands of euros tucked in the side pocket of my black bag would necessarily disappear, I was sure of it.

"What now? La Héronnière de Haut is at least twenty minutes from here," I said.

He didn't say anything but led me to a cab waiting on the street. I maintained the silence, sat back, and watched the town disappear behind me. The buildings in the distance that we approached didn't look like houses; they looked like dilapidated factories or warehouses.

I knew the stretch between Cherbourg and Paris very well; I could draw it on a map. We were coming into La Héronnière de Haut.

"Oui, c'est là," my captor said, pointing to the house.

The house was within a cluster of other houses, a farm of some sort with an unpaved driveway and a multitude of dogs running about the place. I saw four within two seconds and hesitated, my fingers on the door handle. I didn't want to be here. There was something wrong.

Two minutes later a man approached. He had two of the dogs in step with him as he moved. "Mademoiselle? Are you here for the meeting? Come."

"What the hell kind of setting is this for the probate of a will? This is Anais's idea of a joke?" I got out and started following him, all the while thinking the town wasn't too far away. I could catch a bus to Paris. Or get a ride, rent a car. My mind was buzzing.

A hand landed on my shoulder. Sandrine's son motioned for me to follow him. The walk through the mud and grass to an outer barn didn't thrill me. My life revolved around pulling up flagstones to reveal the filth underneath.

He slid a sheet-metal door open and shut it behind us. *"Asseyez-vous,"* he instructed, pointing to a chair in the corner. It was cold, but hay dust was still floating in the air. It smelled of grain and freshly tilled earth. Not unpleasant.

I sat down as he instructed. Then he left me there wondering if I'd lost my mind. The sheet-metal door slid open again, and a short man in a suit approached and sat next to me.

"So glad you made it, Ava. I know it was a bit much."

"A bit much? Really? Getting me on that train under pretenses I'd find my father. What's the issue? I don't want whatever Anais left me, and this isn't exactly a professional setting. Who are you?"

He smiled. It wasn't a terrible smile. "Milo Rotton, your grandmother's lawyer. Of all the people on the Acte de Notoriété, you were the most important. Anais insisted. You refused, so I had no other choice. But you're here."

I raised my arms. "Fabulous. Let this thing begin so I can get on my way."

"Why'd you go to Cherbourg? What were you looking for in Anais's cottage?"

"Some photographs. But it seems someone knew that and left me what I was looking for—a picture of my father. Wait—why are you asking? Exactly?"

"I can't say much at the moment, but I'll tell you more as we go on."

"When is Sandrine coming? I'm a little pissed at her about all this."

"She asked you nicely? And you refused?"

"She was getting a little pushy. Like she was my grandmother or something—"

"Ah, and how many of those do you have? Let's count. Well, Anais Lavoisier, and then Philomena, she's relatively new to the grandmother circuit, and then Francesca Tosi, though she's probably not the cookie-baking type. Should we add Sandrine to the list?"

"You seem to know me well." I crossed and uncrossed my legs. He was making me nervous. "So what do you want?"

"For one, you were looking for your father, Davide Tosi. That's why you got on the train. Yes?"

"He disappeared July twentieth, nineteen—"

"Your father is dead, Ava. He was killed—"

I stood up. "How do you know that? You can't know that. Thanks for the miniadventure, but I want to leave. This whole thing's got me back to a great hotel I haven't been to in years."

"I know you were hoping to hear something else."

"If my father's dead, none of what I'm doing should matter. To anybody."

"In nineteen sixty-eight—or maybe sixty-nine, I don't know—your grandmother—Anais, I mean—Philomena, and Tommaso Lacroce were in Vietnam. They went north one day, the three of them, and Tommaso's little sister was with them. A whole Vietnamese family was killed—mother, father, and baby. And the sister, Tommaso's little sister—she disappeared. Tommaso told his mother she got lost in the crowd. Bad timing to have a missing child. Nobody cared because the country had bigger fish to fry."

"So?"

"Well, as it turns out, at the farmhouse, Tommaso did the cutting—stabbed the man and his wife. It was less certain who killed the infant and what exactly happened to Tommaso's sister, Na."

"Wait . . . what? That's not possible. Anais, maybe, but Philomena? Never ever. Not ever would she do something like that."

"Hmmm. The bigger question that remains in all of this is what happened to Tommaso's sister."

I lifted my hands out to my sides. "Well? What happened to her?"

"That's the question. She had her throat cut—not there at the house. Down the street a bit."

"By Tommaso? Is that why he was killed?"

"That's the interesting part. Nobody knows who of that little trio did what. They kept it to themselves."

"So how does anybody know the rest of it, then?"

"They all kept their little secret, maybe quietly blaming each other. Until threatening letters started to arrive."

"From whom?"

"From someone claiming to be Na."

"So she's alive? That's good to hear. None of this has anything to do with me. Nothing."

"Oh, but sweet Giada—"

"Ava," I corrected him. I hated him calling me that name.

"Sweet Ava, then. It all has to do with you. You're the personification of the greatest book ever written."

"Which one? The Bible? *Return of the Native*? *Ivanhoe*? *Wuthering Heights*? I think I might be a few IQ points too slow for this little story."

He laughed out loud and then stopped. "Your father died that night he disappeared. But there is a bright spot for you. Your grandmother—Anais, that is—might be very much alive."

"No. I found a picture of my father at my grandmother's cottage. He was older. Older than nineteen. And Anais had a stroke that night I showed up at her house. Me just being there killed her."

"You found what you were supposed to find. And there was a benefit to her dying then. For her. For you. For everyone. She was so upset you'd returned to her house that night. Because you were dead. You were supposed to stay dead. Coming back made you a target again."

I felt my eyes narrowing. "A target of what? Who are you? I thought this meeting was about Anais's will."

He stood up and straightened his suit jacket. "You'll see very soon what your grandmother left to all of you."

CHAPTER 57

JOANNE

Bu Non, Vietnam

The restaurant in Bu Non was only half full, so she picked the seat she wanted, in the corner so her cereal box would be less conspicuous. Russell looked exhausted but picked over his xoi with a spoon. Joanne curled her nose up at it when they put it in front of him.

"It's just sticky rice with sausage, onions, egg. Some mung beans. Perfect fast food," he said, putting a chunk into his mouth.

She poured her cereal into the bowl and dipped her spoon into it dry. "Looks fabulous, like a clog in my drain. Not for me. I'm glad I brought my cereal with me, just in case. So, you paid the driver to wait with us? And take us back?"

"Yeah, he'll be here in about thirty minutes. So eat up. And don't eat so much cereal that it ruins your appetite for dinner."

She nodded. "I'm kind of excited, if that's the word. It was a surprise. The farmer offering to take us to the adoption center. If this girl lived and was adopted out to someone in Europe or the States, where is she?"

"More interestingly, he said he'd talked to her. We didn't get a chance to question that. Do you think that's true?"

"So, if Na knows who she is, what happened to her, why hasn't she contacted her mother?" She put the last spoonful of Rice Krispies into her mouth and chewed. "Finish that up. Let's go." She pushed her bowl into the middle of the table and started to stand up.

"When we finish this little quest, you want to stay on for another week? Take the train north? Maybe see Hue or Hanoi? Halong Bay?"

She smiled. "Do the trip you were supposed to do with Juliette? I don't think I brought enough cereal for that. I'm going to the bathroom; meet me outside in five minutes."

He watched her stand up. "You're enjoying yourself; you'll just never admit it. And I think we're going to stay. You'll see."

The guide's car was right outside the doors of the restaurant. He smiled but was mostly quiet, probably wondering how he'd gotten involved in this. Once the city began to spread out, transforming slowly into country, he became chattier. "I was surprised the old man offered to take you to the adoption center. I didn't think he was going to. I thought he was going to tell me not to ever bring you back again."

"Why?" Joanne asked.

"The way he was talking. It was almost a last-minute thought. The war has been over, and the Vietnamese have forgiven but not forgotten. Why dig up the past if you don't have to?"

"But he'll take us to where we need to be?"

He smiled. "I will stay with you. If he asks for a large sum of money, this deal is off. Understand? No matter how much you might want this, it's not worth it."

"Thank you," Russell muttered.

They sat in silence until they pulled up in front of the farmhouse. The guide got out and disappeared. A few minutes later he returned with the same man and woman as before. Joanne jumped out and slid into the front seat, and they squeezed into the back.

The man, who they soon learned was named Hanh, began speaking rapidly in Vietnamese. When he was finished, he motioned for the guide to go. The car pulled out, moving slowly.

"He had time to think. This might not be the best idea."

"Oh no, no, no, please—" Joanne started, but the guide put his hand out for her to stop.

"He is going to answer whatever questions you have while we drive, and then I will drop you off where you need to be. There's a woman you should talk to—he will give you her name and describe her—but he doesn't want to be involved any more than that."

"Okay," Russell said. "That sounds fair."

"When did he last see this woman, the one that had her throat cut?" Joanne asked.

"Two years ago. She came to his house," the guide translated.

"How did you speak to her? Did she have a translator?"

He shook his head. "She speaks Vietnamese. Not fluently, but well enough. He speaks some French. And English."

"And you're sure it was her? How does he know?" Russell asked.

"She had the same markings as the child—"

Joanne was turned around in her seat. "But how does he know the child's markings? Was he that close to her when all of this happened?"

The man bowed his head and spoke rapidly to the guide. "He was the one who found her, took her to the hospital."

"Where, where was she when you found her?" Russell asked.

He pointed at the road. "In a ditch. She was in a muddy puddle with reeds. He was walking, following the Europeans, because of what happened at the house."

"They just left her there?" Joanne asked. "The two women and the boy? With her throat cut?"

The two men talked back and forth. "He says they weren't speaking a language he knows. It wasn't French, so he doesn't know what they were saying, and he was a half mile behind, just curious where they were going. He was afraid—if they could kill Binh and Boa Le, who had weapons, he didn't know what they were capable of."

"They never had time to use their weapons," Russell muttered. "They never saw it coming. Tommaso's father sent civilians to do this. His son nonetheless."

Joanne was watching Russell's mind twist the information. "His thirteen-year-old son."

"Maybe," Russell said before turning his attention back to Hanh. "So, the girl's markings?"

"A mole behind her ear. He saw it at the hospital when they were cleaning the wound. And this woman that showed up had the scars from what happened too."

"What's her name?" Joanne asked.

"She didn't tell him the name she was going by. She said she grew up mostly in France. But the adoption people would know more."

"She came back here, so she knows, she remembers? Who cut her neck with the knife?"

"She said she was cut from behind, that only the boy Tommaso and Philomena were there. That she's known for a long time what happened. That none of them, not even Anais, were safe from what happened, even though it was a long time ago. Not even now."

"What else did she say?"

"That she was living under Anais's nose, and she had no idea. The day would come to make things right. With both of them."

CHAPTER 58

MARIE

La Héronnière de Haut, France

The flight landed roughly, the wheels bouncing off the tarmac, shaking the plane so that she had to hold on to the armrest to steady herself. She thought briefly that if the plane crashed and she died, this would all be over. She'd been in an almost panic waiting for Bridgette to appear to check off the necessary boxes on her freshly minted parole forms.

Bridgette had arrived at three in the afternoon. Way too late. Marie calculated in her head. She needed to be in Newark no later than seven, and that was cutting it close. And it took over an hour to get there. Any later, she risked missing that flight. She'd made coffee and paced, waiting for Bridgette to show up for her home check. No bags to pack; she'd wing it with just a few toiletries. Nothing suspicious. Leaving her house, getting transport to Newark wasn't against the rules. If she got caught, she'd have no luggage. She'd slipped her passport into the side pocket of her purse, praying she wouldn't be asked to surrender it.

Bridgette wanted to take her time, accepted the offer for coffee. Walked through the house commenting on how lovely it was, how it had good bones, with a little sprucing up, it could be something really special. She wasn't in any hurry to leave. She sat at the kitchen table and pored over endless forms, having Marie sign on the dotted line.

"You're going to report weekly. Every Tuesday at ten in the morning. Parole office. You know where it is. Market Street, Camden. I will be making random checks to your home for at least the next year. It doesn't mean you have to be home. You can get a job. You can have a life. But I'm going to shoot for times you should be home. When you get a job, give me your schedule. Random drug screens—it's part of this process. I know it's not an issue for you. If you miss, Marie, if you mess up, leave the state without permission, leave the country, your parole will be pulled, and you'll be going to Edna Mahan in Clinton. Five years. No negotiation. You'll appear before the parole board—"

"I know this all already. I agreed to it in court this morning."

"I'm going over it again."

Marie checked her watch. She needed to move things along. "Okay."

Bridgette dropped her pen and looked at Marie. "Do you have somewhere to be? Am I keeping you?"

Marie shook her head and kept quiet. Exactly fifteen minutes later, Bridgette left the house, but she was suspicious. Marie hadn't played it cool enough, and now she was certain that the woman would circle around tomorrow morning and do another check. Except Marie wouldn't be here.

When the car disappeared down the road, she waited ten minutes, then she grabbed her purse and locked the house up. She wasn't calling a cab, Uber, or any other driving service. She wanted no record. She wasn't even going to drive Ava's car sitting in the driveway. She was going to do this as safely as possible. Speedline to Camden, then River Line to Trenton, changeover to NJ Transit train to Newark. Much longer.

She made it to the plane by only minutes, but her mind wouldn't let go of the image of Bridgette charging her for this violation. When she debarked from the plane in Paris, she got through immigration without even so much as a glance at her passport. Just a stamp, and "next."

The bus to Cherbourg took so much longer than the train and had few if any luxuries. She'd only done this once in her life, and that was when the train line was down due to track construction. She climbed on, her purse in her lap, looking out the window. The road was bumpy, and it occurred to her that she hadn't gotten any information about how she would return home. She'd gotten so caught up in the threats that she was stuck. She had little to no money for the trip back.

She got off the bus at the stop and realized she really was in the middle of nowhere. She'd worn her sneakers for walking but had no idea which way to go. There were dirt paths cut through the countryside, nothing more. "Ask directions, ask directions. To the house with the red roof in the middle of fucking nowhere," she muttered, choosing one road and heading out.

It was chilly, the sun was getting higher in the sky, and she was exhausted. She hadn't slept at all, tucked into a seat that only reclined half an inch. Her head hurt, her stomach was empty. It didn't get worse than this. And then there it was. A cluster of farmhouses up ahead. A house with at least three outbuildings, one of which had a red roof.

Her feet ached, and she was almost in tears when she arrived at the driveway. She saw the dogs before she saw anyone. Two were at her feet, watching, not barking but not tail wagging either. Marie saw the barn door slide open, and a man approached her that she recognized immediately as Sandrine's son. She hadn't seen him in a few years; he'd filled out, but it was definitely him.

"Family is almost all here for the gathering. Come on in," he said, motioning to her. Something told her to run, to turn and get back down that dirt path as fast as she could, but that option was gone. He held her arm and ushered her forward into the barn and slid the door shut behind her. That's when she saw her.

Ava was sitting in a chair in the corner. She nodded when she saw Marie enter. "Sit. Make yourself at home. They've been so hospitable. Giving me a meal. Just waiting for you."

She sat down, though she felt prickles all up her spine. "I want to leave."

"It's not time." Marie was startled; she hadn't noticed the round man standing there. She recognized him as Anais's lawyer—Rotton or something was his name. He turned and shut the metal door behind him, leaving them alone.

"Marie," Ava said, "are you violating parole again?"

Marie put her finger to her lips. "Not because I wanted to. They blackmailed me here," she shot back.

Ava's arms were folded. "They tricked me—said they had info on my father."

"Ava, I need you to listen. Philomena is not who you think she is. She's been lying about everything."

Ava was at attention now, sitting closer to her. "About what exactly?"

"About who she is. Her part in everything that happened in the past. That's what Anais told me."

"You believe it?"

"I just do. Whatever this meeting is about? Follow my lead. I have a feeling someone is going to die—leave it to Maman to have a dramatic reading of her will."

"Is Anais alive? I thought I saw her. She is, isn't she?"

Marie was startled. "Who told you that? She died. Sandrine had her cremated."

Ava moved her chair closer. "Now is not the time to fuck with me."

"Fine." Marie's face was only inches from Ava. "Fine. I was never completely sure. Sandrine called me to say that Anais was in the hospital. Then she died. It was all handled so fast. I never knew Maman wanted to be cremated. We never talked about it. It seemed so rushed."

"Marie . . . how'd you get here? Who exactly arranged for you to come?"

CHAPTER 59

Joanne

Ho Chi Minh City, Vietnam

Joanne was sweating so much it was seeping through her clothes. It was over ninety degrees and humid. Her hair was drenched, clinging to her scalp. She wasn't complaining, but she had her big bottle of San Pellegrino water she'd purchased at the hotel in her hand, pulling on it every so often as if her life depended on it.

The adoption center wasn't a center at all. It was a house. A house set back a bit from the street, on ground level this time, brown with a slanted roof made of straw. The guide knocked on the door, then pushed it open. Russell was surprised that it really was an office of sorts with a waiting area and a reception desk.

The guide once again took control of the situation, but several minutes later he turned back to them. "This is not an adoption center now. It's a medical clinic, but there's a woman here who said someone can help you. She said to take a seat."

It was hotter in the house than it was outside, even with a ceiling fan turning at low speed. Joanne put the back of her head against the wall and tried to breathe. "It's going to rain soon, they said. We're lucky—if we stay here long enough, we'll be getting into monsoon season—lots of flash flooding, whipping winds. I hope it cools something off. Because if it's hot rain, we're screwed."

Russell patted her hand and felt her skin was wet with perspiration. "It's almost over."

Just as those words passed his lips, a woman came out from the back. She was small, with good posture, but she moved slowly with age. She smiled at them and sat down. The guide introduced her as a doctor in the facility.

"She says she only comes in two days a week now. You're lucky she was here. This office is now used for some medical appointments for children. It was a clinic before the American War. Some orphans were housed here, and some were adopted out."

"Ask her about the little girl," Joanne said.

As their guide spoke to her, Russell watched her head move back and forth, as if to say no. Then she appeared to be asking questions.

"She said the records they kept of adoptions from this office were mostly destroyed or moved or never existed in the first place. When you have so many children displaced at one time, it becomes hard to keep good records. No computers. She remembers the girl because of her wound."

"What does she remember?" Russell asked.

"The wound was severe. If she hadn't gotten here when she did, she might not have survived. It wasn't so deep that she needed intubation, but she was here for almost four months."

"Here?" Joanne asked.

"No, they had a hospital down the road that's gone now. This office is all that's left."

"Did she talk at all when she was here? Talk about where she came from? Who her parents were?" Russell asked.

"She doesn't think so, or they would have connected her with them. I think she was mostly mute. Not even old enough to write at the time."

"Her parents were probably looking for her. Didn't anybody think to try and connect her?" Joanne jumped in.

The woman seemed angry when she heard these words translated. "That road out front? A mile up the road, bombs were going off. So many people were killed. Bodies everywhere. We did the best we could during terrible times. The girl wasn't our primary concern."

"If you remember the girl, do you remember who adopted her?" Russell asked.

She spoke to their guide, for what seemed like forever. "A French couple. Man and wife. They took her in nineteen sixty-eight or nineteen sixty-nine. They worked for the embassy."

"The French embassy?" Joanne was incredulous. "That cannot be right."

"She says it is. She remembers them well. Or she remembers the case well, because of all the children orphaned, very few were European. Vietnamese, Cambodian, Thai, Eurasian—many Eurasian but very few Europeans. They took her right away, as soon as her wounds healed."

"What were their names? Please tell me you remember their names."

"The last name was Sinclair. That's all she remembers. But she says you can check the embassy records to find them."

Joanne jumped up. "Thank you. I'm ready for the car now."

When air conditioning was blasting in her face, and she could sit back and relax without feeling the humidity was going to shut her lungs down, she started talking. "What are the chances of someone from the embassy adopting the girl without the Lavoisiers knowing about it? From what people have said, they were the most important family around. What's going on, Russell?"

"Maybe they did know. Maybe they didn't. A routine adoption probably wasn't newsworthy. Maybe they had gone back to France by then. Things were getting pretty heated here."

"But the embassies stayed open during the entire war. The French, the American—"

"Yes. And the French embassy is open now too. Let's go. I need to know now who this family is and where they took the girl."

The building was exactly what they thought it would be. A bureaucracy. There were many offices, and no one in charge. Just lines and departments. Eventually they found someone with a computer and the interest to sort through old records.

"Sinclair. Sinclair. Late nineteen sixties? Hmmm." They were relieved he was speaking English. "I don't see a Sinclair family attached to the embassy. I see a woman, Sinclair, who was employed here from nineteen sixty-seven to nineteen seventy. She married during her time here, registered a name change in the system. Then she was no longer a Sinclair."

"What was his name? The husband's name?" Joanne asked.

He seemed to be going over records, pulling down pages on the computer. His mouth twisted. He looked up and spit out a name. Russell and Joanne looked at each other.

"Oh my God," Joanne said.

"Is there any other information on them?" Russell asked.

"They left service together in the late nineteen sixties. They went back to Switzerland. That's the notation on the file here. There's an address in Geneva."

Russell's eyes were moving back and forth, a sign he was thinking hard. "It's Olivia Lacroce's maiden name. Rossi. But seriously? If Olivia was adopted, it means . . . she married her brother?"

She felt worn out, exhausted from days of travel, from the heat that seemed to sink all the way down to her bones. "Russell, I don't feel good." Then she fainted.

CHAPTER 60

Ava

La Héronnière de Haut, France

"How did you get out of the States?" I hissed at Marie.

Before those words were even out of my lips, the metal door started to slide open. Sandrine's son came in and stood in front of them. Anais's lawyer was with him, carrying a briefcase.

"Do you need to use the bathroom again? We can do this in shifts. I have something for you to eat too, when you're done. Not much, but it should hold you. Speak now. You're going to be busy in a little bit. There might not be time," Rotton said.

I shook my head. I wasn't hungry, and I hadn't eaten enough that I needed to use the facilities. The door was still open; I could see the outside grass, part of the path that led me here. Freedom was only a few feet away. There was a car pulling up. Sandrine's son went to the door. "She's here."

"Thank God," the lawyer responded.

Sandrine walked in and just stopped. She didn't come over to where we were sitting. She tried to stand near the door, unsure if she wanted to enter or not. She lingered, her fingertips clinging to the doorjamb. "Please, sit, Mum. This is what you wanted," her son said, closing the door behind her. She nodded and slowly moved to an empty chair but kept her purse in her lap. "This is what Anais wanted."

Nobody looked at her or said anything. It's almost as if they feared what was going to happen next. The air stood still, and then the barn door slid open again. I could see a car pull up. Dark-blue SUV. A woman got out of the passenger seat and came toward us. I couldn't see her face until she passed through the door. "What am I doing here?" Philomena asked. "This is supposed to be a probate meeting. In a barn?" Philomena looked at Marie and at me and then back at the door. "Wrong place," she said, and started to walk back out. "I drove all those hours for this?"

"Have a seat," Rotton said and pulled a chair out for her. "We're just getting acquainted." She sat down and stared from one face to the other. "This is a complicated puzzle, and we all have a piece. That's why you're all here."

The chairs were set in a circle with Philomena, me, Marie, and Sandrine looking at one another. There were three empty chairs. "When is the rest of the party arriving?" Marie asked.

"You'll see. They'll be here very shortly." Not even a minute had passed after he said those words and a tall woman walked in. She had short hair, reddish, and was dressed in a camel-colored coat. She seemed startled, looking around her, and started to back up. I had never seen her before.

"Here, Signora Lacroce. You really need to be here—you're important in this. Pick a chair." She obeyed but kept her eyes on the door. Signora Lacroce had to be Olivia, Tommaso's wife.

Ten minutes went by, and another figure appeared. This time it was Francesca Tosi. She looked annoyed and confused, dressed in the same outfit I'd seen her in before. Black trousers and a black shirt. She didn't even look in my direction. "Oh, another guest. We're almost there," he said, pointing to a chair.

"I got a letter from a lawyer." He put a hand on her shoulder and guided her to her seat. We all sat and stared from face to face, but still nobody was speaking.

"I am Anais Lavoisier's lawyer. I am here to fulfill her requests and probate her will. You were all on her Acte de Notoriété. I want to start by saying none of you are being held captive. But you might all want to think before you leave. Because you all have something to lose. Something to hide. Whether it's a legal concern or just personal information you'd rather be kept quiet, think before exiting the doors. Once you leave you cannot come back."

"Are you going to tell us to put on a play?" Olivia quipped, but she shut her mouth when an old woman came through the door. She was using a walker, unsteady on her feet. She took her time in sitting down.

"We're going to tell a story," the lawyer started without introducing the newcomer. "It's a story that needs to be told. You're all connected in some way. Some of you know each other; some of you think you've never met. But you're all connected. Please know that we are not going to notify authorities unless we have to. As we shall see.

"Now that you are all comfortable, I want to go over the rules. Rule number one—you are all here of your own volition. You can leave at any time, but think carefully before you do; there may be consequences, and you cannot come back. Rule number two—this is a confidential probate of Anais Lavoisier's last will. But there is a larger reason you were all called here, as we will see. Rule number three—if you should choose to leave, remember that what is said in this meeting is confidential. If you report information about others, there will be consequences to you and your families.

"Anais Lavoisier wanted you all here, not just to discuss her assets, but to discuss the past. Things that have happened that have affected all of you in one way or another—"

"My son, Tommaso, was killed. Is that what this is about? Someone here killed my son? And she wanted it revealed?" the old woman said. That answered one question for me. At least I knew who she was.

"An interesting question to start things off. Marie? Let's start with you. Did someone in this circle kill her son? Do you know anything about it?" Rotton was running the show. He'd jumped right to the heart of it.

Everyone looked at Marie. She dropped her head. "Unbelievable. Leave it to Maman to do something like this. I think I'll pass. Let someone else go."

"You have to answer it, Marie. That's part of the rules of this game. Say what you know. If you don't want to play, you'll be removed," he said. "You might not want to be removed. Like I explained before, it comes with consequences."

"I'm not playing," she said. Abruptly, Rotton stood, grabbed her arm, and pulled her out of the chair. She was shoved through the open barn door, and it shut behind her.

He sat. "That was an unfortunate choice on her part. But let's keep going. Yes, someone in this circle killed Tommaso, to answer your question."

I looked around me. I knew I didn't do it. I was three years old at the time. I went around the circle to my left. Sandrine, Francesca Tosi, the older Mrs. Lacroce, Olivia, and Philomena. They were all looking at one another. "So I'm guessing it wasn't Marie. Since she's been removed?" I asked.

"For this round, yes. But she'll be back," he said. "I might give her one more chance before I call her parole officer."

"And I doubt Tommaso's mother killed him, did you?" She shook her head. "So that leaves only four people. Sandrine, Francesca Tosi, Olivia, and Philomena." I sort of liked this game. A pack of vipers being cut open. "Why would Sandrine want to kill him? Did they even know each other?"

The man smiled. “Did you, Sandrine? Did you know Tommaso Lacroce?”

“I did know him,” she said quickly, afraid to suffer the same fate as Marie. “He came to see Anais more than once. So, I knew his face. I knew some of his story. But I had no reason to kill him.”

“Did Anais tell you she thought he might be blackmailing her?” Rotton asked. “With some information from the past?”

Sandrine’s eyes darted around the room. “She might have.”

“Did she ask you to help her with that problem? Maybe offered you money to help her? Or something else in return?”

“No. No, never.” Her voice was panicked.

“That’s probably not the whole truth, but let’s keep moving. We’ll come back to her. Rather than pointing out one person, I want to discuss the relationship each of you had with Tommaso, the connection you share, ” Rotton said.

“So, does that mean Sandrine didn’t do it?” I asked. Rotton didn’t answer. “Of the three left, then, I’d guess Philomena. They knew each other well, from years before. They went on some killing spree in Southeast Asia. That’s where I’d put my money,” I volunteered. “Blackmail gone wrong?”

“Wrong, Ava. You get only one more guess, and then you’re out. But I think it’s time to let someone else take a turn. Philomena, you’ve been so quiet. Who do you think killed Tommaso?”

She was crying silent tears. “I want to go home. You don’t have anything on me.”

“Home to your husband with a gash on his neck? Who slit your husband’s neck? Be a sport, play along for a little bit. Take a guess at who killed Tommaso.”

Philomena raised her shoulders and dropped them. “If it wasn’t Sandrine. And it’s not me . . . she thinks it wasn’t Tommaso’s mother, but it was twenty years ago. She was certainly capable of it, physically. Did you kill him?” She looked at the old woman.

"I met you nearly fifty years ago in Saigon, and you're acting like you have no idea who I am. It's because of you that my daughter is dead and my son is too. Maybe you didn't put the knife in his back that day in the park, but you killed him just the same. The three of you that day when he was only thirteen years old—"

Milo Rotton put his hand on the old woman's back. "I'm going to call that a no. She did not."

"That leaves only two. I have no idea why either of them would want to kill him, but I'd guess Francesca Tosi," Philomena said.

Francesca Tosi stood up. Her wiry frame was quicker than Philomena anticipated so that when the woman lunged at her, she couldn't move fast enough. We all watched it without moving in to help. When they separated, Philomena had some blood on her lip.

Francesca Tosi was shoved back into her chair. "I can't stand her. I hate her. I hated her daughter. I even hate—" She looked at me. "Yes. You too."

I felt my heart drop. I barely knew this woman. She'd never given me the chance.

"So, this is actually moving forward faster than I thought. This seems to be a difficult subject for you, Mrs. Tosi, but can you tell us why you hate Ava?" Rotton said. "She was just a baby when you last saw her."

"Davide should never have been with your mother. Never." Her voice went up. "It almost killed me to see them together."

"So let's not get off track here. Your guess, Philomena?"

She covered her face with her hands. "That was my final guess."

"Eh. Right and wrong. Care to explain, Olivia?"

Olivia had been quiet the entire time. Just then the door opened, and Marie was escorted back in. "Marie was convinced to join the game again. Go ahead, Marie," Rotton urged her on. "Do you know who killed Tommaso Lacroce?"

Marie dropped into her seat. "Let's all just refuse to play." She looked up at the lawyer. "If you take us all down, there's going to be repercussions."

Rotton didn't respond. He took out his phone and pressed a button. "Parole, Camden County Division. Give me a minute." He turned his back to the group.

"Okay, enough," Marie said. "It was her. Okay. Enough games. It was Olivia. I saw her that night in the park. Tommaso came at my car; there were other people there too. I was only there to give him an envelope. Someone was chasing him. But I saw the hair. I saw her face. She looked right at me. It was her. I'm sorry, Olivia, but I need this to be over. I need to go back to the States before they revoke my parole."

CHAPTER 61

Ava

La Héronnière de Haut, France

All eyes turned to Olivia. Tommaso's mother was pushing to get to her feet.

"You hired some detective to solve the case?" Mrs. Lacroce said. "Or did you hire him to mislead the rest of us and keep an eye on the investigation?"

"I didn't want this to happen. I didn't go after him to stab him. I didn't," Olivia said.

"So, what happened, then?" I asked. "You followed him out of the house and just happened to have a knife in your hand?" I was still enjoying this. It was one of the few times in my life that I wasn't guilty of anything.

"Well, I know Tommaso probably left the house to meet me," Marie said. "I don't know if he knew he was meeting me specifically, but I had an envelope for him from Anais. Filled with information she'd gathered. Anais was looking for a woman. Adopted out through Catholic Charities back in the late nineteen sixties, Saigon." Marie didn't look like she was enjoying this part. She looked anxious and angry.

"Ah, now we're getting to the crux of the matter, aren't we?" Rotton said. "Olivia, did you have some interest in keeping your husband from getting information about this adopted woman? You knew what was in the envelope?"

She refused to answer.

"Olivia?" Rotton asked.

"I had no choice. I didn't ask for any of this—" she responded.

"But you did. Tell us where you met your husband, initially. Was it serendipity or a calculated meeting?" Rotton asked. "Where'd you meet?"

"We met in his accounting office. I made an appointment to see him. I'm sure you know that already if you know everything else."

"So, you knew who he was?"

"I needed an accountant. My family gave me money."

"Who are you protecting? Yourself?" Philomena asked.

I was watching them all. Sandrine seemed nervous, a seeming witness to all of this just like me, but she was clearly on edge. Marie was hopping in and out of the commotion, unburdening all her secrets when she found the opportunity. Mrs. Lacroce had stopped following the conversation. She'd finally found out who killed her son, and it had taken its toll, leaving her weeping in the corner. Philomena was twisting her hands in her lap, still clinging to a pretense of innocence, but the perspiration on her forehead gave away another truth. Davide's mother was the most curious of all. I wasn't clear why she'd been included in all of this unless they were going to move on to Davide's disappearance that night and tie it together. She looked angry. Annoyed. Sad. Worn out. I didn't relish watching her learn the fate of her son.

At that moment, I hated Anais. This was all for her amusement, and she wasn't even here to see everyone crumble. Rotton thumbed through some pages in front of him. "So, enough of the questioning. You made the initial contact with Tommaso. You then asked him to lunch. You knew who he was. You knew his family's history in Vietnam. You knew what happened there, didn't you? And not just the basics—down to the exact details of Dong Xoai. And yet you pursued him and chose to marry him?"

"I chose to marry him because I loved him."

"I'm sure you did, but it was an awkward marriage, wasn't it? For many reasons. But let me ask you this. Do you know Sandrine, Anais's neighbor? Have you ever met her before?"

Olivia looked at Sandrine and then kept her eyes glued on the door as though someone was going to come walking in. "You know I do."

"How?"

"I helped get her the house in Cherbourg."

"So, Sandrine is looking to buy a house, and you convince her the one two doors down from Anais Lavoisier might do the trick? Did you know Anais at all during this transaction, Olivia?"

Olivia jumped up from her seat and rushed for the door but was stopped in her path by Sandrine's son.

"If you leave, I have no choice but to pass on information to the authorities. So, let's just cut to the chase. Olivia needed someone to watch Anais, and she found what she was looking for in Sandrine. A spy willing to work for the highest bidder. And that's probably how Olivia knew about the paperwork Marie was trying to deliver to Tommaso that night. She knew everything," he continued. "So, the only question left is why she was interested in all of this. What was her gain? Anyone?"

They all looked at one another. "She's connected somehow to the Vietnam situation. But I don't know how. I don't remember her. She'd have been maybe four then?" Philomena asked.

"You're fifty? Fifty-one?" Rotton asked Olivia.

Her arms were folded. Her face crumpled. "Fifty-one."

"Do you know everyone in this room, Olivia? You know Philomena, Mrs. Lacroce, Marie only in that she witnessed you murdering Tommaso. We've covered Sandrine. What about Francesca Tosi—do you know her?"

"I'm going to jail anyway. I'm not saying another word."

"Nobody is calling the authorities. But you might want to jump in. Or I'll fill in the blanks for you. Where'd you grow up, Olivia?"

"Geneva mostly. And Paris too sometimes." Having dried her tears, the elder Mrs. Lacroce was back in the game, answering for Olivia. "Tommaso told me that. Unless she lied about that too."

"Mrs. Tosi, where'd you grow up?"

"My parents were both professors at Université de Genève," Francesca said. "I lived in Geneva. I lived in Paris, Milan. I lived all over, depending. My father was an earthquake engineer, so we traveled with him sometimes. I even lived in Turkey for six months. New Zealand in the summers."

"You and Olivia went to the same college, then? Both the same year? You're close in age? So you know one another?"

I was staring at the two of them. It was starting to make sense. I couldn't take my eyes off Francesca Tosi. I stared for so long I was starting to get dizzy.

"Yes," she responded.

"Did you grow up in the same neighbor—"

"Cut the shit, we're sisters. Okay, she and I are sisters," Olivia said. "And I've spent most of my life taking care of her. Trying to keep her life in order. She spent all the money left to her; she's alienated everyone around her. She drove her son away. I can't take any more."

"One biologically born to the Rossi family, and one adopted," Rotton said.

The air sucked out of the room, and it seemed nobody was breathing. I put my head down and almost started to cry. Davide's mother was *the* girl. Na.

Francesca stood up. "You want to play a game. Let's play. Everyone in this room is connected to me, you're right. She was there when my brother cut my neck. That one." She pointed at Philomena. "And left me to die in the mud." Her voice was going up. "Tommaso and her," she said, still pointing at Philomena, "smothered the baby. Her name was Ngoc; I learned that later. That baby was crying, and Philomena smothered her. But that wasn't enough. My brother stabbed me while she held me." She pulled down the neckline of her shirt to reveal the scar that ran along her neck to her ear. Jagged, thick white scar. You might not see it if you weren't looking. "She ran after me and caught me. Held me there until my brother reached us. Even if she didn't know what he was going to do, she watched it. And then she left me there, lying in the mud. You need to die, Philomena. I just waited too long to kill you."

It didn't escape my notice that my father's mother was me. She'd suffered something traumatic at a young age, been adopted, but remembered it all. Sought revenge her entire life, even enlisting those close to her to help, leaving bodies in her wake. Now I understood the comment that Rotton made that I was the continuation of the greatest story ever told. Philomena's daughter ended up dating the son of a woman she'd helped try to kill. Romeo and Juliette. And then there was me.

I was in the middle, and I knew exactly why I'd been brought to this meeting. And that before this was over, I was going to have to choose. But how? Should I choose the woman who would understand everything I'd ever been through, intimately? Who would accept my killing the people who'd hurt my mother? Someone who would truly accept me when all the dust was settled? But was torn, bitter, and angry. Or would I choose the family that raised me? Anais, Marie, or even Philomena, because they'd somehow protected me from a worse fate despite screwing me over every step of the way?

"So what about Davide? And Victor." The sound of Philomena's voice brought me back to the present. "What happened to them?"

CHAPTER 62

Ava

La Héronnière de Haut, France

The world did split in two at that moment. I felt alone more than ever. In this room full of screwed-up people, I was the center of it. All eyes were on me. Milo Rotton didn't answer Philomena's question. The important question that had started this quest. Where was my father? I waited for the lawyer to start his panel discussion again, but it didn't happen, and I could only imagine it was because he didn't know. All of this, and he didn't actually know what had happened to my father.

Mrs. Lacroce was just standing in front of Francesca, not touching her, not saying a word, just staring as if she couldn't believe this was the little girl she'd lost sixty years ago. Francesca wouldn't return her gaze. She kept her eyes on the floor, as if just the sight of her was bringing back too many bad memories.

"I started playing a stupid game. I thought it was interesting. I thought they deserved it. I started sending them letters so they'd know I was alive. To make them afraid. Every time I was in Geneva, I'd send one out. I didn't count on them figuring out where I was, who I was. But three of the four were smarter than I thought. I'm talking about all of them but you, Philomena."

"So, you stabbed Victor and followed me to Paris? To the bank?" I asked.

She shrugged. "You were an unexpected witness. Was I supposed to let you go? After you left, he fought me . . . we fought all the way up the stairs. I thought I'd left him for dead. But little Philomena showed up to revive him."

"Who was texting him before he was stabbed?" Philomena looked at Olivia. "They said it was a phone—someone by my name bought it. But it wasn't me. And my blood in Victor's car? How?"

Francesca had her head down. "The phone was easy; the blood in the car was a happy coincidence. A fluke, really, that you must have bled in that car in the past, and they discovered it now. By the way, I'd call the hospital and check on your husband. His condition might have changed since you last saw him."

Philomena looked startled. "Maybe a month ago I fell. I cut my hand, but how could the blood still be on the steering wheel? I wiped it off."

"I don't think blood just disappears," Milo Rotton said.

"And what do you mean Victor's condition has changed? I just saw him before I left. He's dead? You killed him?"

She shrugged. "Maybe." Philomena bent over in her chair and began weeping. "I'm no worse than any of you," Francesca continued. "You think you're better? You're not. And Olivia, stop looking so upset. I told you I was coming here. I told you on the phone. I also told you someone was going to die, didn't I? I just haven't decided who."

"Wait, which one of you was sending me the threatening notes while I was in jail? Was that you too?" Marie looked at Francesca. "Or was it you, Sandrine? You were taking my phone calls while I was in jail, carefully planning this meeting—did you think you needed to threaten me too? Was that part of Anais's revenge on all of us?"

Nobody answered.

"Somebody sent me these letters. They knew I'd been near the park when Tommaso was killed. Who did it?" Marie looked at all of us one by one, waiting for a response. "I deserve answers like everybody else."

"Enough. Take all of them to the main house. Let them eat, and explain the rules of this game to them again. I'll be in soon. I want to talk to Francesca, Ava, and Philomena," Rotton said. Sandrine's son moved next to Marie.

In that split second after everyone had filed through the door, in that second when I wasn't paying attention, Francesca found the rage in her that had been bottled up, never satisfied, and I saw what nearly fifty years of the deep gnawing hatred had done to her. I saw in her face what my own would look like in so many years. She'd found a knife. I don't know if she brought it with her or discovered it here. She had Philomena from behind, the knife to her neck hard enough that I could see the indent the point was making against her skin, and the slightest trickle of blood.

"Tommaso is dead. Victor is dead. Anais is dead, though I didn't get to her in time. Everyone is gone but this one."

The moment was here that I'd known was coming. Philomena was begging for help from me.

"Ava, I'm your grandmother. I raised you until you were three," she said. "I loved you. Help me. Don't let her do this."

"What happened to my father?" I asked for the third time.

"Davide called Tommaso. He wanted to meet him that night. He knew his mother was Na Lacroce. He and Adrianna had figured it out. It was all just coming together at one time. He wanted to talk to Tommaso—get the whole story. Tommaso said to meet him in the park. And Davide stumbled onto his murder."

"A murder you orchestrated through your sister," Philomena said.

"I lost Davide because of you," Francesca said. "Did you think I cared when you lost your daughter? I was glad. Maybe your granddaughter will be next." The knife went deeper, and I saw the blood start to slide down Philomena's neck.

I was strangely detached. Torn. Rotton was standing with his back to the wall, like a weasel, ready to exit through the door at the first opportunity. "Move another inch, and I'll slice her wide open," Francesca said to him. "We're going to settle this here, for good. Isn't this part of Anais's game?" she said. "Philomena took my life. Then her daughter ends up with *my* son. It was like taking my life a second time."

"You chose to live around there. For what? To watch Philomena, prey on her? Torment her? So you could eventually kill them all. You had some sort of plan. It backfired. You could have moved on. Started a new life," I said. "I'm you. And you're me. You killed one? I've killed so many more. Those memories of my mother being killed haunted me. They still do. The anger just took everything from me. It's all I wanted. I loved the anger. So here I am. Nothing. I have nothing."

Those words seemed to jar her. She stared me down, loosened the knife slightly, and I thought she was going to drop it. "Let go of it all, Giada. Or you'll be me." She took the knife from Philomena's neck and sliced her own, the scar from her old wound splitting open again.

She dropped to the floor; the knife skittered to my feet. I picked it up.

I sat down hard on the chair and heard the voices around me, rushing to her side, arguing about calling an ambulance. Had everything I'd gone through to find the truth, find my family, been pointless? My maternal grandfather, Victor, was presumably dead; Anais had used me for her own purposes, and she was gone; and my other grandmother, Francesca Tosi, was dead at my feet.

"So what did happen to my father?" I said again.

Nothing. Nobody said a word.

I heard the sound of my phone ringing in my bag. My cell phone was spitting out a string of strange numbers across the screen. I couldn't think of a better time for an interruption.

"Ava, listen. It's Russell. I'm in Ho Chi Minh City. Joanne and I. We traced the adoption of Na—"

"I know. I'm in this little legal conference of sorts. Complete with a dead body and everything. The only question unanswered is what happened to my father. He's dead, I assume."

"There was a message for me at the hotel desk when I returned from the French embassy. Don't ask. Ava. I think you need to come here. Get a flight. Hotel Reverie Saigon. We'll be waiting."

CHAPTER 63

Ava

Ho Chi Minh City, Vietnam

The flight was long but so much better in first class. I'd been wise to stop in Paris and withdraw the money from Anais's account there. I gave Marie her half. It was the first time we didn't have any desire to outmaneuver each other. She was in a hurry to get back to the States before her absence was detected. I needed to move on.

I'd left the barn without looking back at any of the others. Mrs. Lacroce had found out who killed her son and then regained and lost her daughter, all in the space of a few hours. She was destroyed. Philomena had a red mark on her neck from the knife to remind her of how close she came to losing everything. Victor was dead; she could keep the money he'd stolen from me. I had so much more.

Sandrine, the double spy, had gotten through it all by blinking and acting stupid; Olivia should have been arrested by all accounts, charged with the murder of her husband, but by the rules of the assembly, everybody had turned their backs and left the ultimate decision to Milo Rotton. The last I saw of Olivia, she was sitting in the corner by herself on her cell phone.

I was still wanted for murder in the United States, but I felt surprisingly free. The tires skidded across the landing strip in Saigon, and I felt strangely scared as to what lay ahead. It had occurred to me it might all be a trap. I didn't think so. I didn't have the energy.

The hotel was gorgeous. It almost took my breath away when I saw the marble, the chandelier, the ornate elevator. Room 2256. I walked down the hallway, my bag bumping along my leg as I counted the room numbers. I stood in front of the room and took a breath. It opened before I had a chance to knock. Joanne was there. She wasn't smiling. She wasn't frowning either, but she backed up to let me in.

Russell was behind her, watching. "You have about three hours. Then we're checking out."

I was exhausted. "What? Why?"

"We're going north. The taxi is picking us up in a bit to take us to the train," Russell said.

I walked to an empty bed and dropped down onto it. That's the last I remembered until Russell shook my shoulder. "We leave in fifteen minutes."

I washed up quickly and gathered my things. Russell was cordial. Joanne kept her distance, a look of disgust on her face. I knew she and Russell had had a disagreement over this, but she had a choice of either staying in Saigon alone or coming with us. She chose the latter but wasn't happy about it.

The train moved north at the slowest pace. Our conversations, stilted at first, became more relaxed. After a day, we were talking about the people at the courthouse. The officers at the jail. The parties at the bar around the corner. Joanne jumping in occasionally to add something. But she wouldn't look me in the eye. Ever.

I didn't know where we were going. I thought it had something to do with my father, but I couldn't be certain. I'd run this ragged maze of a race too long to hope for anything. I just knew we were headed north toward China and that I could stay on the train forever, I thought. It was a holding pattern to nowhere with people I actually liked, even if they didn't like me. I didn't have to think. I didn't have to worry. I didn't have to ruminate about anything. The game was done.

But it ended in Hanoi when we debarked. Russell had it all planned out. A car was waiting for us. "Five more hours, Ava, till we get to the end of the earth."

And we did. It was hard for my eyes to adjust to what I was seeing. Limestone mountains covered in vegetation climbed out of green water in every direction. "Ava, do you speak any Vietnamese?" Joanne asked. "I haven't heard you jump in to help us out."

"No. It's a tonal language I could never grasp. You lose the ability to hear the subtlety in sounds after a certain age. I took a class once, just to see, but gave up. Sorry, I won't be of any help."

"Her superpowers are gone, Russell. I love it."

We got onto a boat and drifted out to sea. And then we stopped, just bouncing on the waves. I lay back on the deck, the sun beating down on me. The breeze was refreshing. And then I woke up. A man was standing over me. Looking at me. Smiling.

I pushed up to a sitting position and stared. I knew his face. I'd seen it in photographs. "Oh my God," I whispered.

"Giada, piccola mia. Sembri tua madre," he said.

I stood up. "I don't look like my mother. I look like you," I responded.

He held my face in his hands. "I'm so sorry. I'm so sorry about everything. I didn't know you were alive. I didn't know. Nobody told me. I thought you died with your mother. I thought about you two every day. Every day."

"Why are you here? In Vietnam. I don't understand."

"Olivia had given me money in case I needed to get out—because of my mother. I decided to use it the day I saw Tommaso killed. I found out who my mother was—" He looked out onto the horizon. "I saw Olivia kill him. I could never get involved. My leaving was supposed to be temporary, Giada. It was never meant to be forever. But Adrianna was gone. You were gone."

"So you knew Olivia, growing up? Knew she was your aunt? And Tommaso was your uncle?"

"No. Nothing at all like that. She was a family friend; that's all I ever knew her as. When my mother needed help, she was there. I never met or saw Tommaso until that day in the park."

He had a pained expression on his face.

"What?"

"My mother was so difficult. Angry, crazy when I was growing up. When I finally got away, it was easier to stay in Hong Kong. I went to a British university. I'm an architect. I made a life for myself. I got married. I have an eleven-year-old son. You have a brother. I just didn't feel a need—to go home—if Dri and you were gone. My life was here."

"Your mother never knew you were alive?"

He shook his head. "I couldn't. I just couldn't—"

"She killed—"

"Herself. I know. Olivia called me." He didn't look upset when he said that. I didn't know what to say. "Olivia and I stayed close. She comes to Hong Kong sometimes. She said my mother was getting worse." His face clouded over. "And she was. It's a story it might take a long time to tell. Not now. Now I just want to sit with you. See you. Spend the time we've lost together. Come." He put out his hand for me.

Russell and Joanne followed behind us. At first I wondered if they were a couple, if she'd stolen him out from under me, but then I knew it was something so much more. Something I'd been looking for my entire life. A comfortable, unconditional friendship. I wasn't part of it, and it hurt me. I never would be. And maybe if my father knew everything I'd done, he'd cast me out too. But there was this little seed inside me that wanted forgiveness. To make things right. To make amends. To start over. To think before I acted. One step at a time.

"I'll be there in a minute," I said. I made my way to my cabin and dumped out my bag, looking for a change of clothes. The box with the brooch Sandrine had given me fell out and landed on the floor. The brooch slid under the bed, and it took a minute for me to retrieve it. The clasp on the back had loosened, opening a small cavity.

A small rolled-up paper fell out into my hand. I unrolled it carefully and read it. *Ava. Meet me in Prague on March 30th. Noon. Charles Bridge. I'll be wearing red. Grand-Mère Anais.* Followed by a series of numbers I could only assume was her cell phone.

I read it twice and laughed. The old woman was alive, out there. I really had seen her on the train. And she'd be waiting for me in less than a month on a bridge in Eastern Europe. Or maybe I was just being lured there so she could kill me or try and get me to kill Marie. I stuffed it back in my bag and climbed the stairs to the deck where Russell, Joanne, and my father were sitting in front of an enormous spread of food. They were smiling and laughing at each other.

"Let go of it all, Giada. Or you'll be me," I whispered, thinking of my other grandmother's last words.

There was a huge meal waiting for me. I decided that maybe it was time to eat.

CHAPTER 64

Anais

Prague, Czech Republic

The hotel was sufficient, not too luxurious, not too seedy. It sat on Old Town Square inside Old Town. It was close to everything and minutes from the bridge. Just what she'd wanted. To hide in plain sight. She stood up and stretched. Her back hurt sometimes now when she moved too quickly. Sixty-six years were taking a toll on her body. She spread her fingers, looking at how some of the bones in her knuckles had swelled. The diamond ring on her left hand, just a showpiece, scattered light across the windowsill. She adjusted her gray dress.

"I know you're going to come, Ava. I know you are. You have to."

She'd been in Prague two days preparing for this. To see Ava again, to figure out where they'd go from here. They had an unbreakable bond. In the eyes of the world, they were both dead now. On the run. Other than the twelve million she'd left for Ava and Marie, she'd set aside another account, here in the Czech Republic. Enough to keep them for a lifetime.

Maybe they'd contact Marie, and maybe they wouldn't. That remained to be seen. Marie had always been a loose cannon, unpredictable. Sometimes too moralistic, too plodding, always too nervous. No, Anais's blood ran through Ava's veins, and it had made sense from the minute she'd figured out their connection. Ava was sharp, resourceful, cool under any circumstances, with enough anger, and enough sincerity, to pull anything off.

She'd crawled from the blood-spattered church after her mother had been murdered in front of her and reinvented herself. Then started exacting revenge on the perpetrators at the unripe age of sixteen. Anais cackled at the thought. "My girl," she whispered. And now the circle had been completed, it was time for a new chapter.

She pulled on her red coat and hat, grabbed her purse, and locked the hotel door behind her. When the warmth of the air hit her face, she suddenly felt hot in her coat. It felt like seventy-five degrees outside—summer already, though April was only a day away and spring had just arrived.

The stroll from Hotel Rott to the bridge would take less than ten minutes. She walked through the square past the tourists already gathering for the spring season to take a gander at the Prague Astronomical Clock. She glanced up only briefly. Her mind was jumping from thought to thought: What if Ava didn't show up? What was plan B? She'd be at a distinct disadvantage. She'd shown her cards before she had assurances they wouldn't be thrown in her face.

When she reached the fourteenth-century structure that crossed the Vltava, the wind was whipping across the river. She checked her watch. Eleven fifty-three. She leaned forward into the stone archway and waited. Faceless people walked by, young couples. College students with backpacks and cell phones in their hands. Anais waited, holding her breath with every gust of air. Her coat was *red* red, the brightest she could find, and the hat to match made her look like the sweltering queen of England out for a walkabout.

Then she saw her. The wisp of a creature came toward her from the castle end of the bridge, dressed in black. Black coat, maybe cashmere, in her arms, black slacks tapered down her narrow legs, ending just at ankle length, and a loose black top. Her hair was pulled back, sunglasses nearly filled her entire face. But it was her. Anais knew from the shape of her shoulders as she moved, the long gait of her walk. Her neck—so long, it made everything she wore look elegant.

When Ava was fifty yards away, she stopped for almost a full minute, just looking Anais straight in the eye, then abruptly turned and headed back the way she'd come. Anais watched in disbelief. Ava didn't look back. It was her; the old woman was sure it was her. A game. She was playing a game. Anais watched her walk away and just stood where she was and waited. She'd come back. She was sure of it. And she did, though it took nearly half an hour.

She sauntered up next to her. "So, you put the secret message in the brooch. I found it." Ava took off her glasses and held them in her hand.

"I knew you would," she responded.

"Why? Just let's get the why over with."

"Why did I want to meet you? Why'd I fake my death? Why did I plan the gathering?"

"You pick."

"Let's walk," Anais said, taking off the coat and flinging it over one arm. The hat was next, stowed in her purse.

Ava shook her head. "I want to stand here. It's so pretty."

"I faked my death for the same reason you did. To get away from all of it. To start a new life. To wipe my past clean. I've been tormented—"

"What did Philomena ever do to you to deserve what you've done to her? You got pregnant by her husband, forced her to give birth in a barn—essentially killed her baby—"

"But I let her raise mine. So it worked out." It was flat, matter-of-fact. "She never knew."

"She does now."

"She wasn't innocent."

"I know what happened in Saigon. I know, but—"

"But nothing. You don't even know the half of it. Philomena never killed the little baby. She thought she smothered it because she had it in her arms. But she didn't. I was there. It was Tommaso. He pressed the baby's face into his chest until she stopped breathing—"

Ava stared, unable to form words. "You let her believe all those years that she killed that baby in Dong Xoai. When you knew all along it was Tommaso. Why? Why would you do that to her? You ruined her life with guilt. It was soul crushing. You destroyed her for no reason."

Anais was looking over the water into the distance and didn't answer right away. "Because I could, Ava. I suffered too. Victor was supposed to be mine—"

"He was never yours, Grand-Mère. Only for two minutes here and there in cheap hotel rooms. He was never yours. He might not have been the best husband, but he belonged to Philomena."

"You didn't know her when she was young, Ava. She wasn't even as pretty as me. She had nothing. Yet she ended up with Victor, and I got an American—"

"You should have chosen better," Ava said. "That doesn't justify it."

Anais bristled. It bothered her, even after all these years. She didn't like losing. "No—"

"So when did you figure out who Francesca Tosi was?"

She shrugged. "Before Tommaso died. I had the information to give to him, the night he died. But after he was murdered?" She smiled. "It was all so delicious, I kept it to myself. It all came to a head when Dri—your mother—and Davide got together. What are the chances? I mean, really. What a pair. It drove Francesca crazy. I mean crazy that her son was dating the daughter of the woman who watched as her neck was cut—and left her to die. Then those two teenagers had you." She started laughing and couldn't stop. She reached out and touched Ava's shoulder. "It was just so—"

Ava smacked her hand away. "So why the gathering in La Héronnière de Haut—that ridiculous town? For what?"

"I wanted a place out of the way. Milo Rotton suggested it. The whole lot of them are rotten, Ava. Sandrine, feeding Olivia all my information—just for money. Everything. Taking stories I told her and letting those two disgusting sisters pick over it. She was the biggest disappointment. She should really die." She peeked up at Ava to watch her expression. "And Francesca needed to be outed—I mean, yes, she had a rough start, but things just spiraled out of control. Though killing herself was good enough for me. And Philomena and Victor, so smug and pompous, full of lies. Philomena might not have killed that baby, but she sure as hell left little Na in a mud puddle to die. It's only a shame Victor couldn't make the probate—"

"The letters to Marie—the ones sent to her in jail. That was you too, wasn't it?"

She smiled. "She needed to feel paranoid, afraid, or she never would have come to the meeting, and she needed to be there. She witnessed Tommaso's murder."

"This was all for your entertainment. You were there—in the barn, weren't you? Watching it all. I did see you on the train."

She tilted her head back and laughed some more. "I saw it all—I was just in the next room. That's why I wanted you here with me. We're so much alike. Now you can have anything you want. We can go anywhere—"

"What about Marie? She's stuck in Camden County for the next five years. On probation. Narrowly escaped getting a violation for leaving the country."

"Marie has a road in front of her that I can't travel with her. It's better she thinks I'm dead. She has a house. She has money. Maybe now she'll be free. No religion to hold her back. It's a blessing."

Ava turned her back and looked in the opposite direction, then she started walking to a lamppost. She leaned against it and said nothing. Anais came up beside her. "What about my father?" Ava asked.

"What about him?"

"He was never at your house?"

She shook her head. "You can fake anything with photos these days. That was Sandrine's idea to drive you on. Get you on the train—to the meeting."

"To taunt me?"

"Encouragement," the old woman said. "Encouragement."

"You destroyed my life, Anais." She didn't call her Grand-Mère. Just Anais. "You took everything from me. Every part of it. It was you. You sent my mother to that church, knowing Ross and the others planned to kill the priest, to get revenge on Philomena. You hid Philomena's whereabouts from me. And my father's. Not to mention the rat race you put me and Marie in for money. Philomena's life was over the day she met you. That's the truth. Victor's too. And it's all a game to you. A big game. You justify it. And it's just incredible to hear you talk. So, you've managed to keep the fact you're alive from everyone except Sandrine and your attorney?"

"No, only Sandrine and you. My attorney had no clue." She moved her face close to Ava's. "Don't judge me so quickly. What happened in Saigon changed me. I was never the same after that. And who are you to judge? You're a murderer. You've killed so many people. How many, really? Seven? Eight?"

"That's true," Ava said. She put her sunglasses back on. Ridiculous-looking things that Hollywood starlets wore. Enormous on her small face.

Ava leaned down and looked at the water below. The move came swiftly. Before Anais could move or catch her balance. The sides of the bridge were exceptionally low. Not even waist high. She didn't have time to scream, or clutch the stone. Nothing. She slipped over without so much as a hint of notice by passersby into the Vltava River below.

She felt the cold air around her as she fell. She had one last glimpse of her granddaughter before she hit the water. Ava was leaning over the low stone parapet, yelling one word and smiling a wide-toothed grin from above. *Devět.* The Czech word for *nine.* That's how many people she'd killed, now, including Anais. And then everything went black.

ACKNOWLEDGMENTS

Many thanks to my family for enduring this journey with me. My daughter, Eva, and son, Ian, you have spent the majority of your childhoods watching me hunched over a computer screen. Though it may seem I squeezed you in, in between editing sessions, it was really the other way around. I couldn't do any of this without you. As I see you growing up and spreading your wings, I am so proud of the people you have become.

To editor Caitlin Alexander, this book was a total mess when it landed in your hands. There was a kernel of something worthwhile underneath, but it was so hidden. I am mesmerized watching you work, or hearing your plot suggestions after I have been struggling for days. I always feel when we're done that the final product is yours. For the endless hours and patience—even when I sent you the wrong manuscript to edit—and for enduring my last-minute panic, I appreciate you more than you know.

Many thanks to Liz Pearsons. You saw the potential in this Ava Saunders story from the beginning. I appreciate your insight and honesty. You gave me a chance, and I will forever be grateful.

To the production manager, Laura Barrett, and copyeditor, Wanda Zimba, I am amazed at the attention to detail and the time involved in poring over this manuscript. You managed to sort out a complicated timeline and made this manuscript shine.

To Yolanda Hughes, thank you for your support and encouragement. Our Sunday life-improvement sessions have boosted us both when we needed it. I might have given up without you. You know that.

To Lisa Field, my proofreader, many thanks for the years of friendship. I appreciate you every step of the way.

To Shawn Graham, thank you for corralling the squirrels when they break out of their cages. Nobody does it quite like you.

To my mother, Edith Green: You have been there for me, whether it was for last-minute babysitting, late-night plotting sessions, or to listen to me cry at life's latest complication. You've endured it all without complaining and always pushed me along when I needed it. Your input is invaluable. My children point out that their happiest memories were when you were present. I hope you know how much you mean to the entire family.

ABOUT THE AUTHOR

Photo © 2017 June Day Photography

Ellen J. Green is the Amazon Charts bestselling author of the Ava Saunders novels (*Absolution* and *Twist of Faith*) and *The Book of James*. She attended Temple University in Philadelphia, where she earned her degrees in psychology, and has worked in the psychiatric ward of a maximum-security correctional facility for fifteen years. She also holds an MFA degree in creative writing from Fairleigh Dickinson University. Born and raised in upstate New York, Ms. Green now lives in southern New Jersey with her two children.